THE FIRST HOUSE

TURN OF THE ZODIAC, BOOK 4

ASHLEY R SCOTT

Published by Ashley R Scott THE FIRST HOUSE

A Turn of the Zodiac Novel Copyright © 2019 by Ashley R Scott

First Electronic Printing: 2019 Ashley R Scott All rights reserved.

ISBN-13: 978-1-951427-91-7

❀ Created with Vellum

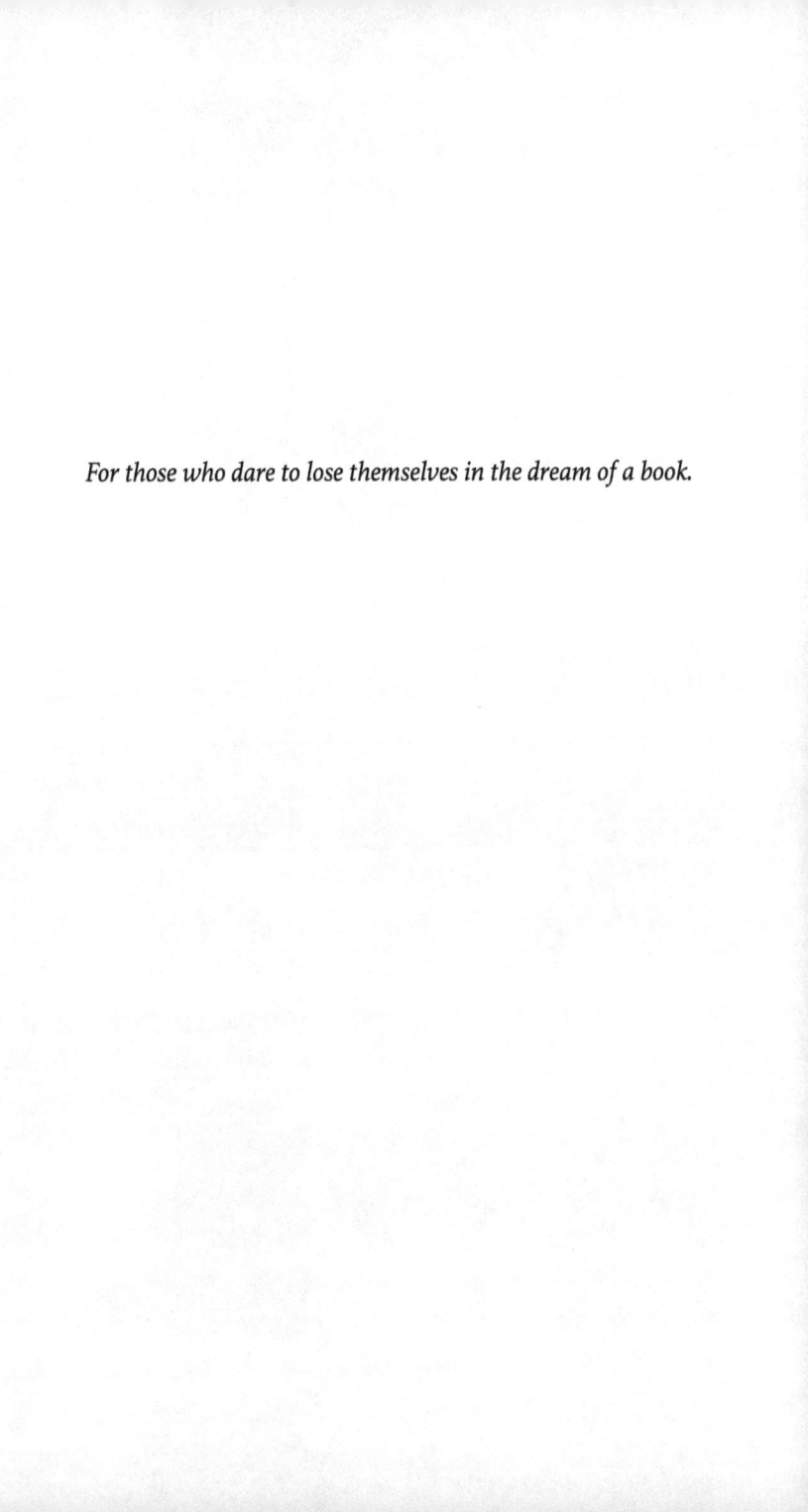

For those who dare to lose themselves in the dream of a book.

THE HOUSE OF ARIES

"What matters most is how well you walk through the fire." *Charles Bukowski*

"Fire that's closest kept burns most of all." *William Shakespeare*

The First House is the fourth book in the Turn of the Zodiac series.

Each house corresponds to one of the Zodiacs. The First House is ruled by Aries and the planet Mars.
It is commonly known as the House of Self and is the home of the Ascendant and new beginnings, which focus on the individual and the discoveries that define a person. It's the house of realizing one's potential and becoming a unique individual, which is one of the most significant contributions to the world.
The First House is about the person we are and will be, both inside and out.

1

___

The forest stretches out in front of me, the very tops of the trees highlighted with the bright silver light of the full moon, and deep shadows fill any space between them. I bend over with my hands on my knees, panting as I focus on getting my breathing under control. I don't know how long I've been running or how far I've gone.

The moon slips behind the clouds, throwing the area into complete darkness. I blink to help my eyes adjust and study the trees in front of me. I have no idea where I am.

I feel like I should recognize the trees in the forest, but I can't recall any of their names. A slight frown creases my brow as I sift through my foggy brain. Still, I come up empty. I don't have time to worry about that now.

Somehow, I know this place, but I don't think I've ever been here. Memories slither around the edges of my mind, like smoke rising around the flame of a candle, visible but not solid and something I can't grasp.

The shadows beneath the leaves are deep, hiding secrets I'm not sure I want to know. A cold shiver runs down my spine, my breath coming in quick pants as my pounding heart refuses to slow. I don't want to go in there, but I have to. If I turn back now, I'll be caught.

Caught by who? Or what?

I turn around, searching the dark field behind me, the grass a gray tint in the darkness. It looks like I'm completely alone, but I know it's out there somewhere. Energy is thick in the air, pressing against me and urging me to keep running.

The grass in the field is tall, up to my waist when I ran through it. Where did that thing go? It's hiding out there somewhere, taking shelter in the grass to keep out of sight. Fear grips my throat, my chest closing so tight, it's hard to breathe. What's out there?

The silence of the night weighs heavy on my shoulders, my mind spinning in wild circles. There's no sound of birds, frogs, or even crickets. It's like the entire world holds its breath with me. Or maybe the other creatures know what lurks in the darkness, and they're smart enough to keep quiet.

The gray of the grass shifts into silver as the moon reappears, and the world around me changes from one thick shadow to many inky pools. The tall blades shiver, and my breath catches in my throat. Did something move, or was that my imagination?

The grass splits as a deep line moves quickly through the field, heading straight for me. The movement is so fast that it's hard to follow. My mouth turns dry, like it's stuffed full of cotton balls, as I force my legs to step backward. It's almost here.

I turn on my heel, racing toward the trees, and nearly trip over my feet in my panic. My instincts tell me not to go into the forest, to keep running and avoid the trees, but from here I can't see any way around them. The trees stretch for miles.

It's the last place I want to go, but it's the only place I might survive.

My feet pound against the ground, muted thuds thanks to the soft dirt beneath my feet. I strain to listen over my ragged breathing, but the night is silent other than the noise coming from me.

The trees grow closer and my heart leaps with the thought of safety. There has to be somewhere in there I can hide.

I throw a quick glance over my shoulder, afraid of both falling and seeing whatever is chasing me. There's nothing in the darkness behind me, but I know it's still out there somewhere. It's behind me and moving faster than me. I can't let it catch me.

Panic pushes my feet faster than they've ever run. The air burns in my throat and lungs as tiny, white lights burst in my vision. Pain stabs in my ribs and my legs grow heavier with each step. All I want to do is collapse on the ground until I can finally breathe again, but I won't let it catch me.

A sob escapes my lips as I finally burst through the tree line, the ancient trunks thick and towering so high, the tops are lost in the dark. I skid to a halt, ducking behind a tree and pressing my body tightly against the rough bark. The wood snags at my clothes as my chest heaves with gasping breaths. I take a deep gulp of air and hold it, listening.

Silence.

My slow exhalation helps to get my breathing on track, but my heart still races, and my body is cold despite my running. A cool breeze brushes against my sweaty face, and it makes me shiver. I swallow the lump of fear rising in my throat, and carefully shift to see around the trunk without exposing too much of myself.

The shadows are thick, barely any moonlight piercing through the foliage. I can't see anything behind me and I don't know if that's good or bad. Movement catches my eye and I gasp, quickly clamping a hand over my mouth, and squeeze my eyes shut as I slide back behind the tree.

A tear slips out of the corner of my eye as I wait, panic wrapping a tight fist around my chest. I've never felt so alone in my life. How did I get here?

I hear whispers behind me, like a thousand voices all talking at once. I can't quite make out the words, and they sound as if they're all coming from the same place. The creature that's after me. Beneath the whispering is the soft crackling of flames.

My feet freeze to the ground, planted like I'm a part of this forest, as my heart beats so fast it might explode in my chest. The voices grow louder. It's almost here. I can feel it searching for me.

I should be able to defend myself. Why am I so afraid?

How can I be so helpless?

The bark beneath my palms slowly begins to vibrate, tickling my hands with a warm, tingling feeling. I gasp, yanking my hands away from the tree, but I can still feel the energy pulsing through my back. What is that? It's like magic.

Magic. I suck in a sharp breath, quickly closing my mouth. Do I know magic?

I close my eyes, pressing myself tightly against the trunk, and the vibration intensifies. My body feels electric, like I'm plugged into an outlet. The forest around me springs to life, and I can feel every tree, every blade of grass and every creature. Even the being that hunts me through the shadows. The energy around me thickens, and I feel it hesitate.

I push my energy deeper, reaching far beneath the surface of the ground until I feel the cold, damp earth in my mind and smell the mud in my nose. I concentrate on the dirt, pulling the energy into my body. Nothing happens.

A frown wrinkles my forehead and I take a deep breath, leaning closer to the bark until I feel it biting into my back through my jacket. I reach for the magic again, but it's as if I've pushed it away instead of pulling it toward me. The magic is there, flowing just beneath the surface, like water rushing beneath a frozen river.

I let out a soft growl, chewing on my bottom lip. For a moment, I was sure I could use magic.

The creature pushes closer, encouraged by my failure. I can feel it coming.

I shove myself away from the tree, running as fast as my feet can carry me over the uneven forest floor. The trees are a blur of wood and shadows, and I weave between their trunks, ignoring each sting of the low-hanging branches that whip across my face.

Behind me, the whispers grow louder, closer. I glance over my shoulder and a black shadow hovers above the ground, stretching ten feet in the air. Faces appear in the swirl of darkness, disappearing so fast that I can't quite make them out. The creature burns with an inner blue fire that crackles in the center of its chest.

My stomach drops. I can feel its hunger and I know it wants me. To consume me.

I cry out as my foot catches on a tangle of roots and sends me crashing to the ground. My hands hit the dirt first, shooting pain up my arms. I grit my teeth and roll onto my back, pulling my arms against my body, gently testing to see if anything is broken.

The creature catches up to me, hovering almost horizontally as it peers down at me. All I can see are two black holes where the eyes should be, but they aren't empty. They're filled with darkness. Cold waves roll off the creature, despite the fire that burns in its chest, and they make my teeth chatter.

I try to push myself back and away from this thing, but my arms no longer work.

It floats down closer, hovering just inches above me.

My legs kick, anything to put some distance between us, but my body won't budge.

The shadow moves, extending one long, bony arm, a skeleton without the skin but covered in a yellow, jelly substance. It reaches for my hand.

"No," I whimper, but I can't seem to make my body move.

The creature touches my skin and a scream rips through me as the jelly burns my hand like acid. It closes its grip on my hand and the pain races through me with blinding speed.

I summon all my strength and kick my legs, connecting with something solid.

"Shit, that hurt!"

I recognize the voice that sounds a million miles away and I hesitate, even as the creature pulls closer.

"Ciara!"

My eyes fly open and I struggle against the grip still tight on my hand.

"Ciara, relax." Aidan sits down on the bed next to me, one hand still gripping my arm as he wraps his free arm tightly around my shoulder.

The sound of his voice and heat from his body calm my nerves, and I take deep, steady breaths to stop the panting. I look around, and tears fill my eyes as I realize I'm at home in my bed.

"You're covered in sweat. Are you all right? What happened?" Aidan asks, his blue eyes narrow as he studies my face.

I take another deep breath, holding it for a moment before letting it out slowly.

"I don't even know where to start," I say, my voice shaking.

"You can tell me." Aidan rubs my back, and I relax into the rhythmic movement.

I swipe at the tears in my eyes. "I was in some forest. I don't know where I was, but something about it seemed familiar. There was a creature that was chasing me, and it was so scary. I couldn't use any magic and that thing caught me. I tried to fight it off but I couldn't, and it was burning me with its touch."

"Is that why you kicked me?"

I look up at Aidan, and his face is blank, but amusement flickers in his eyes. I groan. "I kicked you? I'm sorry."

He squeezes me tight. "Tell me about the creature. What did it look like?"

"I'm not sure." I shake my head, trying to clear away the fuzzy edges.

"It was a massive shadow and it had blue fire burning in its chest. Similar to the fire around the portal but brighter. It was freezing and its hands were covered in a yellow jelly that reminds me of the stuff that the pieces of Leo's birthstone were sealed in. But that's not the worst part. It was like it had people trapped inside it. I could almost see their faces, but not really. They were just swirling in the shadows of the creature."

I wrap my arms around myself and glance up at Aidan, and the look in his eyes sends a shiver down my spine. "Do you know what I'm talking about?"

He shakes his head slowly. "I've never seen anything like that before."

I wait for him to continue, but he only reaches out and pulls a strand of hair away from my face. My gut says he isn't telling the whole truth. I open my mouth to ask him, but he shakes his head, kissing me softly.

"Lie down. Let's try to get some sleep, and we'll figure this out in the morning. It's probably nothing more than a bad dream." Aidan settles down on the bed, holding his arm up and waiting for me.

I sigh but lie back down, snuggling beneath the warmth of his arm. He's been staying most nights at my house to make sure I stay safe from the mages, and I'm glad he's here tonight, even though my mind continues to swirl. Somehow it felt like more than a dream, but Aidan's steady breathing calms my fears, and before long, sleep takes me again.

My eyes slowly peel open, and I blink them to clear my sight. The edges of my vision are blurry as my bedroom slowly comes into focus. My eyelids feel heavy and my eyes burn like I haven't slept in a week.

I sit up slowly, my head aching with a dull pounding, and I squeeze my eyes shut, feeling like something ran me over in the middle of the night. I rub my hands together, sucking in a sharp breath between my teeth. My wrist is raw and has a red spot that wasn't there yesterday. My stomach turns with the thought that maybe last night wasn't as much of a dream as I want it to be.

I throw the cream-colored comforter off my legs and swing my feet over the edge of the bed. My head swims with the movement, and I take a second to swallow down the sickness threatening to rise in my throat.

"How do you feel? You don't look so good," Aidan says softly from his spot near the window.

"I don't think I feel that great." My throat feels like I swallowed a handful of rocks, and talking makes me cough.

Aidan silently crosses the room, picks up the glass of water I keep on the nightstand and hands it to me.

I take a small sip, grateful for the cool liquid sliding down my throat. "Aidan, what happened last night? That wasn't just a dream, was it?"

He studies me closely, an inner struggle fighting itself out in his eyes.

"Whatever you know, you have to tell me. I need to know." I quickly duck my head so he can't see the angry tears filling my eyes.

Aidan gently takes the glass of water from my hands and sets it on the table before squeezing my fingers tightly in one hand and using the other to tip my chin up. "I'm honestly not sure what to tell you. Was it a dream? Yes, but was it just a dream? I don't think so."

"What was that creature that was chasing me, do you know?" My heart thumps against my ribs as I wait.

He looks away for a second before meeting my eyes again. "I'm not sure what that creature is or if it's real. There have been rumors on Polaris, chatter among the servants mostly about an unknown creature. One of the girls caught sight of something that matches that description floating on the edge of the Daruchta Forest. She ran back to the compound and told the Zodiacs about it. They're investigating. That's all I know."

"Is there any way to control these dreams, or are they some kind of vision, like Morgan's gift? I didn't think I had that kind of magic." I stare at him, both hoping that I have a new magical gift and afraid of having another one of those dreams.

Aidan frowns. "It's hard to know. Your powers are still developing, and no one knows what kind of magic the union of an Aid and Guardian can produce. You're the first."

I grit my teeth at his words, swallowing down the bitterness that coats the back of my throat.

"I know. Just like Kyrell and Slade said, I don't know how to use my magic." My words come out sharper than I intend, and I immediately regret them when he flinches.

"That's not what I meant at all," Aidan says softly.

I sigh. "I know. I'm sorry. It's just that I don't know how to use all of my magic and I couldn't do anything in my dream last night."

"But that was a dream."

"Was it?" The dull ache in my head turns into a steady pounding. I lean my head into my hands, rubbing my temples.

Aidan carefully sits down beside me, and I lean into him. "Remember that magic takes time to learn. Most Guardians have their whole lives to learn to work with their element, and you're already more advanced than some Guardians I've seen. Plus, the more you work with the earth, the stronger you'll connect with your magic. You will develop gifts for the rest of your life."

Deep down I know that he's right, but I can't help feeling that I'm behind and somehow letting people down. My mom and I have a better relationship now than ever, but some of my childhood resentment bubbles to the surface.

"I didn't have anyone to teach me magic growing up. The only magic I can use is in the heat of a battle, and I can't always control that. I can't even control my house plants," I mumble.

Aidan chuckles. "And you were just thrown into all of this a few months ago, but you've already come so far. You've produced some amazing magic that other Guardians can never create. You also have a gift for connecting with the earth that I've only seen in Capricorn himself. Don't be so hard on yourself."

I open my mouth to argue when I'm struck by a bright idea. I sit up so fast, Aidan stares at me with wide eyes that quickly narrow into a frown at the look on my face.

"I'm not going to like this, am I?" Aidan asks.

"Of course you will." I pop up from the bed and wobble a little on shaky legs, but my excitement keeps me standing. "You're going to teach me to use my magic."

Aidan rolls his eyes. "I'm not exactly a teacher."

"It'll be fine. You grew up around the magic for all four elements, and you know more than anyone else in my life about this stuff." I reach down, grabbing his hands, and pull him reluctantly to his feet.

"We'll start today." I practically squeal with excitement.

He groans, but he can't hide the smile that tugs on the corners of his mouth. "I'm pretty sure this is going to be a bad idea."

"It'll be great. I'm so excited. Thank you so much." I lean in and kiss him before dashing off to my closet and leaving him laughing behind me.

The tires of the Jeep crunch and pop as the vehicle lurches back and forth, rocking us violently over the uneven dirt road that leads deep into the trees on Mt. Rose.

I grip the handle of the door, my knuckles turning as white as Aidan's as he hangs on to the steering wheel.

"Where are we going?" I ask through my gritted teeth.

Aidan throws a quick smile my way, even though it looks like more of a grimace. "We're almost there. I wanted to make sure we were far enough away to keep anyone from seeing our magic."

"Right." Another bump in the road almost makes me bite my tongue. "Let's just hope we make it in one piece."

I do my best to focus on the trees passing by my window, anything to take my mind off the potholes in the road.

The peak of Mt. Rose is still covered in snow, even in April, but at our elevation, I can only see patches of it still clinging to the ground in the deepest shadows. Leaves are growing on the aspen and oak trees, thickening the forest around the pine trees. The ground is muddy and slick with the snowmelt running down the mountain.

There's a small break in the trees, and Aidan steers the car off the road and stops in the turnout. He switches off the engine, pocketing the keys as he turns to look at me. "The place I want to take you to is just a short walk from here."

I smile at him, and I can feel it filling up my face. "Thanks for this."

Aidan snorts. "Wait and see if you feel like thanking me later."

I roll my eyes and slip out of the Jeep, following Aidan as he weaves through the trees. "How do you know where to go?"

"I know every inch of this mountain." His voice is soft

and filled with awe. "It's very important to the Zodiacs, and so we're taught everything they know in our training."

My eyes roam through the forest as I try to memorize every detail. "Why this mountain? I'm sure there are thousands of places around the world that meet the same elemental requirements."

Aidan slips his hand into mine, and I feel the familiar tingle. "That's a story for another time."

"But—"

"Just be quiet," he says softly. "Lesson number one. I want you to reach out with your magic and feel the forest. Feel the mountain. Pay attention to every leaf and blade of grass. Close your eyes."

"How can I close my eyes when we're still walking through the forest? I'm going to fall on my face." I'm always falling on my face, but I keep that last part to myself.

He raises his eyebrows but doesn't answer my question.

I sigh and close my eyes, trusting him to keep me on my feet, and take a deep breath as I reach out to the energy around us.

Old energy, rooted far beneath the surface, races like the current of a rushing river. The air vibrates around me and goosebumps run up my arms. My steps slow but my feet keep moving forward on their own.

I reach around, feeling for the grass, the dirt, and the leaves, anything that has the energy of the earth running through it. Every detail is clear in my mind as if I'm actually seeing it, and I'm surprised to see tiny green sparkles swirling around the plants. I gasp as my eyes fly open.

Aidan watches me closely, the edges of his blue eyes crinkled. "Tell me what you see."

"Everything." I look around the forest as if seeing it for the first time.

"I could see everything even with my eyes closed. The trees feel different now. I sense their energy without reaching for it. What are the green sparkles?"

He stops walking, his mouth hanging slightly open. "You can see green sparkles?"

I nod, searching the trees, and I think I can still faintly see them. "What are they and why do you look so surprised?"

"Those sparkles that you see are the raw elemental magic. You can actually see the energy of the earth. That must come from your dad, because I thought only Zodiacs and Aids could actually see the magic." His words are filled with pride.

My cheeks warm and I duck my head, but he quickly tips my chin, forcing me to look at him.

"Ciara, that's amazing. Don't be embarrassed. If you can see the magic, it will be that much easier to tap into and use." He smiles brightly and tugs on my hand, leading me through the trees.

"Why couldn't I see it before?" I rush to keep up with him on the uneven ground.

"That kind of thing is easier when you're surrounded by your element. When I first started seeing the water magic, it was easier near the ocean than by a pond. Earth magic is in its prime here, so you can see more energy than you could in the grass of your yard." He pulls me into a small clearing and stops. "Here we go."

I let go of his hand and look around the small clearing, not much bigger than a house. The grass is green and lush, like fancy carpet, without a single weed. The trees around the edge stand tightly together, making the whole area feel private. "This is beautiful. And perfect."

"I thought you'd like it here. It's one of my favorite

places." He lowers himself to the ground, tucking his legs beneath him and motioning for me to do the same.

I sit down beside him, running my hands over the tops of the cool blades of grass, and close my eyes as the magic tickles my palms.

"That's good. Keep the connection strong," Aidan says. His words startle me, and I open my eyes.

"What?"

Aidan chuckles. "I can feel your magic humming around your body. Getting and maintaining that connection is going to be the easiest way to learn to control your magic. See if you can make the grass grow."

My eyes close again, and I can see the grass clearly in my mind. I hesitate for a moment, wondering if this grass is going to have the same temperament as my house plants, but decide to try it anyway. I concentrate on the blades, coaxing them taller. The grass tickles my arms and I'm encouraged to keep them growing.

"You can stop now." Aidan chuckles.

I open my eyes and gasp. The grass around us is nearly up to my chin.

"I did it!" In my excitement, I lose hold of the energy, and the blades shrink down to their normal height, making me groan.

"That's okay, it's a good start," Aidan says.

"Why didn't the grass stay tall?" I do my best not to pout.

"Because you have to finish the magic if you want it to stay." He raises a hand when I open my mouth. "We'll get to that lesson."

"Let's try something harder." I waggle my eyebrows at him.

He rolls his eyes, but a smile spreads across his face. "How about we try the grass again?"

I wrinkle my nose at him but I close my eyes, holding the grass in my mind. Beneath the grass, the rushing current of energy tugs at me, and I push my energy beyond the green blades. The magic rushes through me, an electrical shock to my body that I'm not prepared for.

My jaw squeezes shut as the muscles twitch in my face and my fingers curl tightly into a ball by my side. I can't let go of the magic, and panic rises in my throat.

"Ciara!"

I hear Aidan shout my name, but his voice is muffled in my ears. My body won't move as the magic holds me, buzzing through every limb. Voices ride the current, but I can't understand what they're saying.

The ground rumbles beneath me and my body rocks with the motion. Strong arms grab me around the waist and lift me to my feet, breaking the connection with the deep river of energy.

It's too late. The earthquake has started.

2

The ground lurches beneath us, sending me stumbling forward, and I trip over my own feet, landing face first on the ground.

Aidan, still gripping my waist, falls hard on top of me, knocking the breath out of my lungs.

"Sorry," he shouts in my ear over the rumbling of the earth.

I close my eyes against the shaking of the ground, swallowing deep to keep from getting sick with the motion.

Small pieces of rock rain down on us from the mountain above, and I throw my hands over my head, praying nothing bigger shakes loose. Aidan pushes me flatter against the ground, protecting me.

"You need to stop this!" His voice is tight and his breath is warm against my ear.

A loud crack rips through the air to my left, but I'm too afraid to see what caused the noise. "I don't know how!"

Aidan grabs both of my wrists, pulling them from the back of my head and placing them firmly against the ground. "Get back to that connection."

I take several deep breaths, pushing back the tears that fill my eyes. A moment later, I can feel the energy of the earth buzzing beneath my palms, racing back and forth, chaotic thanks to the unnatural earthquake.

With my eyes closed, I can see the green sparkles of the earth magic, swirling so fast they blend together. I concentrate on their movement, willing them to slow down, and at first, they fight against me, the earth groaning as it shakes. But piece by piece they split apart, returning to their lazy floating, and the earthquake subsides.

I lie plastered to the ground, panting with the effort of controlling the raw magic. My fingertips tingle with the energy.

"Well, that was exciting." Aidan rolls off me, landing with a soft thump on the grass by my side.

I roll my eyes before lifting my head to look at him. "I'm not sure exciting is the word I would use."

Behind him, an uprooted tree catches my attention, and I groan. "Look what I did."

He props up on his elbow, following my gaze over his shoulder. "I'm glad that didn't fall on us."

I pull myself up to my knees, my legs shaking beneath me as I stare heartbroken at the tree.

"That's it? You're glad it didn't fall on us? I killed that tree. It had to be ancient." My chin trembles, and I squeeze my jaw together to get my emotions under control.

Aidan turns back to me, sympathy in his eyes. "It was an accident, and yes, I'm glad it didn't fall on us. That would have killed us, too."

He has a valid point, but that still doesn't make me feel any better about the situation. Slowly, I climb to my feet, testing my footing on my wobbly legs. Once I'm sure my legs won't betray me, I rush over to the fallen tree, running my palms along the rough bark.

Aidan walks up behind me, laying a hand gently on my shoulder. "I know you feel bad, but there's nothing you can do about it now."

"There's always something." I chew on my bottom lip, staring at the tree, and hope that the crazy idea forming in my head might actually work.

"What are you going to do?" One eyebrow shoots high on Aidan's forehead.

"I'm going to save it. Put it back in the ground." I settle into a seated position next to the tree, my hands still flat against the wood.

Aidan clears his throat, running a hand through his dark hair. "I'm sorry. I don't think that's possible. I've never seen anyone be able to do that. I know you want to help."

I raise my hand, cutting off his argument.

"Just because you haven't seen it doesn't mean it can't be done. Watch and learn," I say, hoping my voice sounds more confident than I feel.

Aidan takes a step back, giving me room to work, but the frown on his face doesn't exactly say go get 'em.

Closing my eyes, I push his doubt and my own out of my mind and focus on the tree. Beneath my hands, I can feel a faint pulse of life filled with fear, but it's getting weaker by the second, and I know that I only have one shot to get this right.

I take a deep breath, pulling in energy from the ground and send it through my hands into the tree. The tree sighs and relaxes a bit, but it's enough to give me hope that I'm on the right track. I pull more energy, my whole body humming, as I continue to pump the tree with life.

With the steady flow of magic keeping it alive, I turn my

focus to the roots, and there's so much pain there that it breaks my heart, nearly making me lose control of the magic. A thin film of sweat covers my face as I concentrate on healing as many of the roots as I can, starting with the most painful.

I can no longer hear any noises in the forest, only the rushing of magic in my ears, like I'm standing next to a waterfall. My hair flutters around my face, but I keep pushing, urging the roots to grow and reach for the hole in the ground.

The roots reach for the dirt, stretching and groaning but eventually digging into the ground and taking hold. Despite the current running through me, my body is getting tired, but I grit my teeth and hang on to the magic. I'm almost there, I know it.

I check on the strength of the grip that the tree has regained in the ground and I'm satisfied that it feels sturdy. One thing left to do. Stand the tree back up. I force a deep breath into my lungs and transfer the energy running through my fingers to the back side of the tree.

I push with everything I have left in me, and I can feel the tree pitching in to help me, and slowly it rises off the ground. A scream rips through me as I give it one final shove, the tree now upright and towering once again.

My eyes open as my body tips over, lying flat on the ground as my chest heaves, gasping for air.

Aidan drops to my side, his hands on my face. "That was the craziest, most incredible thing I've ever seen. Are you all right?"

I blink my eyes to clear my blurring vision.

"I think so. Is it done?" I reach for his hand and he gently helps me into a sitting position.

"We just need to pack the dirt in around the base, and I

think it's going to be fine." Aidan stares at the tree with wide eyes.

I frown as I concentrate on the dirt around the roots, pushing it back into place, and slump against Aidan.

He wraps his arms firmly around my shoulders, and I can feel a tingle in the air. Water rises to the surface around us, collecting around the base of the tree, and his thoughtfulness warms my heart.

I climb slowly to my feet with Aidan's help and stumble over to the tree, placing my hands against the bark. I'm overcome with a feeling of gratitude and happiness that makes me smile. Dropping to the ground, I lean against the tree and I feel it twitch as if it's hugging me.

Aidan sits down beside me, unzipping his jacket and pulling a small bag of chips and a granola bar out of his inner pocket.

"Here, this junk is for you." He smirks, handing me the granola bar.

I snort. "It's not junk."

"It's not chips." He rolls his eyes, pulling open the bag and groaning. "They're all broken."

"They're easier to chew that way." I laugh at his glare. "Why can I only work with earth magic?"

"It's the original rituals the Zodiacs went through. When a piece of their essence was removed, they were assigned an element to rule over. If three of the Zodiacs each ruled over the four elements, then they'd have a balance of power. When people are born to each of the Zodiac houses, they have a natural connection with the element." He stuffs more chips in his mouth.

I fidget with the granola bar in my hands. "How's that different than the other magic? Mierna, Jocelyn, the mages. They aren't confined to the elements."

He shrugs his shoulders and tilts his head back, dumping almost the entire bag into his mouth.

"Their magic is less of a connection and more an ability to conjure magic. They need spells and other things that help create the magic, where you naturally have the ability. Tell me what went wrong with the earthquake." His voice is muffled around a cheek full of chips.

I slowly tear into the granola bar wrapper and take a small bite, chewing carefully as I watch him devour his bag of chips. "I'm not really sure what happened. I was connecting with the earth like you told me, and beneath the first layer of energy, I could feel something deeper, like a river flowing inside the earth. The power was intense, and when I reached into it, it felt like I'd grabbed an electric fence. I couldn't let go."

Aidan stares at me, his mouth hanging slightly open and his hand gripping the chip bag.

"What? Why are you looking at me like that?" I frown at him.

He shakes his head, dumping the last of the chips in his mouth. "You tapped into the primal energy of the earth."

I shift against the tree. "So? What does that mean?"

"It means you're lucky to be alive." There's a shadow of fear in his eyes, and I also can't help but notice the hint of pride. "Most Guardians never experience anything like that, and some have died from it."

I chuckle to cover the icy shiver running down my spine. "That sounds ridiculous. It was just right there below the surface."

"That could have been bad." Aidan slowly shakes his head.

"At least it wasn't bad." I shrug my shoulders and give him a half smile.

Aidan frowns at me. "I'm serious about this. Some of this stuff is really dangerous until we figure out how your powers are going to grow and what exactly you can handle."

I reach out and take his hand in mine, squeezing his fingers as I hold his gaze. "That's why we're out here and you're teaching me to control my magic."

He pulls my hands to his lips, kissing them gently. "I won't lose you. You know I'll do everything I can to keep you safe, but there are some things that I might not be able to protect you from."

My heart skips a beat and a warm blush floods my cheeks.

"I know you'll always keep me safe," I say so softly, I barely hear my own words.

Aidan leans forward, brushing my lips with his, then kissing me deeply. I lose myself in the kiss, my heart pounding wildly against my ribs. He slowly pulls away, holding my gaze, and I get lost in the blue as I struggle to catch my breath.

I sit, frozen in my spot for a long time, staring at his handsome face as my mushy brain works feverishly to decide what to do next.

"We should probably get going. You've been through a lot today." Aidan squeezes my hands and pulls his legs beneath him to stand.

"Wait. What?" My words come out faster and higher pitched than I mean for them to. "I'm not ready to go. There's more I need to learn."

He lowers himself back to the ground and pinches the bridge of his nose. "You can't learn everything in one day. It's a building process. But you've done great."

I fold my arms across my chest.

Aidan sighs. "Fine. We'll work on a little more, but we

keep it simple. You may not realize how much you've put yourself through now, but you will later."

I smile so bright that it stretches my face, and I have to stop myself from bouncing. "Thank you."

Leaning forward, I throw my arms around his neck and kiss him again, losing some of my excitement as my heart leaps.

"Are you sure you want to work on magic?" he asks, his lips still against mine.

I hesitate, lingering in the kiss. "Sorry, but yes."

He groans, pulling away, but the corners of his mouth tilt up as he tries to hide his smile. "Simple magic, okay?"

Another hour passes, growing flowers and grass, and coaxing mud into different shapes, including weapons I can use in a fight. Even though I still have a lot to learn, I feel more in control thanks to Aidan's instruction.

Aidan and I walk silently back to the Jeep, hand in hand, and I wish we could stay out here forever in the peace of the mountains.

I lean back in the passenger seat and close my eyes, thinking about the progress I made today using my magic. My body tingles, and I can still feel the power of the earth running through every part of me. Fatigue is setting in, but I've never felt so alive, and a soft smile slides across my lips.

Aidan glances over at me as he backs the Jeep out of the small clearing. "Are you happy? You have a glow about you I've never seen before."

I roll my head to the side and meet his eyes, my heart full for the first time in a long time.

"Thank you for helping me. I know that I still have a lot

to learn, but I feel good about today. Like I have some control over my magic. It won't be long before no one can say that I'm not using my full potential." The smile slips from my face as Draven's words echo through my head.

Aidan grits his teeth as he hangs on to the steering wheel, the Jeep bumping roughly over the uneven path. He takes his eyes off the road long enough to frown at me. "Don't let them be the reason you're doing this. It's your birthright. It's who you are, down to your very soul. This isn't about war or vengeance. You can do some real good with the earth. Think about that tree you saved earlier. That was incredible, and I've never seen anything like that. Ever."

I sigh, turning my attention back to the forest that slides by my window. "You're right. I know that, and I know my magic isn't just about fighting. But damn it, I hate that they think I'm weak."

Aidan snorts. "Who ever said anything about you being weak? Draven said he thought you had more potential. The way I remember it, he sounded pretty relieved."

"You've really never seen anything like what I did with the tree?" I ask, my voice soft as I dare to hope that I did something special.

He reaches over and gently pats my hand, then quickly reaches back to the wheel as the vehicle lurches out of a deep hole. "Honestly, no. I didn't think anything like that was even possible. Not only did you give the tree enough energy to hang on, but you helped it replant itself. The word miracle comes to mind."

Aidan chuckles as a warm blush spreads quickly over my cheeks.

"I can't wait to tell Capricorn. I wonder if even he can do something like that." His eyes narrow as he stares out the windshield.

My head jerks away from the window as I study his face. "He has to be able to do something like that, right?"

Aidan shrugs, letting out a deep breath as he turns out onto the paved road of Mt. Rose Highway. "It's rare, but sometimes Aids or Guardians develop magic that the Zodiacs can't do."

I chew on my bottom lip, my mind spinning with questions. "Is there anything Capricorn can do with magic that I can't?"

"Definitely, although I can't give you specifics because I have no idea exactly what magic he wields. Always remember that no magic is more powerful than the magic that the Zodiacs can cast." He shoots a quick smile at me and it warms my heart, knowing that he's always happy to teach.

"What about the mages? Is their magic not as strong as the Zodiacs'? So far, they've been able to steal magic from Guardians, capture Pisces, split Leo's stone, and make Aries sick. That sounds really strong to me." I wrinkle my nose, grumpy to even bring them up.

A shadow crosses Aidan's face as he frowns, and I know he's just as frustrated to talk about them as I am. "There isn't a lot we know about the mages and the magic they use. They seem to have an affinity for fire. All the mages we've fought can wield it."

He pauses, and I wait patiently for him to collect his thoughts. "I don't believe their magic is stronger, especially facing all twelve of them and the Aids and Guardians. But they have access to arcane magic that hasn't been seen for centuries, and no one seems to know where they found it. It's also very dark magic."

Dread settles like a rock in the pit of my stomach. We may never know how many of these types of spells they have, and they definitely don't have any problems killing to get what they want. The thought of being subjected to one of those spells like Delia suffered sends a cold shiver down my spine.

I push away the thoughts and decide to switch back to lighter questions. "Is there any magic you have that Scorpio doesn't?"

He turns his head to stare at me with wide eyes, looking at me so long that I have to point to the windshield to remind him he should be watching the road. He shakes his head but turns his attention back to his driving.

"What? That's a fair question. You said sometimes that happens." I try to hide the amusement in my voice, but I know I'm busted. I can't imagine what Scorpio would be like, knowing Aidan had magic that he didn't. The Zodiac isn't intolerable, but he isn't exactly the most pleasant.

Aidan shoots a quick glare in my direction. "As far as I know, I can't work any magic that Scorpio doesn't possess. I work best with water in its liquid form, but Scorpio can work with the element in any form."

I get lost in my memories, thinking back to the day that Scorpio saved Jocelyn and I on the mountain by covering Wesley and Slade in snow and freezing them inside. "You can't work with ice or snow?"

"I can. I'm just not as good." Aidan navigates the Jeep off Mt. Rose Highway and onto 395 north, heading toward my house.

I fidget with my seatbelt as too many questions flood through my mind. "How did you become an Aid?"

He weaves through the traffic, taking a long, slow breath before answering my question. "I'm not sure exactly why I was chosen. The Zodiacs are aware of the people that are born under their sign even if they don't know them individually. They know when someone is born that's special, as in that person has a natural magical ability. When it's time to pass on the duties of the Aid, a boy that's deemed special is brought to Polaris to undergo the ritual and train until it's time to take over."

My heart is heavy with the idea of him being taken from his family. "Do you miss your family? Do you ever get to see them?"

Aidan shakes his head. "The Zodiacs choose their Aids at such a young age that I don't even remember what they're like. Polaris is all I've ever known."

He looks over at me and I quickly try to blink away the tears in my eyes as he smiles. "Don't be sad. Scorpio explained to my family what an honor it is to be chosen. Even though the boys aren't always chosen from the same family, more than one Aid has been chosen from mine, so they understood. Besides, it has some perks."

My face heats as he winks at me, making my heart skip a beat. "Are Aids always male?"

"Yes, just like Guardians are always female."

I frown, shifting in my seat to face Aidan. "But we're all from the same family line. Why? And were we chosen the same way? Was my ancestor, the original Guardian, special somehow?"

Aidan chuckles, holding the wheel with one hand and reaching with his free hand to lace his fingers in mine. "Your ancestor was among the first group of people to populate the Earth."

I suck in a sharp breath, trying to wrap my mind around his simple statement.

"Once there were people here, the Zodiacs decided they would come to Earth and mingle with them, learn about this new race. But there was a risk that they'd stay here or get too power hungry and use their sign to control the humans. The Oracle forced them to go through the ritual to keep them from staying on this planet. She chose the original Guardians and performed their rituals in order to allow them to tap into their magic and have the strength to protect the birthstones that had been created."

"I'd really like to meet the Oracle," I say, my voice soft and filled with awe.

Aidan shakes his head. "No one alive has seen her. She hides somewhere in the mountains of Polaris and only reveals herself if she wants to be seen. Only the Zodiacs and Violet have seen her."

My stomach drops, and I hang my head. "Doesn't she know how much she can help us with the mages?"

He sighs. "She rules over everything but only steps in if she thinks it's necessary. And even then, her messages are more cryptic than Violet's help."

I groan as Aidan turns down my street. "We can't be home already. I have too many questions to ask."

Aidan slips his fingers from mine, using two hands to pull into my driveway. "There's plenty of time to ask questions, and you know I'll always tell you anything I can. I'm sure it's tough learning so much when your life is in danger, but you're very strong."

I smile and open my mouth, but my words die on my lips as I see Jocelyn sitting on my front steps.

Jocelyn's flaming red hair is pulled into a soft ponytail at the base of her neck, and it slips over the shoulder of her blue sweater. Her legs are pulled in tight on the step beneath her, and she rests her chin on her knees as she watches us.

As soon as the Jeep stops, I slip out of my door and cross

the yard with Aidan right behind me. "I didn't know you were coming by. How long have you been here?"

She stands up, slowly descending the steps to stop in front of me.

"I haven't been here very long. Where have you guys been?" She smiles, but it looks forced.

I look closer at my friend and realize she looks pale, with blue circles beneath her eyes that her normally perfect makeup can't even hide. "Are you feeling okay?"

Jocelyn sighs, playing with the hem of her sweater. "I'm fine. I've been working with Mierna to learn how to use some of my magic. It's hard, since I haven't gone through my ritual yet, and it's taking a lot out of me. My powers weren't supposed to be activated until my ritual, but Aries messed that up when he used me. I can't just ignore it because it can build up inside me, so Mierna says she's going to move up my ritual soon."

Her chin quivers slightly, and she clenches her jaw to hide it.

"What happens if they don't move up your ritual?" I squeeze my hands into fists, leaning into Aidan for support. My stomach turns as I watch my friend try to hold herself together.

Jocelyn lets out a shaky breath. "Apparently, the magic can kill me."

"What?" My question comes out higher and louder than I intend, and I quickly shut my mouth, wrinkling my nose.

She snorts. "It's going to be fine. Where did you guys go?"

I feel like I should keep pressing, but the look in her eyes says she's done with this subject for now. "We went up to Mt. Rose. Aidan is teaching me to connect better with my magic, so I'll have more control and fewer accidents."

Jocelyn looks past me to Aidan, one eyebrow raised high on her forehead and amusement dancing in her hazel eyes. "And how'd that go?"

Aidan chuckles but quickly stops with my glare. "Other than the earthquake, it went fine."

Jocelyn rolls her eyes, laughing. "You started another earthquake?"

"It was a small one." I fold my arms across my chest, daring her with my gaze to keep making fun of me. "And it didn't even last very long."

Jocelyn presses her lips together, but she can't keep the smile from her face. "Well, that's good. Anything else?"

I glare at Aidan, wishing he hadn't mentioned the quake, but he just shrugs his shoulders. "That's it. I grew some grass and some flowers and tapped into the primal source of the earth's magic."

"You what?" Jocelyn's eyes grow wide. "The primal what?"

"The primal magic that runs beneath the earth. I guess I'm not ready for it, because that's what caused the earthquake."

"Don't forget about helping the tree replant itself," Aidan says, his chest puffed up with pride.

Jocelyn looks from Aidan to me, her eyes even wider if that's possible. "You helped a tree?"

I feel my cheeks heat and I push past Jocelyn, heading for the stairs. "It fell over in the earthquake. I'll tell you about it inside."

I pause with my hand on the railing and look back at Jocelyn. "Why were you waiting out here? You have a key."

Her eyes flicker to the door before meeting my gaze. "I know, but when I got here, I had some kind of weird feeling, so I decided it was better to wait out here."

My stomach drops and my hands grow cold. "What kind of weird feeling?"

Jocelyn shrugs, now staring at the door. "I'm not sure. I just didn't want to go in there."

Aidan pushes past both of us, taking the stairs two at a time. Without a word, he slips the keys from his jacket pocket and turns toward the door. He pushes the key into the hole, but the door swings open without being unlocked. Aidan slips inside with me and Jocelyn right behind him.

I'm quickly stopped by his arm across my middle as he holds me back. I sway on my feet with Aidan and Jocelyn both grabbing my arms to help me stand as I stare at the disaster that used to be my living room.

3

"Stay here," Aidan whispers so softly, I barely catch his words.

I shake my head, angry tears threatening to spill down my cheeks. "I need to see what happened."

Aidan places his hand gently on my shoulder, meeting my eyes. "Just let me do a quick sweep and make sure whoever did this isn't still in the house. Stay here with Jocelyn, but be ready just in case. Do that for me."

I stand there, staring at him, fighting my need to rush through the house to make sure everything is okay, and wanting to give him this opportunity to protect me. I also want to go along to make sure nothing happens to him either, but after seeing the determination in his eyes, I slowly nod, stepping back closer to Jocelyn.

Jocelyn brushes against my arm as she surveys the damage of my living room. "What are we supposed to do if someone comes down here? You have any weapons?"

I shake my head, my heart skipping a beat at the thought of the turquoise dagger hidden in my room, and I hope that it's still safely tucked away.

My eyes linger over the broken furniture, the stuffing ripped from the couch cushions and the pictures yanked from the walls, lying in a bed of broken glass. The rug lays in a heap where it was carelessly tossed, exposing chunks of shredded carpet. My stomach twists, and I know it had to be the mages looking for the birthstone. I just hope that I hid it good enough.

A sigh escapes my lips as I glance into the dining room, very aware of every tick of the clock as I wait for Aidan to come back. I can see that the chairs have been smashed and the table tipped over onto the floor. I hope they left me something that I can break over their heads the next time I see a mage.

I press my lips tightly together, morbid thoughts spinning through my head. The mages are going to pay. The sound of boots on the stairs breaks through my thoughts and I look up, relieved to see Aidan coming down the stairs. "Is everything okay?"

"I don't know if it's okay, but there isn't anyone else in the house. I can feel a magical residue, so whoever was here used magic, although I'm not sure for what." He glances at Jocelyn as he stops in front of us. "I'm assuming you can feel it and that's why you had a weird feeling from the house."

"Probably," Jocelyn says softly.

I step forward to head up the stairs, but Aidan grabs my wrist, holding me back. "What? You said it's safe. I have to go make sure the birthstone and dagger are safe."

"Ciara." Aidan holds my gaze as his fingers linger on my arm. A frown creases his brow as he struggles with his words.

My heart pounds against my ribs, wondering what could be so bad that he can't just tell me. "Out with it. Like a Band-Aid."

He tilts his head to the side, his frown deepening. "A Band-Aid?"

I snort, wishing my bad joke would actually make me feel better. "You know, quick, so it doesn't hurt as bad."

"I've never heard that." He raises one eyebrow.

I shake my head. "Never mind. What is it? Why don't you want me to go upstairs? Is the birthstone missing?"

I hold my breath, hoping I can handle whatever he's about to tell me.

"I can't feel the birthstone." He grabs my arm again as I head for the stairs.

"You have it hidden good, and I can't ever really feel it. But Ciara, your whole house is trashed. It all looks like this, and some of it, like your bedroom, is worse." The corners of his mouth tilt down as he presses his lips tightly together.

My heart drops and the room tilts a little before I catch my balance. I pull my arm from his grasp and run for the stairs, taking them two at a time, with Aidan and Jocelyn rushing to keep up. I burst through the door, stopping so fast that they bump into me from behind.

The sheets have been torn off the bed, piled onto my favorite cream comforter that someone sliced in half, exposing the deep cut running diagonally across my mattress. The nightstand drawers have been emptied on the floor and dumped beside their contents. The curtains are shredded and my clothes tossed from the closet.

My knees buckle, and Aidan and Jocelyn rush to keep me from hitting the floor. I sag in their arms as my stomach churns and tears spill down my cheeks. "How could they do this?"

"We'll find whoever did it. They won't get away with this." Jocelyn's voice is hard and filled with tears.

I fight the urge to lie down on the floor and cry, pushing

away from them with a deep, shuddering breath. The only important thing is that the birthstone and dagger are safe. On shaky legs, I walk to the closet, breathing a sigh of relief that the shelf in the back hasn't been moved.

I hesitate, glancing over my shoulder and locking eyes with Aidan, and take a deep breath. Turning back to the shelf, I drop to my knees and pull out the bottom drawer, surprised that my clothes are still folded neatly and in place. I slip my hand inside, pushing past the shirts, and feel for the latch at the back of the door, pulling it with a soft click as my fingers touch the cold metal.

The bottom of the shelving unit swings open, including the entire draw, and I shift to the side, giving it room to open all the way. I reach into the back, feeling for the secret door cut into the back of the unit that isn't visible against the wood. My fingers brush against it and I hold my breath as I push it and it pops loose.

Inside, I find the tiny box and pull it out into the light. It's highly polished, with a goat carved into the top and a piece of turquoise in place of the heart.

Jocelyn slips a necklace from the front of her shirt, rubies held together with silver in the shape of the Capricornus constellation. She pulls it over her head and hands it to me.

I flip the box over, using the necklace as the key, and push the lid as it creaks open. My breath whooshes from my chest as I see Capricorn's birthstone lying on a bed of green velvet. Tears blur my vision as I carefully lock the box and place the stone back into its hiding spot, making sure that everything is back in place.

I stand up, handing the necklace back to Jocelyn, who slips it back around her neck. The three of us step out of the closet and I silently move to the nightstand beside my bed. I reach into the space created by the missing drawers and feel for another compartment in the back, grateful that I'd taken the time to modify some of my furniture with hiding spots.

I slide a small panel to the side and reach in, closing my eyes as my fingers wrap around the cool hilt of the dagger. I pull it out, squeezing it tightly in my hand after replacing the panel. "At least they didn't get what they came for. I'm not letting this out of my sight."

I unzip my jacket, ready to put the dagger inside the inner pocket, but freeze at the sound of my front door opening. I adjust my grip on the hilt, heading for the top of the stairs, but Aidan stops me with a hand on my shoulder.

"Come down here, girl." A familiar voice floats through the house.

I pocket the dagger and walk down the stairs, both relieved and nervous that Capricorn is paying me a visit.

The Zodiac waits just inside my front door, tufts of fur barely peeking out around his hands inside the pockets of his pine robes. The ghostly outline of his horns curls around his head as I stare up into his eyes that swirl with green and gold.

I fold my arms across my chest, waiting for him to tell me why he's here. "I'm sorry that I can't offer you anywhere to sit down right now."

Capricorn raises his narrowed eyes above my head, surveying the damage that is my house. "What happened here? Is my birthstone safe?"

"Someone broke in while I wasn't home. Of course, we're assuming it's the mages. The birthstone and the dagger are safe."

I frown at him, moving my hands to my hips. "And we're all fine too, by the way. Thanks for asking."

He looks down at me, the hint of a smile tugging at the corners of his mouth. "I can see that you're all fine."

"You still could've asked," I grumble.

Any trace of the smile disappears from his face as he tugs on his goatee. "I've come with instructions."

I roll my eyes. "Of course you have. Why don't you ever stop by for a cup of coffee and a chat? Doesn't that sound better?"

"You know that we're only supposed to be on Earth one night of the year, and that standing here now, I'm breaking the rules." Capricorn frowns, his silver brows tightly knitted together.

"It was a joke, but never mind." I sigh, wishing I had somewhere I could sit down and brace myself. "What are your instructions?"

Capricorn straightens his shoulders and smoothes the front of his robes. "Tomorrow, you will report to Polaris. We need you to go to into the Beinn Dorcha Mountains and collect a magical fire for us to heal Aries."

"What?" Aidan steps forward, his eyes wide. "She can't go out there. The Zodiacs don't even go out there."

I shake my head, not sure I heard him right. "Where am I going?"

"The mountains. We need your help to get the fire." Capricorn's face softens as he fidgets with the fur around his hands.

"What's so bad about the mountains?" I ask, afraid to hear the answer.

Aidan stares at Capricorn as he answers my question. "The mountains are wild and dangerous. They're steep and covered in snow. They're also home to creatures you've only seen in fairy tales. Or nightmares."

He finally looks at me, his eyes narrowed. "If the mountains don't kill you, the creatures will."

A cold chill races down my spine. "If the Beinn whatever mountains are so dangerous, why doesn't one of you go get this magical fire?"

"Believe me, I would save you from this trip if I could. It won't be safe and it won't be easy. The decision to send you is out of my hands, and the fire can only be handled by those who control the element. Leo and Aries are sick, and Sagittarius cannot go."

I chew on my bottom lip as I frown at the Zodiac. "But you know I don't work with fire."

"That's why Zoe will be going with you." Capricorn holds up his hand as I groan. "As his Guardian, she is best suited to help him."

I swallow back the urge to argue with him, knowing it won't do me any good. "What do I do when I get there?"

"It doesn't matter. You're not going." We all turn raised eyebrows to Aidan as he steps in front of me. "I've promised to protect you."

Capricorn stares at Aidan, his face carefully blank other than his eyes crinkling around the edges. "We are all aware of that promise. That's why you're going with her."

Aidan's shoulders slump, the bravado suddenly missing.

"It's dangerous," he mumbles.

"And you'll keep her safe." Capricorn shakes his head when Aidan opens his mouth again.

"What about me?" Jocelyn speaks up for the first time since we came downstairs.

Capricorn shakes his head. "I'm sorry. You must stay here and prepare for your ritual. It will be sooner than any of us thought."

Jocelyn nods, her eyes on the floor.

"Someday you will come to our realm and you will be an honored guest." Capricorn smiles as she looks up at him, then turns back to me, tucking his hands in his pockets again.

"Bring your dagger and cold-weather provisions. We'll provide you with food and further instructions when you show up tomorrow. You'll have to get to the mountains and back as quickly as possible."

"How am I supposed to do this when I can't survive very long on Polaris? We can't make the journey that fast?" I hold on to a sliver of hope that I won't have to go.

"You have the necklace I gave you for your birthday?" Capricorn asks.

I nod, my hand absently rising to my throat, and my heart skips a beat as I realize it's not there. "I took it off yesterday. Why?"

"Don't come without it." Capricorn's words are blunt. "Why?" I ask.

Capricorn blinks out of sight before answering my question.

I glance at Aidan, my eyebrows raised high, but he shrugs his shoulders with a slight shake of his head. "Why would I need that necklace? It's just jewelry, isn't it?"

Aidan scrunches his face as if tasting something sour. "I have no idea. The Zodiacs never tell me more than they think I need to know." His tone holds a bitter edge.

"I've never felt magic on it when you wear it, but if Capricorn wants you to bring it, then it has to be more than just jewelry."

A deep sigh escapes my lips, and I roll my eyes. "I don't know why it's so hard to answer my questions. I hate it when he ignores me and poofs out of here."

"Maybe he had somewhere important to be," Jocelyn

says, absently straightening a piece of furniture from the corner of the room.

I watch her work for a second, my eyes narrowed. I didn't even see her move. "It's always something important."

It's my turn to sound bitter. My shoulders slump as I let my eyes wander over the chaos in the room. "How do they expect me to pack my stuff and leave for a few days when my house was just robbed?"

Jocelyn picks up a pillow and pushes the stuffing back inside before setting it down on the couch.

"I'll keep an eye on your house, since I can't go." She lets out a huff, bending over for another pillow.

"You don't have to straighten that up, you know. Half this stuff is trash now, anyway. You won't have time to watch the house, since you have to get ready for your ritual. We don't know what that's going to take." I fold my arms across my chest.

"What about Julia?" Aidan asks, also picking up pieces of the wreckage.

"Will you two knock it off?" I frown as Aidan drops the picture frame back onto the floor, breaking the rest of the glass. "I guess I can ask Julia, but I hate to put her in any extra danger."

Jocelyn glares at me from across the room.

"What?" I put my hands on my hips.

She wrinkles her nose. "I said I'd watch the house."

"I know, but what happens if you're not ready for your ritual?" I arch one eyebrow, daring her to argue.

A cool breeze flows through the living room, soft whispers riding the wind as it ruffles my hair. I quickly close my eyes, sinking into the stream as quiet words form in my mind.

"Do not worry about your home, Ciara," Capricorn's

voice echoes softly in my head. "I will send an Aid down to make sure that no one else gets inside."

I take a deep breath, relaxing my shoulders as an image of my dad floats through my mind.

"No, it will not be Donnelly. He has a more important task," Capricorn whispers.

The frown is back on my face.

"What's more important than helping me protect your birthstone?" I form the words carefully in my mind. I'm still getting used to this whisper speak, and it's weird to have a conversation with someone else inside my head.

"You will have answers soon." And with that, the wind dies out, my hair falling limply around my shoulders.

"Yeah, it's always later or sometime soon," I mutter.

"What did they say?" Jocelyn asks, her voice right beside me causing me to jump. She must have moved while I was in my trance.

I open my mouth to answer her, but I'm struck by a thought that makes me grit my teeth.

"Are you eavesdropping on me?" I raise my eyes to the ceiling, shouting at what I imagine to be the Zodiacs.

"How did you know to tell me that?" I wait, tapping my toe. I don't really expect an answer, but it makes me feel better to yell at Capricorn in case he's still listening.

"Tell you what?" Jocelyn raises her eyes to the ceiling, trying to figure out what I'm looking at.

Aidan chuckles. "That was Capricorn telling her he's going to send someone to watch her house."

A growl escapes my throat. "I thought you had rules against that!"

I turn my glare to Aidan. "Don't they have rules against that? How come he can answer that and not tell me about the necklace?"

Aidan holds his hands up in defense. "Don't ask me. The Zodiacs do what they want."

The corners of his eyes crinkle and the sides of his mouth twitch as he fails to hide the smile from his face.

I sigh, knowing he's right, and give up on the losing battle. "I guess we should get ready to go tomorrow. I don't even know what to pack."

Aidan steps forward, taking my hands in his, and gently squeezes my fingers. "I have to go back to Polaris to get ready."

He shakes his head when I open my mouth to protest. "I'll be back later tonight after I pack. The journey will be hard, so pack as much as you can but make it as light as you can."

I roll my eyes. "That's helpful."

"I wasn't finished." Aidan matches my eye roll. "The mountains will be freezing. They have snow on them all year. Wear hiking boots and bring layers and a blanket or something to sleep in. A change of clothes in case you get wet, but make sure you keep everything as minimal as possible."

I chew on my bottom lip, running his list over in my mind to commit it to memory. "What about food and water?"

Aidan shakes his head. "Don't worry about that. Capricorn will have the servants make us food to take with us."

"Servants? Never mind." I search my brain to see if I'm missing anything. "Is that it then?"

"Oh, and make sure you bring weapons if you have them. Bring your turquoise dagger, but don't use it if you don't have to. Some creatures there will be happy to kill you for it, even if it isn't the true dagger that belongs to Capricorn."

"Weapons?" My voice squeaks out a little higher than I mean for it to sound. "I thought we were just going to collect that fire?"

Aidan presses his lips into a thin line, studying my face and taking a deep breath before answering me. "There are things in those woods, creatures that humans can't even imagine in their craziest dreams. All of them can be dangerous, and some of them are deadly. You can use your magic as a weapon, but remember that almost all the creatures there have some kind of magic of their own."

"That's cheerful. Thanks." I sigh.

Aidan slips his hands away, sliding them over my shoulders and pulling me so close, I can feel the heat from his body. "I'll be there to keep you safe."

"I know," I mumble into his chest.

"I'll be back as quick as I can." He presses his lips to the top of my head and slips out the door as it shuts behind him with a soft click.

Feeling suddenly empty, I turn to Jocelyn. "Will you help me pack?"

"You are pretty terrible at it." She winks, the first hint of a smile on her face since she got here.

I snort. "Gee, everybody is just so comforting."

Jocelyn giggles, brushing past me and heading up the stairs.

I follow her into the room, immediately collapsing on the ruins of the bed.

"That's a great start to your packing," Jocelyn says, her voice thick with sarcasm.

"I know." I cover my face with my hands to muffle my

groan, and sit up as she tosses an empty backpack at my feet. "I'm nervous about going to Polaris."

"Why?" Hangers scrape across the bar in the closet as Jocelyn sifts through my clothes.

"My trips to Polaris haven't exactly gone well." I pick up the backpack and unzip it before dumping it on the bed next to me. "And you heard what Aidan said about the mountains and the creatures."

"At least you get to go." Jocelyn reappears, dumping a handful of clothes in my lap, pointing at the backpack before returning to the closet.

I wad up the clothes and shove them into the bag without even looking at them. "I wish you were going and not Zoe."

Jocelyn brings out a couple pairs of wool socks, a scarf, and hat. "What's your problem with her?"

I hold open the bag and she frowns at me, but I wait patiently until she drops the stuff in the backpack. "I don't have a problem with her. She has a problem with me. I just don't think she likes me. You heard her that night at the gathering."

Jocelyn stares at me for a second then heads into the bathroom, returning with a small first aid kit, and drops it in my lap. "You're right. She wasn't very friendly. Good luck with that."

I snort. "Thanks. That's very helpful."

She waits with her hands on her hips until I put the kit inside the backpack. "What else are we missing?"

I frown, chewing on my bottom lip as I think. "Other than weapons, I think that's it."

I pat my jacket, feeling the weight of the dagger inside my pocket, and smile. "I already have the dagger."

Jocelyn shakes her head slightly, her fiery red hair

swinging with the movement. "It doesn't sound like that dagger is going to be enough."

My mouth hangs open as I stare at her. "You don't think that will be enough? Even with my magic?"

Jocelyn scrunches her face as her hazel eyes sweep around the room, searching for anything that remotely resembles a weapon. "You heard what Aidan said about everything having magic. Why don't you have anything around here that you can fight with?"

I roll my eyes. "That's because I wasn't fighting anything until a couple of months ago. I'm sorry I haven't had time to go shopping for swords."

She glares at me and I duck my head to hide my snicker. "Maybe there's something in your kitchen that you can take." She taps her foot absently.

"I'm not taking a kitchen knife with me." I fold my arms across my chest. "The dagger will have to do, and I'll get something when I get back."

Jocelyn crosses the bedroom, kicking my broken things out of her way, and pulls the heavy stick from the window, testing the weight in her hand. "Or maybe Capricorn will have another little present for you when you get there."

"Maybe." I join her by the window, pulling the stick from her hand and putting it back in the window.

"I'm not taking that with me." I shake my head at her frown.

Sighing, she walks back over to my bed and plops down on the edge. "Do you ever think that I'll be able to go to Polaris with you? I got to go to the mage realm. What's the difference?"

I lean against the wall, my heart sinking at the sadness in her voice. "You'll get to go and you're going to love it. There are lots of cool things."

Jocelyn shakes her head, a soft smile crossing her lips. "Don't ruin it. I want to see that for myself. I don't need your terrible descriptions messing it up for me."

I glare at her but let her comment slide. There's no use in arguing if she's right.

She sighs as she stands, pausing by the door, the smile gone from her face. "I guess we head downstairs and kill some time until Aidan gets back."

She stretches her hands high over her head. "I could use a cup of coffee."

"That sounds good." I push away from the wall, freezing as a thought hits me. "I almost forgot to get the necklace."

"Yeah, don't forget your necklace."

Rolling my eyes, I cross to the dresser, grateful that all the drawers are still in place. I pull open the top left drawer and my heart skips a beat. I shove everything around, spilling some of the contents on the floor as a cold chill races down my spine.

I turn to Jocelyn, my mouth almost too dry to speak. "The necklace is gone."

4

Jocelyn stares at me with wide eyes, her mouth hanging slightly open. "What do you mean it's gone?"

I lay my arm on the top of the dresser, leaning over until my forehead rests against my hand, and take deep, slow breaths, wishing that the room would stop spinning. "I mean it's not here in the drawer. I mean it's gone. Missing."

"I know what gone means." I grimace at the frustration in her voice, and I don't have to lift my head to know that an eye roll went with the statement. "Are you sure that's where you left it?"

I groan into my hand before standing up straight and shuffling through the drawer again. "I'm positive. We have to tear this place apart and find it."

Jocelyn glances around the carnage already littered across my floor. "Even more?"

"Jocelyn!" My voice comes out high and dangerously close to a shout.

She snickers, quickly slapping a hand over her mouth to stifle the grin. "Sorry," she mumbles.

It's my turn to roll my eyes. "I'm serious. It has to be here somewhere, and you heard Capricorn, I can't go without it."

Jocelyn nudges some clothes across the floor with the toe of her brown leather boot. "I'm sure it's still here somewhere."

I drop to my knees, close to tears, shoving the bedding out of the way to search the floor, my breathing close to a pant as I search under the bed. After finding it bare, I sit back on my heels and glare at Jocelyn. "Are you going to help me or not?"

"I'm helping." Jocelyn quickly moves over near the closet to dig through another pile of clothes. "Maybe you should just take a minute and think about where you might have left it. It's possible you didn't put it back there, right?"

I press my head back to the floor, looking under the bed again even though I know there's nothing there, but hoping that I missed something the first time.

"The few times I've taken it off, I've always put it in the same place. Why would someone want to take that necklace?" I crawl across the floor, shoving things out of my way.

"It has Capricorn magic."

Her statement is so matter-of-fact that I bang my head on the dresser, trying to look beneath it. I sit back, rubbing my forehead, and stare at her with a frown. "Do you think it's magic they can use?"

Jocelyn shrugs her shoulders. "It could be. Didn't you ever ask or notice anything about it?"

I chew on my bottom lip, sifting through my memory of the times I've worn that necklace. "I've never noticed anything specific about the necklace, but maybe you're right. It wouldn't be the first time Capricorn has forgotten to tell me something." I don't mean to sound bitter, but it just slips out.

Jocelyn chuckles as she sits on the edge of my bed. "You know I'm right."

I glare at her, crawling across the room and into the closet. "If you're such a genius, why aren't you helping me look for the necklace?"

She stands, slowly crossing the room, and disappears into the bathroom. "All I'm saying is why would Capricorn demand that you bring it with you if it doesn't have some of his magic? Do you think it'll let you do the poof thing?"

"Seriously!" This time I actually shout at her. Finding nothing on the floor, I stand and let out a frustrated growl.

"Sorry." Her voice echoes through the wall.

"Where is the damn thing?" I yank an armful of clothes that managed to stay untouched during the break-in, and rip them from their hangers, tossing them out of the closet.

Jocelyn squeaks as the pile hits her square in the face. She kicks the shirt at her feet back at me. "That's helpful."

I brush past her, ignoring her comment, and head for the door.

"Where are you going?" Jocelyn asks, her hands on her hips.

I pause at the door, swallowing down my impatience. "We have to keep looking. Maybe whoever tried to take it dropped it downstairs. We have to search the whole house."

Jocelyn sighs. "I think you were right the first time. I think it's gone."

Her words freeze my feet, and a sick feeling swirls in my stomach.

"We have to figure out where the necklace is. Capricorn's magic or not, I won't let the mages keep it." Before she can answer, I head out of the room, taking the stairs as fast as I can without falling.

Her boots pound on the stairs behind me. "Wait a minute. Where are you going so fast?"

I reach the door, pausing only when she grabs my arm. "What? I have to get that necklace back. I won't let them use their dark magic on it and let's not forget that I need it. Tomorrow."

"We'll get it. Just wait a minute." Jocelyn chuckles, raising her hand as I open my mouth to argue with her. "This is funny. Normally, you're the common sense stopping me from rushing out the door."

I narrow my eyes at her, and she quickly sobers. "We're wasting time standing here talking about this."

Jocelyn raises her eyebrows, folding her arms across her chest. "Fine. At least tell me where we're going to go."

My mind races with possibilities, my lips pursed as I think and turning into a scowl as I fail to come up with any answers.

Jocelyn continues to watch me, refusing to back down. "Well?"

I throw my hands up, letting them slap against my legs. "I'm thinking."

"I thought you already knew the way you were headed out that door." The corner of her mouth tilts up in that "gotcha" look.

My nose wrinkles. I brush by her and plop down on the couch, narrowly avoiding being stabbed by a spring poking out of the cushion. I drop my head into my hands and swallow back the tears that threaten to fill my eyes.

"I have to find that necklace. How can I tell Capricorn that I lost it?" I take a shaky breath, clenching my teeth to keep my chin from trembling.

Jocelyn walks over beside me, her lips pressed tightly together. She eyes the loose spring before deciding to sit on the end of the couch. "We'll find it. I just think we need to figure out where we need to go before we head out of here, ready to shred some mages." She chuckles to herself as I watch her, one eyebrow raised high on my forehead.

"I'm so sick of those mages. Why won't they go away and leave me alone?" I groan, dropping my head into my hands.

"Where's the fun in that? At least you hid the dagger and the birthstone good enough that they couldn't find them."

I peek at her through the space between my fingers. "Why won't you just go away and leave me alone?"

She winks at me, a slow smile spreading across her face until the corners of her eyes crinkle. "Because you need me. Without me, you'd be out wandering around the city, searching for your necklace and probably falling on your face, tripping over some pothole in the street."

Jocelyn keeps talking, but I don't hear any more of her words. My mind races as I feel the first swell of hope since I came home to a trashed house. "Jocelyn, hush."

She pauses mid-sentence, frowning at me. "I'm just teasing. You don't have to be rude."

I sit up straight, staring at her as I work the last pieces of what I hope is a brilliant idea through my mind. "I said stop talking."

Jocelyn scoots to the edge of her seat, her back straight as she tilts her head. "Do you hear something? Is someone here?" she hisses.

"What?" I stop to listen, then shake my head. "I know where the mages took my necklace." I can't help the smile that covers my face.

She frowns at me. "How do you know that? Did one of

the Zodiacs do that whisper talk? I didn't see your hair move."

I roll my eyes. "Nobody whispered anything. You gave me an idea."

"I did? How'd I do that?" She wrinkles her nose, twisting her lips back and forth.

"Because you won't stop talking." I snicker, my excitement causing me to bounce in my seat. "You said I might be out there and trip on a pothole."

Jocelyn raises her eyebrows with that look she's given me all our lives that says she thinks I'm crazy. "So? You're always falling on your face. How's that an idea?"

I give her my best glare, but it doesn't last long. "When you said pothole, it made me think of a hole in the street."

"That's what potholes are," Jocelyn says as she rolls her eyes.

"I said stop talking. Let me finish." I sigh as Jocelyn leans back on the couch, motioning with her manicured hand for me to continue.

"A hole in the street made me think of the tunnels. We know the mages were using them, and they're probably still using them. There's an entrance just a couple of blocks from here."

Jocelyn sits up straight, her eyes narrowed. "You really think it's down there?"

"It has to be. We just have to get there before they move it to some new place." I jump up, heading straight for the door.

Jocelyn jumps up behind me. "Wait a minute."

I stop, tilting my head up and staring at the ceiling as I take a deep breath and swallow down my irritation. "Now what? I think we need to hurry."

"I know." She takes a step forward but hesitates, clasping

her hands tightly in front of her. "Don't you think they have new spells down there? There was a magical alarm the first time, and they know we know where at least two entrances are located."

I turn my eyes toward her and study my friend. She's right, even if I don't want to let myself think about what might be waiting for us in the tunnels. "And what if them stealing my necklace is the bait for a trap?"

Her eyes widen as the color drains from her face. "I didn't even think about that," Jocelyn squeaks.

I take a deep breath and hold it as I weigh the possibilities. It could be a trap. Or maybe the mage that wrecked my house ran to the safety of the tunnels. Maybe he isn't there anymore or I'm wrong and he never went at all. I let my air out slowly, knowing that it's still our best option. "We have to try."

Jocelyn nods, but she doesn't look convinced. "Should we call for backup? Wait for Aidan?"

"No time." When Jocelyn sighs, I turn for the door, yanking it open as I rush out. I jump, letting out a squeal as I step back, bumping into Jocelyn.

"Ow." Jocelyn pushes me forward.

I grab the door to steady myself as I look into Aidan's smiling face. He takes a good look at us and quickly sobers. "Where are you going? Did something happen?"

"Whoever broke into my house took the necklace that Capricorn gave me. I think they went to the tunnels, and that's where we're going." Aidan studies my face but I hold his gaze, daring him to talk me out of it.

Aidan shakes his head, leaning around me to toss his backpack to the floor just inside the house.

I shake my head at the sound of chip bags squeaking inside the pack.

"We better go and make it quick. We have a long journey over the next few days, and you need to rest." Aidan turns around, leading the way down the steps.

I take a deep breath and follow him, hoping that I'm right about the necklace and wrong about the trap. The last thing we need is to get caught. Or killed.

With that cheery thought running through my mind, I watch Jocelyn lock the door and we head for the tunnels.

We stand over the metal cover in the street, forming a semicircle as the three of us silently stare at it. My heart thumps in my chest, each beat feeling closer to breaking through my ribs as I rub my cold fingers against the hips of my jeans, desperately trying to restore the feeling in my hands.

I question myself for the millionth time since we left my house and walked the short blocks to this tunnel entrance. What if it is a trap?

Aidan sighs a heavy breath, sounding tired. "We should get this over with. You need to get some rest for the journey after we have dinner."

He glances up at me with a sparkle in his eye that makes me laugh despite our situation.

"You and your food." Even though he shrugs his shoulders at me, that bit of normal conversation helps to calm my nerves. I take a deep breath, squatting next to the metal cover.

"Are you sure this is a good idea? I mean, it's probably a trap or something." Jocelyn's legs fidget beside me, her tennis shoes shuffling on the pavement.

I glance up at her face, her eyes mirroring all the

questions and feelings that run through me. "I have to find that necklace. For whatever reason, it's important. If you have any better ideas, I'm listening. Otherwise, we need to get down there before that mage gets away."

"He's probably already gone," Aidan says absently.

I glare at him, but he doesn't seem to notice, so I turn my attention back to Jocelyn. "You don't have to go. You can stand here and keep watch."

Jocelyn rolls her eyes at me. "You know I'm going down there with you. I just don't think it's a good idea, that's all."

"It's not anything close to a good idea, but right now it's the only thing we have." I frown at the metal cover beside my feet.

"How are we going to lift that? Nobody brought any tools, right?" Jocelyn asks.

"Ciara," Aidan says abruptly, scanning the street with narrowed eyes.

"Me? I can't lift that, and no, I didn't bring any tools." I stare at him from my crouched position, cursing myself for rushing out without thinking this through a little better.

Aidan glances down at me. "Use that fancy magic you've been practicing."

He whips his head up, searching the shadows of the growing darkness. "You should hurry. I think we're still alone, but I don't like standing out here in the open like this."

My heart skips a beat, and I swallow hard to keep the butterflies in my stomach. I quickly glance up and down the street then close my eyes, forcing myself to focus on my magic. My breathing slows and I feel the essence of the nearby trees and grass reaching toward me, weakened by the effects of the city but still there.

The earth magic hums through my body and the nerves

are replaced by an energy so deep and ancient that it fills my heart. I lean forward without opening my eyes and place my palms flat on the metal cover. There's nothing but silence.

Frowning, I push my magic deeper into the metal, searching for some essence of the natural metal left. I'm about to give up when my hands begin to tingle, and I can't stop the smile that slips across my face.

My happiness doesn't last long as the essence of the metal seeps deep into me, filling my heart with overwhelming sadness and loneliness at being ripped from its home in the earth and molded into something new, then left alone on the street.

A single tear slips down the side of my face, and I know that I'll never look at commonplace items the same way again. My mind slips back to the lock, and without thinking, I promise to save the cover too, if it can just help me lift itself out of the street.

'When we come out of the tunnel, I'll need to put you back for a while. If you can help us give the mages trouble, that would be awesome, and I promise I will come back for you,' I whisper in my mind, somehow knowing that it understands me.

I feel a moment of hesitation through my fingers before I feel the essence of the metal shifting to one side. I slip my fingers into the holes on the empty side and lift the cover so much lighter than it should've been. I roll it to the side, giving us enough room to get through the opening.

Jocelyn watches me with one eyebrow arched high on her forehead. "Are you going to be able to put that back?"

I shrug. "I'm sure it'll be fine." I glance at Aidan and my heart swells at the pride in his eyes.

"Here we go." With a quick smile, Aidan slips into the hole and down the ladder.

Jocelyn sighs and follows him into the damp tunnels.

With one more glance around the street, I scoot in behind them, sliding the cover into place and hoping that no one was watching out of a window.

I would have been perfectly happy to never set foot in these tunnels again, and my body shivers as I splash down from the ladder, my shoes instantly soaked by the inch-deep water covering the floor. I pull my jacket tighter around my body as my eyes wander through the tunnel.

Bricks lay scattered around the floor, the broken evidence of our magical battle with Draven a few weeks ago. Not that I expected anyone to clean it up, but seeing the tunnel the way we left it makes me both hopeful and afraid that the mages aren't using this underground system anymore.

Aidan leads the way deeper underground, sending bricks clattering to the sides with his boots.

"Do you think you should be making that much noise?" Jocelyn asks, her words barely above a whisper but still echoing off the walls.

Without looking over his shoulder, he shrugs, kicking another brick. "Do you want to trip over this if we have to run out of here?"

Jocelyn looks at me with wide eyes, and it's my turn to shrug. "Fine," she grumbles.

I snicker but quickly sober, knowing that I need to be on high alert for any noises.

We weave deeper into the tunnels, with the light growing dimmer the farther we walk. I repeat our steps in my mind with every new direction we turn, hoping that I can remember the way out of here.

We're long past the damage of the fight, and the only sounds I hear are the soft squishing of our footsteps, water dripping from the ceiling, and the occasional scratching of feet that I can only assume are rats.

"We're lost down here, aren't we? I'm lost. Are you lost?" Jocelyn groans over her shoulder at me.

I shake my head. "I don't think we're lost."

"Think? That's super comforting." Jocelyn kicks at some trash, squealing as a rat dashes out of the pile. "Holy shit. Did you see that?"

I do my best to keep from laughing at the look on her face. "I saw that. You scared that rat to death, poor thing."

"Scared the rat?" Jocelyn scowls at me.

"Ciara."

I look up at the sound of Aidan's voice, surprised to find that I can't see him. "Are you okay? Where are you?"

"Around the corner to the left. You should see this."

My heart sinks at the sound of his tone, and I force my feet forward. I turn the corner, holding my breath, afraid to know what he's found.

Aidan looks up at me, his lips pressed firmly together. Draped over his arm is my emerald sweater, my favorite because it's the same color as my eyes.

My face flushes as the heat of anger fills my cheeks. "Why would they steal my clothes? That's really weird, right?"

Aidan opens his mouth then closes it, fidgeting with one of the sleeves. "Not really."

He scrunches his face as I stare at him with my mouth hanging open. "They're probably trying to see if they can get some of your magic from it."

"They can do that?" Jocelyn's high-pitched question echoes through the tunnel before I can get the same words out of my mouth.

Aidan nods slowly. "It's not much, but every time you

work magic, you leave a type of residue around you. I'm not sure what they'd be able to do with it."

"Is there any way to get rid of it?" My chest tightens at the thought of leaving a magical trail.

He shakes his head slowly. "There's no way to stop it, but it fades away. You wear this a lot, and they must be watching you to know that."

A cold chill runs down my spine, and I clench my jaw to keep my teeth from chattering. The more I learn about the mages, the more I hate them. My skin crawls at the thought of them watching me all the time, especially when I don't know about it. The muscles in my face twitch, and I force myself to take deep breaths.

Aidan reaches over and lays a gentle hand on my shoulder. I fight the urge to shake him off and concentrate on the warmth in his touch.

"Ciara." Jocelyn says my name so softly, I almost don't hear her.

I search around and find her standing by a tunnel leading off this section. She squeezes something small and green in her fist and I rush over to her, my heart pounding in my chest. I hold out my hand and she drops the tiny jewelry box into my outstretched palm. With shaking fingers, I flip it around and pry open the lid. My stomach twists, sick at the sight of the empty bed of green velvet.

"That's the box that you keep your necklace in, right?" Jocelyn searches the ground around her feet.

I squeeze the box tightly in my fist before shoving it into my pocket.

"Yeah, that's the box. You don't see it anywhere, do you?" I know the answer to my question before I even finish asking it.

Jocelyn shakes her head, making her fiery hair bounce.

I glance over my shoulder to find that Aidan has disappeared around another corner. Jocelyn and I jog to catch up before we get split up in the maze.

"At least you know you were right about the mages stealing your necklace," Jocelyn says, panting as she slows down beside me.

"You're not helping." I chew on my bottom lip as we follow behind Aidan, scanning the floor for anything that looks like my stolen necklace.

We twist through the tunnels, as the silence weighs heavier on my shoulders with each step. It feels like we've been down here for hours. Who was it that broke into my house? Was it Draven? The thought of him being inside my house sends goosebumps racing up my arms. What do they want with my necklace? Do they know it's important to Capricorn?

Aidan stops, jarring me out of my thoughts. His body is so still, he could be mistaken for a statue.

Jocelyn and I freeze as I strain to listen for any noise in the tunnel. My heart races, but I'm afraid to ask questions. After a long pause, Aidan slowly turns around.

"It looks like we need to go back. The tunnel ends up here. I think we should just go home. I'm sorry the mages have your necklace." His voice trails off to a whisper.

I blink back the tears filling my eyes and put my hand in my pocket, gripping the small box. "We can't go back. It has to be here somewhere."

"I think he's right," Jocelyn says softly.

I hang my head, not sure that I'm ready to accept that my necklace is gone. "Capricorn is going to be pissed."

5

I peel my eyes open slowly and immediately slam them shut against the early morning sun that streams through the curtains in my bedroom window. Groaning, I roll over and bury my face in the pillow.

"Come on, Ciara, it's time to get up and head to the Polaris." Aidan's voice is soft and coming from somewhere near the door.

I twist my head around and peek at him with one eye. "I don't think I want to go."

The corner of his mouth tilts up on one side in a half-smile. "I don't think you have a choice. It won't be so bad. I get to show you more of my home."

He sounds genuinely excited about the last bit. I sigh, pushing myself into a sitting position.

"I think that part will be nice." I force a smile to my face and I hope it looks more convincing than it feels.

Aidan rolls his eyes. "What is it, really? Are you afraid of the creatures we might see?"

"It's more like I don't want to tell Capricorn I lost the necklace he gave me." I hang my head, my hair slipping from my shoulders to hide my face, while all kinds of crazy scenarios of his reaction zip through my mind.

"He should understand. It was stolen from you." Aidan folds his arms across his chest as he leans against the doorway.

"Should understand?" Another groan escapes my lips as I flop backwards to lie back down on the bed and cover my face with my hands.

"I'm not going. I should've never taken it off. I can't tell him it's gone." I blink back tears while my face is still hidden beneath my palms.

The bed moves gently as Aidan sits beside me, prying my hands away as he leans over to softly kiss my lips. "It's going to be fine. Get dressed. We have to go soon."

I hold my hand up and he pulls me to my feet as I glance out the window at Mt. Rose. Her peaks are still covered with several inches of snow, even though spring is blooming here in the city. Something looks off with the mountain. It's shadowed instead of shining in the morning light. My stomach tightens, and I sway on my feet.

Aidan reaches out a firm hand and steadies me, holding me close to his chest. "Are you okay? What just happened?"

I frown at the mountain for a moment longer and shake my head to clear it. "I don't know. Something feels weird when I look at Mt. Rose. Does it look dark to you?"

Aidan rests his chin on the top of my head as he looks out the window with me. "Dark how?"

"Never mind. It's probably just a trick of the light or something." I push away from him but he hangs on to my arms, studying my face with knitted brows over his blue eyes.

"Whatever you think it is, tell me," he says, gently rubbing my arms.

I pull away and walk toward the closet. "I'm sure it's nothing. I'll be down in a few minutes."

"I'll go start the coffee." Aidan hesitates, then disappears out the doorway.

I stand in the closet, staring absently at the clothes hanging in front of me. How do you dress for a place you've never been? I'm supposed to pack light and be prepared, and that seems impossible. I run my hand along the hangers, wondering if the mages took anything else.

"Ciara." Aidan's voice floats up through the floor.

"I'm coming," I shout back. Sighing, I pull on a pair of jeans and hiking boots, layering the top from a tank top all the way to a sweatshirt. I quickly throw my hair into a ponytail and jog down the stairs.

He frowns at me as I step into the kitchen. "Your breakfast is getting cold."

On the table sits a plate full of eggs, toast, and the little hash brown patties I love so much. Next to it is a travel coffee mug. My heart beats a little faster at his thoughtfulness, but I can't help myself. "Sorry, Mom."

Aidan glares at me and I snicker, sitting down in my chair. "You can make your own breakfast next time." His voice sounds stern, but he can't hide the smile that tugs at his lips.

I hold my hands up in defense. "That's okay. I'm sorry."

I shove in a mouthful of eggs as he sits down across from me with a bag of sour cream and onion chips.

"Is that all you're eating?" My question is muffled around my cheeks full of breakfast.

"No." He pops a few chips in his mouth and chews, sighing. "I had some donuts earlier that I found in the pantry."

"Donuts and chips. That's what you're having for

breakfast?" I stare at him, my hash brown hovering halfway between my plate and my mouth.

Aidan shrugs, stuffing more chips in his mouth. "What's wrong with that?"

"Don't you need something a little more sturdy than just junk food?" I take a sip of coffee and dive back into my food.

He stares at me with a look that says I might as well have told him he could never have another chip again, but after a moment he rolls up the bag and heads to the stove.

He sits back down with eggs and a piece of toast on his plate, and pushes the food around with his fork without eating it.

I snort. "It's not like you have a plate full of vegetables. You'll be fine, I promise."

Reluctantly, he takes a bite, but he still doesn't look happy.

We finish breakfast sitting in comfortable silence, with only the clanking of the silverware on the plates to fill the space. When we're done, I quickly wash the plates and stick them in the dishwasher.

"Are you ready?" Aidan asks from the doorway, his backpack already slung over his shoulders.

"No. Yeah, I guess." I fidget with the sleeve of my sweatshirt. "No."

Aidan smiles softly, holding out his arms for me, and I walk into his embrace. "I can't wait for you to see Polaris. I think you might really like it there."

"Except that every time I've been there, that realm has tried to kill me." My words sound a little more bitter than I mean for them to, and I grit my teeth as he flinches.

"I'm sorry. I'm just nervous. I'm excited to see more of Polaris, and I'm glad you're going to be the one to show it to me. I wish it could be just the two of us." The bitter tone is back.

"We need Zoe, or Capricorn wouldn't insist that she come with us. Come on." He squeezes me, then guides me toward the front door.

I search my mind to see if I can come up with any excuses to drag my feet a little longer, but sadly I come up empty. I make sure that the turquoise dagger is zipped into the inner pocket of my jacket and throw it over my arm. Grabbing my backpack, we head out the door, and I jump at the sight of a man standing in my front yard.

He waits, still as a statue, with his pale hands clasped lightly in front of him, stretching the arms of his brown corduroy jacket. His copper hair hangs in ringlets, gently brushing his shoulders as he watches me with chocolate eyes.

I glance from the man to Aidan, who doesn't seem alarmed, but I take a step back, putting more distance between us. "Who are you?"

The man dips his head in a nod. "I am Doran."

"Okay, Doran, what are you doing here?" I fold my arms across my chest as Aidan looks at me with eyebrows raised, but I don't care. I'm not taking any chances.

Doran chuckles, glancing at Aidan. "She's every bit what they say about her."

I sputter. "They? Who? What are people saying about me?"

"Relax." Aidan reaches out, grabbing my elbow and pulling me closer to him. "Doran is the Aid of Sagittarius."

I narrow my eyes and look him over. "That doesn't tell me what he's doing here."

Doran smiles, wide and toothy. "Capricorn has sent me

watch over your home while you're gone. I hope you're okay with that."

"She's fine with it, thank you." Aidan smiles, squeezing my arm.

I frown at him, but I breathe a sigh of relief. "Thank you. Make yourself at home."

Doran nods, brushing past us on his way into the house, closing the door softly behind him.

I lean in close to Aidan. "I can trust him, right?"

"Capricorn and Sagittarius have always been close. Besides, Capricorn wouldn't have sent him here if he didn't think it was a good idea." Aidan slips his arm around my shoulder, guiding me toward the Jeep.

"I think I remember Julia saying that too, when she helped us escape." I get inside and Aidan closes the door, hurrying around to climb into the driver's seat. "Why are some Zodiacs closer than others?"

Aidan shrugs as he starts the ignition and backs out of the driveway. "It's like any family, I suppose. You like some better than others. Some relationships have changed over the thousands of years and some haven't."

We drive along the side streets, eventually making our way onto the highway as I try to wrap my mind around living for thousands of years. It's probably a good thing they're immortal, or they might've killed each other by now. If they had, would we all have personalities, or would we be more like robots?

"What are you thinking about so hard over there?" Aidan glances over at me, chuckling.

His question startles me out of my thoughts. "What it would be like to live that long?"

"It would be harder than you think," he whispers.

I watch the buildings slide by my window, deciding how to ask my next question.

"Since you have part of Scorpio's essence, are you immortal too?" I hold my breath, not sure I really want to know the answer.

Aidan reaches over and squeezes my hand. "No. The Aids live a normal human lifetime. Going through the ritual ties me to the Zodiac and allows me to live on Polaris full time."

I let my breath out slowly, my eyes wandering from the buildings to Mt. Rose. Cold spreads through my body, and I shift in my seat. I've always found comfort in looking at the mountain, and the uneasiness I feel now shakes me to the core. I blink my eyes as I swear a shadow shifts across the peak.

"Did you see that?" I sit up a little straighter.

"I'm watching the traffic. See what?" Aidan shoots a quick frown in my direction.

"There was a shadow." I chew on my bottom lip, waiting to see if anything else moves.

Aidan glances up at Mt. Rose as he guides the Jeep toward the mountain highway. "What kind of shadow?"

"I don't know. I saw something like that earlier when I was looking out my bedroom window. I have a bad feeling that something is happening up there that shouldn't be." I press my face against the cool glass, twisting to get a better look.

"We'll have to check it out when we get back from Polaris. There isn't any time right now." Aidan grips the wheel as he pulls off the highway.

I lean back in my seat, watching the trees thicken as we drive deeper into the forest, bouncing over the muddy road. Even though I can't see what's happening, I can feel it in my bones. I can feel it from the earth, and I'm not sure I want to know what it is.

Aidan stops at the end of the road and shuts off the engine. "Here we go."

I give him what I hope is a bright smile and slide out of the vehicle.

I search through the trees, not really knowing what I'm looking for, but the shadow I saw on this mountain has me feeling uneasy. The morning sunlight breaks through the thick canopy, leaving the forest floor cloaked in spotted shade. Patches of snow still cling to the ground, but they aren't deep on this part of the mountain. The air is fresh and cold, making me shiver, but I don't think it's entirely because of the temperature.

I grab my jacket and backpack, slipping them on before locking the Jeep. Stepping around the front, I lean against the hood, still trying to put my finger on whatever is bothering me.

"You okay?" Aidan stops beside me, shrugging into his pack.

What is it that's bothering me? Something is missing. I chew on my bottom lip, trying to decide how to answer him. "I'm okay, but something feels off. Don't you feel it?"

He stands perfectly still, closing his eyes.

"You're right, but I can't tell what it is either." He opens his eyes, frowning at the trees.

"It's too quiet out here. I don't hear any birds or animals or even any wind." I hold my breath, straining to hear any sound at all, but it's completely silent. Aidan takes a step closer to me and I can feel the heat from him.

"I don't hear anything either," he says so softly, I almost can't hear him.

I suck in a sharp breath as I'm suddenly struck by the

real reason I think I feel uneasy. "I can't feel the energy of the earth."

Aidan looks sharply at me, his eyes wide. "You can't feel anything at all?"

I shake my head, my heart hammering against my ribs. "Nothing. Do you think the mages did something to me?"

He grabs my hand, wrapping it tightly in his warm fingers, and the tingle races up my arm. "I can still feel your magic. It's something else. Something going on with the mountain itself, but I'm sure it's the mages. We should hurry and get to Polaris before anything happens."

Still holding on to my hand, Aidan leads me down the path and into the trees.

We walk for a while, holding on to each other without talking, only the crunching of our boots over the uneven trail breaking through the heavy silence. A thin film of sweat covers my forehead from the walking, and I use my free hand to unzip my coat a little. My breath comes out in pants thanks to the elevation, and pain stabs me in the ribs from walking so fast.

"Let's sit for a second," I say between ragged breaths. I pull on his hand at the sight of a large tree trunk lying across the ground.

He nods as I plop down on the tree and pull a bottle of water out of my backpack. Aidan walks along the edge of the trail, scanning the forest.

"Do you see anything?" I ask, afraid to know the answer.

"Still nothing." Aidan glances over his shoulder at me, his brows knitted. "We should get moving."

My legs are heavy, but I know he's right, and I slip the water back into my pack and sling it over my shoulders.

A shrill shriek rips through the air, followed by a thunder of wings.

I cry out, nearly slipping off the trunk, and Aidan drops to the ground, his eyes on the treetops.

A murder of crows fills the sky like a black cloud, racing away from the forest.

"What the hell?" I swallow thickly, my throat dry and my heart pounding in my ears. "I didn't think anything else was here."

Aidan grabs my hand, pulling me to my feet. "I'm more worried about what spooked them. Let's go."

I let him drag me through the trees, my eyes focused on the trail to keep from tripping. What is with this trail to the portal? Why can't I ever make this trip without something chasing me or scaring the crap out of me?

A twig snaps to my right, somewhere in the trees, and I whip around so fast, I almost fall. I bump into Aidan as he slams to a halt, and he reaches out a hand to steady me. "What was that?"

He shakes his head, his narrowed eyes scanning the forest. He turns to keep moving but freezes at the sound of another snap.

I step toward the sound, hoping to get a look at whatever is making the noise before it sees us, and frown as Aidan puts himself in front of me. I reach for the energy of the earth in case I need to use my magic, but I still can't feel it.

A figure slips out from behind a thick trunk, and I immediately breathe a sigh of relief.

Mierna weaves gracefully through the trees, wearing jeans and a blue silk shirt that brings out the blue tint in her black hair. Capricorn once called her the raven-hued witch, and that's exactly what she looks like with her pale skin and black eyes.

"What are you doing here?" I ask as she stops in front of

us. We got off to a rocky start, and while I trust her now, I'm not exactly ready to call her my friend.

"I'm glad I caught you before you made it to the portal." A smile slides across her face as she places her hands on her hips.

"How did you know we're going to the portal?" I ask, suddenly wary.

Mierna's smile broadens. "Relax. Violet told me where to find you."

"What is it, Mierna? We need to hurry and get to Polaris." Aidan glances through the trees in the direction of the cave.

Mierna looks up at the sky. "Yeah, your time is running short. Violet sent me to tell you to be as quick on Polaris as you can."

I frown at her. "I already know that. Humans can't stay there."

She shakes her head. "There's something happening on this mountain, and you'll need to get back here as soon as you can."

I suck in a sharp breath through my teeth. "What's happening? You can feel it too?"

"She didn't say. Just that you need to hurry." Mierna hesitates for a second before the confident smile returns. "Have a safe trip."

"That's it? Just hurry up?" I stare at her, my mouth hanging slightly open.

Mierna tilts her head to the side, studying my face, and again I'm reminded of a raven, and I wonder what else I should probably know about this woman that's helping us. "Yes, hurry. And I think you know that we're moving forward with Jocelyn's ritual while you're gone."

I nod slowly. "I heard."

"Good." Mierna turns to leave and stops.

"Oh, and one more thing I almost forgot." She slips her hand into the pocket of her jeans and pulls out something clasped tightly inside her fingers. She holds her fist out to me, waiting.

I look at her hand for a second before holding up my outstretched palm. She drops a silver necklace in my hand, and I struggle to swallow as I look at the small silver goat with a piece of turquoise in place of the heart. "Where did you get this?"

Mierna winks at me, mischief glimmering in her eyes. "I was on my way up here to find you and I found one of the mages slinking through the trees, causing trouble. So I kicked his ass, then searched him. I found this in his pocket, and I assume it belongs to you, since it's a goat."

My heart skips a beat, and I find it hard to even speak. "You have no idea what you've just done for me."

Without thinking, I rush forward and wrap her in a tight hug.

Mierna stiffens, then reaches around and pats my back, laughing as she steps away. "Glad to help."

As soon as I slip the necklace on, Aidan gently grabs my hand. "Time to go."

"He's right," Mierna says.

I follow Aidan down the path, turning to wave at Mierna, but she's already gone.

We walk down the sloping path, past the first cave where Scorpio hid us. My legs and lungs burn from the walking, but my heart is light now that my necklace hangs securely around my neck.

The trees break, giving way to the small, perfectly round meadow that never fails to take my breath away. Clumps of snow still frost the edges near the trees, but the grass in the center is already turning the first shade of green. It feels magical and peaceful, like it's straight out of a fairy tale.

I stop for a second, squeezing Aidan's hand as I soak in the serenity of this place. "Some day when the world isn't in danger, we should come up here and have a picnic. I love this place. It's beautiful."

Aidan scoots closer, slipping his arm over my shoulder, and takes in the full view of the meadow. "Bring chips and I'm in."

I snort, rolling my eyes. "There will always be chips."

He kisses the top of my head and guides me through the meadow. I feel a pang of guilt for walking across the grass; it seems too perfect to disturb with my footsteps. The peace of being in the meadow slides away the further we walk through the trees.

The path takes one final slope down, and we find ourselves standing outside the cave entrance.

"Are you ready to see more of my home?" Aidan's smile stretches from ear to ear, and I can't help but return it with a smile of my own.

"I'm ready." I pop up on my toes, kissing him gently on the lips.

"Are you two coming?" An irritated voice echoes out of the cave, ruining the moment and my mood.

I wrinkle my nose and sigh, stepping onto the rock.

Zoe waits next to the rock pit with the blue fire blazing in the center of the cave. She folds her arms across her chest, staring at me with amber eyes as she taps the toe of her boot against the stone floor. "You're late."

I take a deep breath before answering, hoping I can keep my mouth from getting myself into trouble. "No one said there was a specific time to get here."

"Capricorn said to get an early start." Zoe raises her copper eyebrows, daring me to argue.

"It is early," I say through clenched teeth.

"Not early enough." The tapping of Zoe's boot gets louder.

I take a step forward. "What is your problem with me?"

Aidan grabs my arm, pulling me back a second. "This isn't helping. You two need to sort this out, because we have a long journey together and we're going to need each other."

Zoe looks at him as if only now realizing he is standing there. "I heard you were involved with an Aid."

"That's it." I don't like her tone. I push forward, but Aidan tightens his grip on my arm.

Zoe raises one eyebrow, a smirk on her lips. "I guess he has a point."

"You know, you don't have to go. I'm sure we'll be fine without you." I pull my arm from Aidan, rubbing the spot where I can still feel his fingers.

Her smirk shifts to a frown. "I don't think you can do it without me."

"Tell me what your problem is." My voice is close to a shriek.

Zoe shrugs her shoulders. "I just don't know why you get to be in charge."

"Capricorn put me in charge. I didn't ask for it." Angry heat flushes my cheeks.

Aidan steps between the two of us. "You both need to stop. I mean it. We have to work together or none of us are going to survive this trip."

Another shrug. "Fine," Zoe says.

"I'll see you on the other side." She hops into the ring of fire, disappearing through the portal.

I stare at the place she was just standing, shaking with rage.

"Are you okay? Can you make this work?" Aidan asks softly.

I tear my gaze away from the fire and look at him. "She started it."

His eyebrows shoot high on his forehead. "Seriously?"

I hang my head. "All right, I'm sorry. I'll behave."

"Thank you." Aidan slips his fingers through mine, bringing them up to gently kiss my fingertips. "You go first."

With a sigh, I step into the portal, careful not to touch the blue flames that are so cold they burn. Energy zaps my body, pulling it in every direction, and a buzzing noise fills my ears to the point of making my head want to explode. I'm tossed around, end over end, through the pitch-black nothingness that leads to Polaris.

6

My feet hit the ground as I'm thrown out of the portal, my boots squeaking across the obsidian floor of the observatory as I bump into Zoe's back. I manage to stay upright, but she tosses a quick glare over her shoulder before turning back to stare up at Capricorn.

The hint of a smile tugs at the corners of his mouth, making his silver goatee twitch slightly. His green and gold eyes sparkle with amusement, and I know he's thinking that I usually fall on my face when I come out of the portal.

I roll my eyes at him but wait quietly for Aidan to join us on this side of the portal.

A second later, he lands deftly on the floor with his usual catlike grace. I both envy and admire his fluid movement. Feeling my eyes on him, he looks at me around a lock of dark hair and winks.

My cheeks instantly flush with heat but I smile at him, my heart fluttering in my chest. Capricorn clears his throat and I whip my head around, blushing all over again as I find him staring at me.

"I'm afraid we have little time, and we have information

that's vital to the success of your journey," Capricorn says, running a finger down the smooth curve of his horns.

I watch the movement of his hand as the fur around his wrists ruffles against his arm. He must've done that a billion times in his long life. My eyes wander down to the floor where his hooves peek out beneath the hem of his pine robes. It thrills and unnerves me, seeing the Zodiac in a hybrid form.

I sigh, meeting his eyes again. "Why isn't there ever any time? Everything has to be right now."

Capricorn frowns, his thick gray eyebrows hanging low over his eyes, but then he softens with a sigh almost as deep as my own. "Someday we'll be victorious over the mages and then you'll have your quiet, but for now, we continue the fight. Before we go, do you girls both have your necklaces?"

I hook the silver chain around my neck with my thumb and slip the silver goat pendant from beneath my shirt, laying it gently against my chest. I take a deep breath, sending another silent thank you to Mierna for finding us in the forest.

Zoe unzips her jacket an inch and withdraws a large bloodstone the size of a silver dollar, dangling from a silver braided chain. The stone is a brilliant green with blood-red specks, and around the sides curl the two silver horns of the ram. She glances at me, with her face carefully blank.

"Very good." Capricorn turns to head down the long hallway, leading to the rest of the Zodiac compound.

"Wait." I take a step forward when he stops walking and turns to face me. "Aren't you going to tell us what they're for? Why was it so important to bring them here?"

Capricorn folds his arms in front of him, slipping his hands into the sleeves so that not even the fur is visible.

"The necklaces are infused with special spells, found deep in the scrolls of our old magic. You are to keep them on at all times because the spell holds the effect of our realm at bay. It will be the only way you can survive on our planet for the time you need on your journey. Lose them and you could die. Is that understood?"

Zoe and I nod in unison.

Capricorn turns to leave again, but I have more questions that I know I shouldn't ask, but somehow, I can't seem to help myself.

"Do all the Guardians have one of these necklaces?" I grab the goat pendant and slip it beneath my shirt again for safekeeping.

Capricorn stops with a clack of his hooves that echoes off the marble hallway. "Yes, but they are not all in possession of their necklace. It's saved for special circumstances," Capricorn says without turning around.

"But you gave me mine a few months ago. Did you know I'd need it now, or is there something else it does?" I shut my mouth as Capricorn's shoulders visibly tighten and I see Aidan give a quick shake of his head out of the corner of my eye.

The Zodiac spins around, his robes twirling around his legs. "No more questions for now. Please, just follow me. Quietly."

Without waiting for an answer, he picks up his pace down the hallway, his shadow flickering in the light of the lavender fire hanging in pans from the ceiling.

"I know, it's always go now and answers later." I grunt as Zoe and Aidan simultaneously elbow me from either side. "Sorry," I mutter.

The three of us rush to keep up with the Zodiac as he pushes through the steel doors and into the main compound. Zoe stares around the walls, covered floor to ceiling with murals of forests, mountains, oceans, and fire. Her eyes widen as grasses blow in the wind, waves roll, and the fire crackles.

"It's pretty amazing, isn't it? When I came here the first time, I hadn't been through my ritual yet, and nothing moved and the colors weren't as brilliant." I smile, thinking about how much my life has changed in the last few months.

"You've been here before?" Zoe's question sounds closer to a hiss.

"Yeah, um, just when, um, just to help with Taurus." I wrinkle my nose as I stutter over my answer.

Zoe narrows her eyes at me but doesn't say anything else.

My cheeks puff as I blow out a breath of air. This trip is going to be a long one, especially if she's going to hate me for everything. I glance at Aidan, but he only gives me an unhelpful shrug of his shoulders.

Capricorn turns a corner and we follow him into a corridor with plain wooden walls, leading into a part of the compound that I've never seen before.

"Where are we going?" I suck in a sharp breath as Aidan elbows me in exactly the same spot as before. I glare at him, rubbing my ribs.

Capricorn ignores my question, leading us to the end of the hallway and stopping next to a closed door with a gold handle that looks like twisted ivy. He pushes open the door, motioning for us to walk inside.

The room is small, about the size of an average living room, but tiny in comparison with the other rooms I'd seen here on Polaris. The walls, floor, and ceiling are covered in the same walnut-colored paneling as the hallway. In the center of the space sit three wooden chairs in a semicircle that face a large map covering most of the back wall, and it reminds me of a small classroom.

Capricorn shuts the door behind us, motioning to the chairs as he passes by them on the way to the map, where he waits for us to seat ourselves.

As I walk into the room, the magic from the wood reaches out to me, tickling the back of my neck. The panels feel different here than they do on Earth, and I get a sudden thought that the trees here volunteered to be used instead of being forced like they are back home. The tickling sensation increases, and I giggle all the way to the center chair.

Aidan and Zoe sit down on either side, with Zoe frowning at me like I've lost my mind. She shifts in her chair, fidgeting with her hands.

"I need you to listen carefully. I'll be brief because you need to get through to the mountains before nightfall." Capricorn looks at each of us and we nod our understanding.

"We are here in the compound." Capricorn motions to the bottom of the map with detailed drawings of the buildings, and I'm surprised at how big it actually is.

"Where's the little red arrow?" I snicker despite the glare from Capricorn.

He continues his lesson without answering my question, sliding his finger farther up the map. "Just outside the safety of our home, you'll climb a hill, and down the hill you'll enter the Daruchta Forest."

I groan, quickly slapping my hand over my mouth, as it sounds way too loud in the small room.

Capricorn pauses, his finger pushing into the map so hard that his finger turns white. "Now what is it?"

I grit my teeth, knowing that I've pushed my limit. "I'm

sorry, but that place is creepy. That's the forest where Pisces tied me up and was trying to summon the mages, right?"

"That's correct, but you were barely inside the forest. There are far worse dangers there." Capricorn holds my gaze, and for a moment, I'm afraid he's trying to look right through me.

A shiver runs down my spine. "Like what?"

"There's no time now to cover the many creatures that call Polaris their home. Trust Aidan to be your guide." Capricorn turns his attention back to the map, illustrating with his hands as he talks. "Once you make it through the forest, you'll climb down the canyon wall, cross the Reite River, and move into the Beinn Dorcha Mountains. It's somewhere in the mountains. You'll find what you're looking for." His voice trails off into a whisper.

"And what exactly are we looking for?" I ask, my voice almost as soft. Any jokes I had are long gone.

Capricorn looks up from the map, meeting each of our eyes, as the tension settles over my shoulders like a thick blanket. "You're looking for a magical fire. It's rumored to be pink, and it's the only way to save Aries."

"It's rumored to be pink? You mean you don't know?" Zoe asks, finally finding her voice.

Capricorn shakes his head. "We've never had a need for such a fire."

"If you've never had a need for it, then how do you know that's what we're looking for?" My stomach twists, thinking about going out there looking for something we're not sure about.

"There's mention of it in the ancient scrolls," Capricorn says.

Aidan opens his mouth, but I cut him off before he can

speak. "Ancient scrolls? How do we even know it's still out there?" My mouth is almost too dry to swallow.

The Zodiac's shoulders slump, and he looks more vulnerable than any time I've seen him before, making me feel slightly guilty for hammering him with questions. "We have to try. We know of no other way to save Aries."

"What do you mean when you say it's somewhere in the mountains? We both know how big the mountains are, and we're already pressed for time." Aidan's voice is low, and his face looks a little pale.

"We do not know the precise location. That's the other reason it's so important you leave right away. Remember your studies well and keep the girls safe." Capricorn turns his gaze from Aidan to me. "I trust you."

I stare at the Zodiac, trying to remember how to breathe with the weight of the task pressing down on my chest. So many questions and no time to ask them. I glance at Aidan. "You've never been out there?"

"We're not allowed." Aidan presses his lips firmly together.

I stand up, wiping my sweaty palms on my jeans. "Great. We're going to a place that none of us have been, and looking for something that may or may not exist somewhere on a mountain. I guess we better get going."

My two companions join me.

"You'll be leaving soon. You'll need the last of your supplies." Capricorn brushes past us, pausing beside the door. He lifts a small piece of rope from the wall and pulls, but nothing happens.

A second later, there's a soft knock on the door. "Enter."

The door swings open and a wisp of a girl enters the room, bending at the waist in a bow so low, her black, curly hair sweeps the floor. She straightens, clasping her hands in front of her gray linen dress that covers most of her blue-tinted skin. She shifts her glowing turquoise eyes in my direction and smiles. "Yes, Master?"

"Holly, please show Zoe to the back hall and help her load the food. The rest of us will be right behind you," Capricorn says.

Holly bows again and slips her tiny hand into Zoe's, leading her silently out of the room.

"What is she?" I ask softly.

Capricorn closes the door softly and turns back to face Aidan and me. "She's a dryad."

"What's a dryad?"

Capricorn sighs as he stares down at me. "A tree nymph. To answer your earlier question, each of the Guardians have a Zodiac talisman, the necklace you now wear. Each talisman is infused with our essence, which is why it's only given when necessary. Your magic is stronger and your connection to the earth deeper with the necklace. I gave it to you anyway because I knew that you'd need it soon, with the mages after you in particular. But you must be extra careful now. Not only are you a Guardian and a human, but you carry two items, the dagger and the necklace, that have a piece of my magic. All manner of creatures in this world will be after you and Zoe, too."

I stare up at Capricorn and shiver at his words. "Why didn't you say this in front of Zoe?"

"Because she doesn't need to know that you have your own dagger. Let her think you're using mine." Capricorn opens the door again, waiting for us to walk through. "Stick together and keep each other safe. Follow your instincts. You'll need all three of your talents before this is over. We can't find out what happens if you fail."

"Gee, thanks," I mutter as I follow Aidan out the door.

The three of us stand huddled together on the top of a small hill that overlooks the edge of the Daruchta Forest. The grass beneath our boots is the healthy green of summer grass, and the mixture of trees all have their leaves, but a freezing wind blows across us, blasting us with tiny pellets of ice.

The shadows of the forest are so thick, I can't see past the edge of the trees. A cold shiver races down my spine, but it's the shadows and not the weather that causes it.

A wild magical current races through the air like lightning before a storm. The skin on the back of my neck tingles, and I scoot a little closer to Aidan. "What's with the mixing of seasons? Why is it so cold when everything else is green?"

Aidan scans the edge of the trees with narrowed eyes. "It's always all four seasons on Polaris. In some places, the seasons collide and in other spots it's more one season than another. It's not like Earth, where the seasons rotate, or the mage realm, where it's always the opposite of Earth."

"That's weird, isn't it?" I ask, pulling my coat tighter around my body.

Aidan shrugs. "It never really matters, since we aren't supposed to leave the Zodiac compound."

"Do you guys feel that in the air?" Zoe's voice is so soft, I almost don't hear her over the winter wind. "It's like electricity, but not."

"What you feel is the magic here. The magic on Earth is tainted, ruined by the people that don't believe in it. Here, it's wild and free, and every creature in this realm has some sort of its own magic." Aidan turns to look at each of us. "Please remember that. Be careful with anything you encounter. Some creatures are helpful, others are just tricky, but most of them would love to find a human."

I sigh, tucking that cheery thought into my memory and hoping that I remember it when I come across anything. "So, who else can't wait to get this party started?"

"Seriously?" Zoe rolls her eyes at me as she starts down the hill. Aidan grabs her arm, squeezing her wrist.

"We need to get going, but I'm first. I will always go first. Keeping you two safe is my responsibility." He frowns at her to emphasize his point.

"Fine," Zoe says quietly as she pulls her arm from his grasp. She glances at me, but I just shrug.

Aidan leads the way down the grassy hill, the footing sketchy even in boots as the bitter wind coats the green blades with a layer of ice. My foot slides in front of me and I wobble, throwing my arms out to catch my balance. I take a deep breath once I'm steady and follow the others a little slower.

We reach the bottom of the hill, and I stare into the darkness of the forest. My heartbeat races as the memory of being tied to a tree by Pisces floods my mind. It was somewhere in these trees that he took me, intending to hand over to the mages. I shudder, reminding myself that he wasn't in control, and take a slow breath, the cold air helping to clear my mind.

"You okay?" Aidan asks, one eyebrow raised high, hidden behind his shaggy brown hair.

"I'm fine. I was just thinking about when Pisces kidnapped me." I shake my head, pushing the thought away.

Aidan gives me a gentle smile, squeezing my shoulder then turning toward the forest and slipping through the trees.

Zoe glances at me with wide eyes but keeps any thoughts to herself as she falls in behind Aidan.

I force my heavy legs to move. Something about this forest has my nerves on edge, and I'm not sure I want to find out what's doing it. I take in my surroundings, squinting into the deep shadows, every part of me on high alert.

The foliage in the canopy of the trees is so dense that sunlight doesn't penetrate this far on the forest floor. It's impossible to tell what time of day it is in here, but at least the air is a little warmer, the trees keeping us shielded from the wind. They glow with a magical light, giving off a nightlight type of glow, and it's the only reason we can see anything at all.

Aidan moves forward, pausing every couple of steps to check and make sure we're alone.

Our boots sink into the muddy path covered with slick leaves as we walk painstakingly slow through the forest. I'm already getting tired from the stress as I rotate my tense shoulders beneath the straps of my backpack.

As I search the trees, I notice the small glowing lights of the earth magic, and I cautiously reach out to them. They dance around my fingers like fireflies in the night, bringing a smile to my lips. Even though I'm still learning my magic, I can tell a difference from the energy on Earth. I touch one with my fingertips, and it sends a jolt through my body, making me gasp.

Aidan and Zoe turn to look at me, both with wide eyes. I open my mouth to answer when a high-pitched giggle breaks the silence from the leaves above us. The three of us immediately push together, standing in a tight circle with our backs against each other as we struggle to scan the tops of the trees.

Nothing moves above us, and we begin to relax into the silence.

"Let's go," Aidan whispers.

Zoe and I nod, falling in line and sticking closer together. Our boots squish in the mud as we walk deeper down the path.

Another giggle, musical like the tinkling of a silver bell, the same laughter as before. We freeze mid-motion, staring again at the leaves.

"What is that?" Zoe presses closer to me, looking up with wide eyes.

"No idea." I glance at Aidan around her.

Without taking his eyes off the trees, he says, "My guess is a dryad."

"Smart is the boy," the voice sings from above us.

"We should go." Aidan grabs our sleeves and pulls Zoe and me down the path.

Another giggle and the leaves rustle above us as the dryad follows our movements.

"You don't want to play?" She sings her question.

I pull my jacket free of Aidan's grip and stop. "What do you want with us?"

"Ciara," Aidan hisses. "Don't talk to it."

"Mean boy. Mean boy. I don't like mean boy." The voice no longer sings her words, and it sends a chill down my back.

I glance at Aidan, giving him a slight shake of my head. "Her. The dryad is female, not an it."

"How do you know?" Zoe asks.

"I just do." My words are quiet, but I know in my heart that I'm right.

The tree rustles above us, and we all turn our eyes to the canopy. The leaves part and my breath catches in my throat as a tiny face emerges, the skin tinted green and shining with an iridescent glow. Bark and leaves frame the edge of her face, covering the top of her head in the place of hair. She tilts her head to the side, blinking her large amber eyes and looking directly at me.

I shift my feet beneath the weight of her stare as I struggle with what to do or say next. My mouth opens and closes several times without a single word escaping.

"You are of the earth like me." The dryad still speaks her words, but the sharp edge to her voice is gone.

I nod, keeping my eyes locked on hers. "I am."

The leaves snap back together as the dryad disappears. A flash of movement catches my eye as she climbs down the trunk, stopping just above eye level. She grips the bark of the trunk like a squirrel, adjusting her leafy dress as she watches me closely. "But you do not live in the trees. I sense the goat in you."

My heart beats faster, and I struggle to keep my breathing even. I don't know if I'm doing the right thing or putting us all in danger, but I decide to follow my instincts. "You are right. I'm of the house of Capricorn."

Aidan sighs, but I ignore him. "Do you have a name I can call you?"

"I have no need for a name." The dryad narrows her eyes. "You are not like the others."

"No, I'm not," I say carefully. "We're just trying to get through your forest. Is it all right if we leave?"

"I like you and you may go, sister of the earth. Let the boy lead you out, but go quickly. I will tell the others not to bother you." The dryad races up the trunk, disappearing in the blink of an eye.

My heart skips a beat at her words. "What others?"

The dryad's giggle echoes from the leaves, but she doesn't answer me.

"Let's go." Aidan grabs my hand, pulling me down the path.

I've lost track of how long we've been walking without any light breaking through the trees. The cold has settled all the way into my bones, and my legs feel like there's lead in my shoes.

"Are we almost out of the forest? I could use a break." I do my best to keep my voice from sounding like a whine.

Aidan ducks under a low-hanging branch, holding it up for us to pass under. "We should be almost out of here. There are rocks on the edge of the cliff that we can sit on and rest."

"Cliff?" Zoe's question comes out more of a squeak.

"Should be?" I pile on, my voice almost as high.

Aidan shrugs. "I've never been this far, and Capricorn told us about the cliff. So yes and yes."

He drops the branch and resumes his place at the front of the line.

I stop at the sound of scratching, like tiny claws scampering over the fallen leaves. "What was that?"

"I didn't see anything," Zoe whispers.

"But you heard it, right?" She answers my question with a nod.

"Run!" Aidan grabs Zoe by the shoulder, pushing her in front of him and reaching for me next. As he grabs my arm, I glance over my shoulder and gasp.

The path we're standing on rolls up, a ten-foot wave of dirt and branches pointing directly at us like deadly spears, and it's heading straight for us.

I hold up my hands, breathing deep and focusing on the

earth. The wave slows but doesn't stop. Aidan yanks me out of the way just as sharp branches crash at my feet.

We race for the end of the forest, stumbling as the ground rumbles beneath our pounding boots. I choke back a sob as I finally see the gray light of a wintry day break through the trees. We surge past the final tree as the mud slams against the trunks.

We throw ourselves behind the rocks, huffing and puffing as we wait for the rumbling to stop.

"What the hell was that?" I wipe the sweat from my forehead as I look at Aidan.

He swallows hard, his eyes still glued to the forest. "Maybe a creature. Maybe some kind of magical trap."

Zoe pulls herself up on a rock, tucking her legs beneath her. "Who would set a trap?"

She pulls a small parcel wrapped in brown paper out of her bag, looking a little too calm considering what we just ran away from.

I lower myself to the ground, pulling out my snack and handing half a sandwich to Aidan. "We know the mages have been here."

Zoe almost chokes on her bite. "On Polaris?"

Aidan rips off a huge chunk and stuffs it in his mouth.

"We're not sure what all they're up to," he mumbles around his food.

We finish our food in silence, my mind racing with a million questions. Where is the fire? Will we find it in time? What others was the dryad talking about?

Aidan stands, interrupting my thoughts.

"It's getting late, and we need to make it as far as we can before nightfall." He reaches down a hand, helping me stand.

I glance up at the silver clouds covering the sky, not sure

how he can tell it's getting late. I suck in a sharp breath as we all turn our backs to the forest and I get my first good look at the mountains.

The snow-covered peaks brush the sky, so tall that they look like they can stab the sun. The sides of the mountains are dark rocks, jagged and sharp.

"That's where we're going?" I whisper.

"Afraid so. We have to get down this cliff first." Aidan steps carefully to the edge, the wind from the canyon ruffling his hair.

Zoe and I slowly join him, staring down into the raging river below, with cerulean waters and the banks lined with sharp chunks of ice.

Without a word, the three of us slip over the edge, clinging to the chunks of rock on the side of the cliff. Icy wind swirls around us, making it difficult to hang on.

I reach the bottom first and hold my breath as my companions slowly scale the last of the cliff wall. They drop to the ground beside me, panting.

Zoe walks to the bank of the river, careful to avoid the ice, and watches with her hands on her hips as the water rushes by, carrying large chunks of ice. "How do we get across?"

"I can help." A femine voice bubbles on the water. An arm slips over the edge, glimmering in the light like an opal and covered in iridescent scales. Long fingers with pointed black nails wrap around Zoe's leg and pull.

Zoe's shrill scream pierces the air, echoing off the rocks in the canyon.

I lunge forward, grabbing her arm in time to slow her crash to the ground. Zoe claws at my arms as I struggle to adjust my grip by slipping one arm around her waist. I dig my feet into the ground and push with my legs, desperately trying to pull her out of the creature's grasp.

Aidan holds his hands up, palms facing toward the sky, and closes his eyes. The waves splash, frothing with white-capped waves as he concentrates on his magic.

The creature cackles but takes her hand off Zoe's leg.

I pull her away from the edge of the river as Zoe kicks her legs, whimpering as we move. "Are you okay?"

"No." Zoe reaches down and grabs her leg, pulling up her jeans to inspect for wounds.

"I mean are you hurt?" I kneel next to her leg to help her look. The last thing we need is an injury this quick into our journey, but other than finger-shaped marks coloring her skin, everything looks fine. I quickly stand and help her to her feet.

Zoe adjusts her jeans and looks past me to the river. "I guess I'm fine. Thanks for grabbing me."

Her eyes grow wide and she points over my shoulder.

I whip around and gasp so suddenly that I almost choke myself on air.

A wave forms out of the river like water shooting up in a fountain, and on top rides the creature, a sneer pulling her green-tinted lips tightly to the side. Her entire body shimmers like an opal in the light, with scales on her arms and framing her face, blending into the white hair that floats around her head as if she's still underwater. She has large, sea-green eyes that are fixed on Aidan.

Her sneer widens into a smile, revealing razor teeth that remind me of a shark. "You think you can use magic on me? I own the water." Her voice pops like bubbles in a stream.

"You attacked my friend." Aidan keeps his voice steady, but his face pales.

Her smile widens as she taps her chin with one pointed black fingernail and bats her eyelashes. "You can make it up to me."

I move in front of Aidan, my anger instantly flaring and flushing my cheeks. "Back off, whatever you are."

"I just want to play with him for a bit. I never get to a toy that can work water magic." She pushes her green lips into a pout.

I take a step closer to the water, ignoring the warning bells in the back of my mind. "He's not your toy. Either help us or leave us alone."

The smile slips from her face with her eyes still locked on Aidan. "You'd do well to mind your manners, child."

She turns her face to me and a slight crease mars her brows, and just as quickly it's gone. She tilts her head to the side, studying me. "What do we have here?"

"I asked you first. What are you?" My hands ball into fists at my sides as I straighten my shoulders.

"Very brave. Or very foolish." The water shifts, moving the creature closer to the shore, and she narrows her eyes. "I am a naiad, or water nymph, if you will."

"What is that?" Zoe asks, then quickly shuts her mouth. "She's a water spirit," Aidan says softly, attracting the

naiad's attention again.

She crooks her finger, beckoning him forward. "So smart. I'm going to have lots of fun with you."

"Leave him alone." I glare at the naiad, not caring that she could probably wipe me out with a flick of her pinky.

The creature rides her wave closer, hovering at the very edge of the river a few feet above my head.

I stare up at her, my heart hammering in my chest, but I force myself to stand my ground. I don't trust anything about this creature, but we're quickly losing time. "We really need to be on our way. We have a very long and very important journey ahead of us."

The naiad cackles, a harsh laughter mixed with popping bubbles. "There is no way around this river. You can pass only with my permission."

She looks from me to Zoe and back. "You two may go. The boy is my price for a safe crossing."

Aidan sputters behind me.

"We all go or none of us go." I fold my arms across my chest, hoping I didn't just make a huge mistake.

The water in the river begins to churn, swirling faster and splashing over the icy bank. The nymph's eyes narrow to barely a slit. "I know you now."

My mouth falls open as I take a step back, bumping into Aidan.

"You have me confused. I've never been here." My voice is shaky, and I swallow hard to collect myself.

"You have his magic." She hisses. "He promised me."

She raises her arms and water rises in front of us, towering high in the air. Throwing her hands forehead, the water crashes toward us as Aidan's magic sends the water splashing around us. The naiad screams.

The three of us huddle together and Zoe leans in close. "What are we going to do? We can't get past her."

"Who promised you what? Who do you think I am?" I shout over the rushing of the river.

"The goat promised me he would take care of them." She sends another wave of water crashing toward us.

I shriek as the frigid water soaks through my clothes.

"You know Capricorn?" My chattering teeth make it hard to speak.

"You carry his magic. I'll kill you for his broken promise. He said he'd send them away. They're still here," she growls.

A stream of water slips out of the water, sliding toward us like a liquid snake. It twirls around our ankles, rising higher up our bodies.

Aidan pushes his hands into the water, squeezing his eyes shut. The water slows but continues to climb.

"You can't kill us. What did he promise you? Maybe he's still working on it." My voice is tight around the panic rising in my throat.

"He said he'd send them away." The water now twists around my shoulders.

Suddenly it clicks in my mind. "You're talking about the mages here?"

The naiad's eyes lock on mine as the water stops spinning. "They think they can do whatever they want. This is my home, and they pervert it with their unnatural magic."

"We are working to stop the mages. They're destroying our home on Earth, too. We're working with the Zodiacs to stop them. It's just taking longer than we want. They've hurt me more than once, and they're planning more." I take a deep breath, holding her gaze as hope swells inside me.

The naiad tilts her head to the side, a slight frown creasing her forehead. "Stange. I do not sense a lie in your words."

"I'm telling the truth. The mages are hurting the Zodiacs too. That's why we're out here." My words tumble out of my mouth, and I can't seem to stop the flow of what I'm saying, but I believe our lives depend on it.

She stares at me, her large eyes unblinking like a fish. The water drops from around us and I breathe a sigh of relief even as I shiver from the cold. "Do you make me the same promise? Will you get rid of those men?"

I rub my arms, trying to get some warmth back in my body. "I can't tell you how long it will take, but I promise that I'll get rid of those men or die trying."

My body shivers, and I clench my teeth to keep them from chattering.

The rushing water slowly parts, leaving a muddy path filled with small rocks along the riverbed.

I hesitate, wanting to run across but also afraid that it's some kind of trick. Aidan decides for us, grabbing Zoe's hand and mine and pulling us along the path. As we climb out the other side, the river sloshes back together.

I turn around and look at the naiad as she floats on her wave. "Thank you."

"You are brave and foolish. Good luck, child." She nods her head.

I tip my head and turn to leave, but stop at the sound of her voice.

"If you survive, you and the boy come back and play." Her laughter rings through the air like a gurgling stream.

I open my mouth, but my voice is frozen as the water flows up her body, turning every part of her to liquid in the shape of a woman. Her form splashes into the river and she disappears.

"That was crazy, right?" Zoe looks from Aidan to me, her lips tinted blue from the cold. "Is everything in this realm crazy like that?"

"I guess we're going to find out. First, we need to find somewhere to get warm." I bounce on my toes, trying to keep the blood flowing.

Traveling in a line, we walk over smooth gray rocks that grow bigger with each passing minute.

"This is what's known as the meadow of boulders," Aidan says from the front of our group.

"Hang on a second." I put my hands on my hips and survey the area. All I can see are rocks that get taller and sharper the closer they get to the mountain, and it makes me groan. "I can't believe we have to climb over all that."

"This looks like a good place to warm up." Zoe lowers herself on a flat rock, holding her palm above the surface until a small fire sparks to life.

"Thank you." I smile as I sit down next to her, holding my fingers close to the flames.

Aidan sits on my other side, placing a hand on my sleeve and closing his eyes as he draws the water out of my clothes. When I'm dry, he does the same for Zoe.

We rest in silence, all of us staring into the flames, and for a moment, it feels like we're just three people hanging out around a campfire.

I glance at Zoe as she sighs, and I pick up on her

meaning. My body protests as I stand up and stretch my legs. "Yeah, we should go."

With a flick of her wrist the fire goes out, a small black spot the only evidence it was ever there. "Climbing these rocks is going to suck."

"Yup." I grunt as I slide off a smooth boulder shaped like an egg.

Zoe pulls herself up onto the rock next to me. "I thought you were part goat."

"Not exactly." I smile to myself as I get the hang of my footing and quickly pass Aidan.

"Don't get too far ahead of us," Aidan grumbles.

I snicker, pulling myself onto a rock that's taller than me, and gasp at the sight of a forest made of gnarled cypress trees with deeper shadows than the Daruchta Forest. "Please tell me we're not going in there."

"Through that forest is the only way up the mountain," Aidan says as he joins me on the boulder, slipping an arm around my shoulders.

Zoe climbs up beside us without even breathing hard and smiles when I catch her eye. "It looks like it'll be good to be in the house of the ram."

We all share a laugh, but it's only halfhearted as we stare at the forest that waits for us.

Aidan pulls his arm free and slides down the side of the boulder. "Once we make it across these rocks and through the forest, we'll have to climb the mountain."

I run my eyes up the jagged peak, tilting my head straight back to see it all. "We don't have to go all the way up there, do we?"

"There's a pass about halfway up if we don't find the fire on this side of the mountain. We won't go any higher than we have to," Aidan says.

Zoe moves across the rocks, catching up to Aidan. "What kind of weird creatures are in those trees?"

"It's hard to say what lives there." Aidan's voice is soft, and he shudders.

I swear I hear a giggle coming from somewhere behind me as I leap off the boulder to catch up.

We huddle together on the edge of the second creepy forest that we have to enter during the few hours since we started our journey. These cypress trees are tall and gnarled, with hanging leaves like a bony hand with the skin shredded and falling off. Inky shadows slide between the trunks, too dark to see what's hidden behind them.

I stuff my cold fingers into the pocket of my coat as I stare up at the trees that tower above us. Every instinct in my body is screaming at me to turn and run, but my mind fixes on Aries and I know I can't, no matter how dumb it seems to go in there. "What is this place called? It's giving me the creeps."

"The Skeleton Forest," Zoe says so matter-of-fact that Aidan and I turn to stare at her until she snorts. "I don't know what it's called, but that sounds good."

I roll my eyes at her, but find myself laughing with her. "That sounds good. Okay, who wants to go into the Skeleton Forest?"

We quickly sober as tension slinks out of the forest, curling around our shoulders like a heavy scarf. A cold wind blows at our backs, and I lean against it to keep from being pushed toward the forest.

I feel a pinch against my cheek and absently rub my face. "Is that Libra getting pushy?"

I turn to the others to find them both staring at me. "What?"

Without a word, Zoe steps closer, raising her hand and swatting at me.

I try to lean out of the way but she catches me off guard, and I end up leaning into her swing, her fingers slapping against my face. I stumble back. "What the hell was that for?"

"Sorry, you moved," Zoe chuckles. "You had a bug or something on your shoulder."

Aidan moves closer, a frown on his face. "That wasn't a bug, and I don't think you should've done that."

"Why, what was it?" Zoe asks.

"I am no bug," a tiny voice whispers past my ear in a light breeze.

I feel a tickle on my shoulder and turn my head as far as I can to see what's on me and gasp. A small creature stands on my shoulder, and I can just see enough of her mostly clear body to make out the shape of her form. "What are you?"

"I am a sylph." Her words whisper through the air like wind through rattling tree leaves.

"What's a sylph?" I twist my head, ignoring a slight pinch in my neck to get a better look at the creature.

"Mistress Libra says you must hurry through the forest. Shadows watch, and they draw nearer with every step you take." She blows off my shoulder like a feather dancing in the wind, reappearing right in front of my face.

My breath catches in my throat as I stare at the beautiful creature, but her words nag in the back of my mind. "What shadows? Who's following us?"

"Hurry." The word dies on the wind as a large gust of air

blasts us from behind and the creature disappears in the current.

"I love cryptic messages," I grumble.

Zoe glances over her shoulder. "At least we got a warning."

"She's right. I can feel something dark, but I don't know what it is." Aidan clenches his teeth so tight, his jaw muscles jump.

I force my jelly legs to carry me up to the edge of the forest and stop beside Aidan. "What's a sylph?"

"Sylphs are air spirits, which is how she can carry messages for Libra. All elements have creatures tied to them." Aidan looks from me to Zoe.

"Let's move quickly through here. Stay close and as quiet as you can." With those cheery instructions, he dips his head low to avoid a branch and disappears into the forest.

The moment I step between the trees, the temperature drops. It was cold already, but now my breath steams in front of me with each shaky breath I take. I pull my jacket tight around me as I follow Aidan into the darkness.

Zoe walks so close behind me she bumps into me as I stop when Aidan holds up his hand. She scoots up beside me, and together we scan the forest.

I want to ask Aidan why we stopped, but I know better than to speak. Instead, I hold my breath, straining to see through the shadows that float through the trees like the wax in a lava lamp.

Aidan reaches for my hand, pulling me gently forward as he starts to walk again, picking his way between the bony branches that hang almost to the forest floor.

I grab Zoe's sleeve and we continue, holding each other like a human chain. I'm so focused on staying close to Aidan that I don't see the large branch stretching across the ground. As I put my foot down, the loud snap as it breaks echoes through the trees. I suck in a sharp breath through my teeth, freezing mid-movement.

Aidan whips around, staring at me with wide eyes, and Zoe gasps behind me. I wrinkle my face and mouth the word sorry.

Suddenly, the air pressure changes around us and my head throbs with the blood rushing between my ears like a raging river. I bend over, pressing my hands to the side of my face, an attempt to keep my head from exploding.

Zoe drops to the ground beside my feet, bending so low that her forehead touches the ground as she whimpers softly.

My eyes lock with Aidan, and he sways on his feet, looking ready to pass out.

My temples throb, and I fight to keep from screaming. The world tilts around me, and I stumble to stay on my feet.

"We have to go!" I shout, but I can't hear my own words and I know they didn't either.

The edges of my vision begin to blur, and I know that if we don't get out of here quickly, whatever is doing this is going to have its prize. I lean over to grab Zoe and bile rises in my throat. I swallow it, trying not to gag.

Zoe swats at my arm, pushing herself closer to the ground, her fingers curling through her hair.

I grab her hands along with some hair and pull with all my strength, yanking Zoe to her feet. When she turns around, her mouth is open, and I know she's screaming even if I can't hear it over the pulsing in my head. I push her in front of me, hanging on to her jacket as I pull Aidan along with us.

I struggle to put one foot down in front of the other and keep the other two in tow. I'm not even sure we're headed in the right direction as the three of us stumble around like drunks after a night of partying.

My stomach churns as everything tilts around me. I'm too afraid to let go of my friends, and let the tears stream down my face unchecked. I see a flash of light ahead, and even though my bleary eyes can't make it out, my jumbled mind thinks it has to be better than these shadows. I push ahead, desperate to get away from the pressure, and stumble, sending all three of us tumbling to the ground.

I push on the ground, but I can't lift my body. Something warm and sticky trickles down the side of my face, but I don't have the strength to see what it is. I feel my body being dragged across the ground as I push open my heavy eyelids in a fight to stay conscious.

Bright light flashes in my eyes and I slam them shut against the assault. They burn as I throw my free arm over my face. The pressure lifts just as fast as it began, and my lungs pull in such a deep, sharp breath that I send myself into a coughing fit.

My arm gets pulled away and I blink, trying to clear my vision, as I squint into the blurry face of Zoe, who leans over me, looking pale and wobbly but in one piece. A thin line of blood runs down the side of her face from each ear.

I reach up to feel my face and pull my fingertips back, covered in blood. "What the hell was that?"

I can hear myself talk again, but my voice still sounds muffled, like I have my head in a box.

"I don't know." Zoe glances at the forest, then looks down at me, a deep frown creasing her brow. "We're even now. You grabbed me from the naiad and I pulled you out of the forest."

"I'm touched," I grumble, propping myself on my

elbows. My heart leaps into my throat when I don't see Aidan.

"Aidan! Where's Aidan?" I push the rest of the way up, moving way too fast and stumble over the uneven ground.

Zoe grabs my arm, squeezing firmly until I quit wobbling, and points.

I choke back a sob as I see him sitting on a rock, his head between his hands.

"I'm over here." He sounds grumpy, and his words are still a little slurred.

I rush to him, collapsing at his feet. "Are you okay?"

Aidan tilts his head back to look me in the face and forces a smile. "I'll be fine. Are you two okay?"

"Yeah, thanks to Zoe." I stand carefully, this time giving myself enough time to catch my balance and pull Aidan to his feet. "What happened back there?"

"I've never heard of anything like that," Aidan says softly, massaging his temples.

"Do you think it had something to do with whatever shadow the sylph warned us about?" I chew on my bottom lip, praying we don't have to go through that again.

Aidan shrugs, then winces.

"All I know is that it all started when you stepped on that branch."

I spin around at the bite in Zoe's tone. "Do you think I did that on purpose? That I wanted to have my head explode?"

She narrows her eyes at me, her cheeks turning pink.

"Not now." Aidan's tone is equally sharp. "In fact, no more at all. No one is trying to get each other killed. We need each other."

As Aidan turns around to survey the mountain, I stare at

my feet, feeling very much like a scolded child. Even though I want to argue, I know he's right, and I glance at Zoe.

She returns my gaze with a blank face but moves closer to us. "Where do we go now?"

"We start up the mountain. Keep your eyes open for any caves or anything that could hide a pink fire." Aidan props one foot on a rock and pushes himself up, moving slow to keep from falling.

"There's a cave right over there," Zoe says.

Aidan and I both turn to look at her, then follow her pointing finger above us and to the right. Just beyond a sharp ledge, I see what looks to be the shadowed opening of a cave.

"We'll try that first." Aidan pushes himself over the next rock.

Zoe climbs past him without even looking at either of us and I scramble to catch up, refusing to let her beat me. I hear Aidan sigh but ignore him as I keep climbing and pull myself onto the ledge at the same time as Zoe. Neither of us say a word as I glance down to see that Aidan is close.

Aidan climbs onto the ledge, taking a second to glare at each of us before walking over to study the mouth of the cave.

I step up beside him, feeling like the child that got scolded earlier. "All right, I'm sorry."

"Then don't," Aidan says without even looking at me.

I close my eyes and take a deep breath to steady the tears when I feel a rush of energy that burns my fingers. I gasp, stepping closer without opening my eyes, and the burning sensation increases.

"What is it?" Aidan asks softly.

"I don't know. I can feel energy coming from the cave,

but it's tainted. It's burning my hands." I concentrate on deep, steady breaths as I feel out the magic.

Zoe's boots crunch on the rock ledge as she moves closer on my right. "Maybe it's the heat from the magic fire we're looking for."

Raising my eyebrows, I open my eyes and stare at her. "You don't actually think we'll be that lucky?"

"We should check it out." Zoe steps closer to the cave. "Maybe we should wait if the energy is tainted." Aidan reaches for her arm but misses as Zoe steps inside the cave.

The rock beneath our feet lurches, and I crash into the side of the mountain, slamming against Aidan. Large boulders rain down from the top of the cave as Zoe screams.

8

"Zoe!" I shout, lunging forward and narrowly missing being squashed by a large rock falling from the side of the mountain.

Aidan grabs my arm, pulling me close to him and pinning me to his side.

"You can't. Those rocks will kill you." He speaks directly in my ear so I can hear him over the chaos.

I push against him, but he holds me tight. "We can't just stand here and watch."

Zoe's screams abruptly stop.

Panic races through my heart, and I'm terrified that she's in there dead or dying. I break out of Aidan's grasp and rush to the pile of rocks that steadily build a wall that blocks the entrance.

I close my eyes, forcing down a deep breath, and reach out with my magic until I touch the tingly sensation of the rock's energy.

"Be careful using your magic here." Aidan's voice breaks through my concentration and I open my eyes to glare at him.

"Thanks, but I think I can handle it." I turn my attention to the piling rocks and swallow the lump in my throat at the tiny bit of space left before the cave seals shut.

Aidan grabs my arm, forcing me to wait. "I know you can handle it, but whatever magic you use is going to be a beacon to any creature in this realm."

"I don't have a choice. We need to get her before it's too late. Just make sure I don't get smashed beneath a rock." I pull my arm free and close my eyes again, reaching for the rocks.

The energy races up my fingers, speeding through my arms and down my body. It feels so much stronger here, and I force down the urge to laugh as the wild magic fills me to the core.

My magic reaches into the rocks, and I pull them one by one from the top of the pile, and slowly the crack opens wider. I reach for another large stone but it pushes back, crashing down the wall.

Aidan grabs me by the waist, yanking me out of the way as it shatters against the place I was just standing.

I stare at it, panting. "That could've been bad."

"I thought you had control," he shouts over the rumbling.

"Something was wrong with that one." The seconds tick away, and with each one that passes, I fear we'll lose Zoe. I kneel on the ground, placing my palms flat on the rocky surface, praying my crazy idea is going to work.

Breathing deep, I send my energy into the earth, until I connect with the rocks, feeling the weight of the boulders building up in front of the cave.

"Hold on," I shout.

"What are you doing?" Aidan drops to the ground beside me.

I ignore his question and send my magic straight into the earth. The rock rolls beneath us, shaking the wall free as the boulders rain down around us. I can see each stone in my mind's eye and send them bouncing around us.

Again, the magic pushes back, and I struggle to hang on to my grasp of the rocks. Each one lands closer to us, and I hear Aidan gasp. A thin film of sweat covers my forehead, and I grit my teeth, straining to keep control. The wall crumbles enough to give us enough room to get inside the cave as I collapse to the ground, panting.

Aidan reaches for me, gently sitting me back up. "Those rocks are still falling, and that's not going to hold long."

I look at the top of the cave, and for the first time I realize the rocks aren't falling from the mountain but seem to appear out of thin air. "I don't think they're real."

Aidan follows my gaze and sucks in a sharp breath. "That has to be some kind of magical trap, then."

I step closer to the cave as another rock tumbles from the ceiling, grazing my arm as it bounces past me. Burning pain shoots through my arm, and it makes me cry out. "They still hurt like hell."

"I have an idea." Aidan pushes by me and I pull my arm against my body as I step out of his way. He closes his eyes and lifts his arms, palms facing toward the sky.

Water seeps from the ground and between the cracks in the mountain wall. It rains down, soaking the edge of the cave. A faint yellow light shimmers over the opening, and to my amazement, the falling rocks subside.

"What is that light?" I walk up to it, reaching out my fingers.

"Don't touch that." The severity in Aidan's tone makes me jump.

I shake my head to clear it; it's as if something about

the light mesmerizes my thoughts. "Sorry. There's something strange about it." My voice trails off, and I can feel my fingers reaching back toward the light. Warnings scream in the back of my head, but I think I need to touch it.

Aidan pins my arm to my side just before my hand reaches the light and gently walks me away from the shimmer. "That's a gate. It pulls you in and the second you touch it, you're on the other side, trapped."

"Trapped?" I frown at him. "But Zoe is on the other side."

"I know." His jaw muscles twitch as he clenches his teeth.

"Zoe!" I hold my breath, listening for a reply that doesn't come. "Zoe!"

A tiny voice giggles behind us.

Aidan and I spin around, searching the rocky debris for the source.

"Who's there?" My voice is strained as my chest grows tighter. "Come out."

Another giggle, but this time farther away.

"Leave us alone." I'm on the verge of screaming as I kick a piece of rock off the ledge.

"Ciara?" Zoe's voice sounds weak and shaky.

My heart leaps and I rush over to the wall, careful not to get too close to the shimmering light. "Zoe? Are you hurt? Can you stand up?"

Zoe groans, and it echoes off the walls. "I'm bleeding, but I don't think anything is broken."

She grunts as she pushes herself off the floor and sways on unsteady legs. "I must've hit my head, because you guys are blurry."

"There's a magical gate locking you inside. We need to

figure out how to get you out of there." I pace in front of the wall, wringing my hands.

"Thanks for stating the obvious." Zoe frowns, then suddenly bends over and heaves.

I squeeze my eyes shut at the sound of vomit splashing across the rocks. "That's gross."

"Again with the obvious," Zoe says, her voice flat and scratchy.

I press my lips together until I think I can say something without being rude. She's trying my patience, but we're running out of time. "What can you see in there? Is there any way out?"

"There's no way out of here," Zoe grumbles.

"I think we need to hurry." Aidan glances over his shoulder, his brows creased. "We don't know what that creature was, and we don't know what type of trap this is."

"What do you mean, what type of trap?" Zoe wipes at a stream of blood running down the side of her face and rubs it on her jacket.

"It could be a holding cell or it might be a portal. It doesn't help that we don't know who or what created it." Aidan shrugs as we both stare at him.

Zoe sighs, moving closer to the wall. "That's helpful. What happens if I touch it?"

"Find out." It's my turn to shrug when they both look at me. I sigh, letting my shoulders drop and my hands hang loose at my sides. "We told you not to go in there but you did anyway. I have an idea if you'll let me try."

"Whatever you can do, we need to get out of here." Aidan scans the sides of the mountains, his hands balled at his sides.

Zoe stares at me, her fingers hovering centimeters from

the shimmering gate. Without breaking eye contact, she leans in, dipping her fingers into the light.

A loud crack rips through the air and she squeals, flying through the air and crashing to the ground on her side. Zoe sits up, coughing, and her eyes widen at the gel oozing from the rocks. She kicks her feet, scrambling to get away. "What is this stuff?"

I suck in a sharp breath through my teeth, reaching out to pull on Aidan's sleeve with my eyes glued to the gel. It's thick and slow moving, a greenish-yellow that makes my stomach turn. "I think that's the same stuff the mages used to cover the pieces of Leo's birthstone."

Aidan lets out a soft whistle. "Then your idea better work."

Zoe squeals as some of the gel touches her hand. "That burns. Hurry up."

I bite my tongue to keep from snapping at her because I know that my sarcasm will just have to wait. Carefully, I work my way to the far corner of the ledge, placing my hands against the side of the mountain and whispering a plea of help to the earth.

As soon as the words leave my mouth, I feel the rock shift beneath my palms and I know that this is going to work. I reach with my magic until I feel the tingling sensation of the rocks and gently coax the stones apart. My breathing comes in short pants and sweat covers my face, but before long, I create a hole large enough for Zoe to climb through beyond the shimmering gate.

I reach my arms through the opening to grab her hands and a small blob of gel lands on my hand. I yank my arm back as my skin sizzles. "Shit, that hurts."

The spot on my hand instantly turns into an angry red

blister. "Can you climb through without getting that stuff all over you?"

"I don't think so, but I'm going to try. The floor is almost covered." Zoe moves close to the opening, bouncing on her toes.

Aidan steps up beside me, holding his hands close to the opening. "Get yourself up there and I'll pull you through as quick as I can."

"It's melting the edge of my boot," Zoe whimpers. She blows out a quick breath, puffing her cheeks, and jumps for the opening, screaming as Aidan pulls her out of the cave.

They crash to the ground, extremely close to falling over the ledge. I place my hand on the rock, silently thanking the mountain for its help as Aidan pulls Zoe to her feet.

"That was close." Zoe strips off her jacket, checking it for the gel, and shrugs it back on.

I fold my arms across my chest. "I guess we aren't even anymore."

"Let's go." Aidan's blunt tone leaves no room for arguing. "It's going to be dark soon, and we don't want to be out in the open when that happens. Especially not after all that magic."

"How can you tell?" I look up at the silver sky that hasn't changed since we left the Zodiac compound.

"Keep your eyes open for caves and creatures. If you see something, we'll check it out. No more rushing into things." Aidan levels his gaze at Zoe.

"All right, I'm sorry." Zoe ducks her head, falling in behind Aidan as he makes his way up a narrow, winding path.

I keep my eyes glued to the ground as I bring up the rear, wondering how we're going to make it out of this realm alive. Movement flickers around the edges of my vision, but I can't bring myself to look.

The travel is slow and tough, as the path grows steeper and the rocks around us get sharper. The sleeves of my jacket snag against the mountain, but I don't dare move closer to the edge. The sky darkens, turning black in an instant, and as the moon shines high above, the temperature drops.

"Has anyone seen anything we can use for shelter?" Aidan asks, stopping to lean against the rock.

"No," I grumble.

"Then let's aim for that low point and see if we can get to the other side of the mountain." Aidan points to a small curve that dips in the mountain before the jagged rock shoots nearly vertical toward the sky.

Zoe pulls her coat tighter around her body, ducking her head against the wind that's starting to blow. "Why? Is it going to be warmer on the other side of the mountain?"

Aidan narrows his eyes at her. "The Beinn Dorcha Mountains are always frozen, but we haven't found any shelter yet and we can't climb any higher."

"You can't." I snicker at his glare. "Lead the way. It's freezing out here."

Aidan pushes himself away from the wall and heads up the path, shoving his hands deep inside his jacket pockets.

I didn't realize how tired I was until we stopped for a quick break. My legs feel as if I have cement in my shoes, and my calf muscles burn with the steady incline. The cold air burns my lungs as I yawn so hard it makes my eyes water, and the wind whips my hair around my face.

Movement on the mountain beside my head catches my eye, and I stop, pressing close to the wall, but I don't see anything. I study the rock, searching for anything, any kind of creature or animal that might be living here. Nothing.

"Ciara, are you okay?" Aidan asks, watching me with his eyebrows raised.

Zoe folds her arms across her chest, studying her nails like she's bored.

I take one last look at the wall and it's still just jagged rock. "I'm fine. I thought I saw something. Let's just keep walking."

Aidan hesitates but continues up the path.

The wind races around us, blowing harder the higher we climb. I pull a beanie out of my backpack and stuff my hair beneath it to keep it out of my face, so I can be on full lookout for anything close to us.

I jump as something brushes across my cheek and whip my head around, trying to find the creature. A high giggle rushes past me on the wind and I turn in circles, my heart pounding in my chest.

"Did you guys hear that?" I struggle to shout over the wind.

Zoe shakes her head as Aidan brushes past her, stopping in front of me. He reaches down and grabs my hands, pulling me close with a frown on his face. "Are you feeling all right? Maybe we should stop and rest."

"I'm good with resting, but I'm fine. You mean you didn't hear that?" My stomach twists, watching his face as he struggles with something to say. Am I going crazy? Did I even hear anything, or was it a trick of the wind?

"What did you hear?" Aidan asks carefully, squeezing my fingers.

"There was a giggle in the wind. Something brushed against my face and I saw something move on the rock earlier. I've been hearing things giggle at me all day long, and it's driving me crazy." My words hold more force than I mean for them to, but the cold and fatigue are setting in and making me grumpy.

Aidan gives me a soft smile that quickly slips from his face as he searches all around us.

"I didn't hear anything, but I believe you. We're probably being followed. If you see anything, shout out, because everything here is dangerous." He leans down, softly kissing my lips.

"Are you two done yet?" Zoe rolls her eyes, but the hint of a smile tugs at her mouth. "Did I hear something about resting?"

Aidan drops one of my hands but hangs on to the other, pulling me behind him toward Zoe.

"Yeah, I saw a large boulder around that bend, and we can sit behind it and have a snack." His eyes brighten and I shake my head, knowing he's thinking about having some chips.

It only takes a couple of minutes to sit ourselves behind the boulder, all of us squishing together, with me in the middle, to block some of the cold. The wind still howls across the mountain, a creepy ghost song as it echoes through the rocks, but the boulder provides a small amount of shelter.

"Zoe, can you give us any fire?" I rub my hands together, already imagining warming my frozen fingers.

"I'll try, but I don't know if it'll stay lit." Zoe holds her hand out, her palm an inch from the ground, and closes her eyes. Heat radiates through her body and a tiny flame sparks beneath her fingers. She pulls her hand back and the flame puffs out in the wind.

Zoe huffs and puts her hand back down, leaving it close until she coaxes the flame into an actual fire that whips in the gusts. "Get warm while you can in case that goes out, too."

I reach close to the fire, relaxing into the heat that works its way through my body. "Thank you."

Zoe nods, her eyes glued to the fire as she pulls a small sandwich out of her bag.

Aidan unzips his backpack, pulling out a sandwich for me and a bag of potato chips for himself, which he happily rips into, stuffing a large handful in his mouth.

Zoe leans around me, smiling as she watches him dive back into the bag. "You call that a snack?"

I chuckle as Aidan has to chew through the chips in his mouth to talk. "He's addicted to junk food. I think we've created a monster."

Aidan swipes his hand clean on his pants, wrinkling his nose at me. "I don't know why you always call it junk. It's not junk. It's good."

I snicker, nibbling at my sandwich. "Junk food is just something we call food that doesn't really have any nutritional value, like meat or fruit or vegetables."

Aidan holds up the bag, reading the front of it. "These are potato chips. Potatoes are vegetables." He smiles at me, puffing out his chest.

Zoe and I laugh as he sits there looking proud of himself. "You're right. You win." I take another bite and hand the sandwich back to Aidan.

"Is that all you're going to eat?" He wraps the food back up and stuffs it back into his bag.

"We should probably get going again." I sigh, not wanting to get up from the heat of the fire. I reach over and manage to snag a couple of chips before Aidan rips the bag away.

"Hey. Those are mine." He rolls the bag up and puts

them away.

I snort. "One day you'll have to learn to share them."

"Not likely." Aidan leans over and kisses my cheek.

Zoe gasps, ruining our moment as she leans in close to the flames, her eyes wide and staring.

"What is it?" I stare at the fire too even though I have no idea what I'm looking for.

"I saw a face in the fire," Zoe says softly. "It was looking right at me. I've never seen anything like that before."

"I've been seeing and hearing things all afternoon. Welcome to crazy land with me." I continue to stare at the fire, but I don't see anything.

"It was there, I saw it," Zoe grumbles.

I stand up, slinging my backpack over my shoulders. "I'm not saying you didn't. Magic is different here."

I slip my hand into Aidan's, waiting for Zoe to join us. "Come on, we should keep going."

She watches the fire for so long that I begin to think she's going to ignore me, but she waves her hand over the flames and they disappear. She slings her bag over her shoulder and falls in behind us.

The bit of rest and food help to make me feel better, but it doesn't take long until I'm forcing my body to keep moving. My eyes are heavy, and all I want to do is lie down and sleep for a week. My heavy legs feel like we've been walking for days and not hours, and it doesn't seem like we're getting any closer to reaching the mountain pass.

"How much farther are we going to walk?" I try to keep the whine out of my voice, but I don't think I'm successful.

"I think we're getting close," Aidan says, giving my hand a gentle squeeze.

I glance up at the dark sky as the first snowflake kisses

my cheek, and it only takes a minute before we're caught up in a flurry of white, whirling on the wind.

Zoe groans. "I can't believe it's snowing."

I whip around at the sound of laughter in the snow, my breath catching in my throat. "Did anyone hear that this time?"

"I did," Aidan says softly.

"What is going on? What's so funny?" I shout at no one in particular.

More laughter, but this time it sounds like it's swirling around my head. I lean against the mountain and shriek as it shifts beneath me, pushing myself so fast that I nearly slip off the edge of the path.

Aidan grabs my arm, holding me steady. "What are you doing?"

"The mountain moved," I say between ragged pants. "I felt it."

"I didn't see anything move." Zoe leans in and studies the rock.

"And I didn't see a face in the fire," I snap at her. My heart sinks as she flinches at my words. "I'm sorry. I didn't mean that. I'm tired of feeling paranoid."

"It's all right, I get it." Zoe hangs her head, her copper hair whipping around her face.

I straighten my shoulders, refusing to let this place get the best of me. "I really am sorry."

She smiles at me, a halfhearted gesture, and I know she's as nervous as I am.

"Come on. We'll walk until we find a cave or another large boulder to sit behind, and we'll camp there for the night." Aidan gently pulls my hand, and my shoulders drop as I fall in behind him.

I stare at the ground as I walk, with the snowflakes

creating a slippery blanket on top of the rocky path, and I'm forced to concentrate on every footstep to keep from falling off the mountain. My body shivers, my teeth chatter, and every step I take is an enormous effort.

Zoe stumbles behind me, bumping lightly against my back as a whimper escapes her lips.

"Sorry," she mumbles.

I steady her with my free hand, feeling like I might fall over too. "I got you. Aidan, I don't think we can walk much farther."

"I think I see something up ahead. Can you make it?" Aidan's face is pale other than the flush in his cheeks, and snow is freezing to his hair.

I glance at Zoe and she nods, but when I turn back to Aidan, the ground tilts. I stumble forward, bumping against him and nearly dragging Zoe with me.

"I'm sorry, I..." My mind goes blank as tiny colored dots explode in front of my eyes.

Aidan speaks to me, but no sound reaches my ears. I reach out with my hand, my fingers scraping against the jagged rock as everything goes dark.

9

"Should we wake her up or leave her alone?" Aidan's hushed voice comes from somewhere close to me.

There's a moment of silence before Zoe answers. "I'm not sure what to do. We don't even know why she passed out."

I passed out? That seems to happen a lot in this realm. I try to open my eyes and tell them I'm awake and that I'm doing okay, but they won't budge. Nothing in my body seems to respond. What's happening?

"I'm really worried. We need her." Aidan's voice breaks, causing my heart to break along with him. "I need her. I love her."

I scream that I'm awake, but it only happens in my head. Why can't I move?

Zoe sighs. "I'm worried about her, too. I've been a little rough on her, but only because I was jealous that the Zodiacs put her in charge when she doesn't know anything. That's not her fault, though, and I'd like the chance to tell her I'm sorry."

I work to pry my eyes open, straining to make anything

move. I push on my arms, my legs, desperate to let them know I'm awake. My heart pounds in my chest as I push harder. Panic weighs heavy on my mind. Can't they see I'm trying to move?

Before I drive myself into a full anxiety attack, I decide to focus on my surroundings. I can feel cold stone beneath my back, and there's extra weight from what is probably a blanket. There's a slight echo when they talk, and I can hear the occasional plop of water dripping. Did they find a cave?

There's a scraping noise on the ground, and I feel a hand gently caress the side of my face.

"How long do you think we should wait?" Aidan's voice is right above me.

"I'm not sure. Is there any change?" Zoe's voice is soft, barely above a whisper.

"Not that I can tell." Again, I feel his hand move over my face. "Her breathing feels steady, but her face is ice cold."

"Here." More scraping against the ground and heat spreads over the right side of my body.

"Maybe the fire will help," Zoe says, sounding closer.

I struggle against my frozen form, ready to scream if I thought it would do any good. Why is this happening? What is holding me here?

Lie still, a female voice whispers in my head.

My heart skips a beat. Who said that? Who could be talking inside my head?

Aidan pulls a strand of hair from my face, and I hear him clear his throat. "I think the fire is helping. Thank you."

"Sure," Zoe says as I feel the heat intensify. "Do you think we should take her back to the Zodiacs?"

"I don't know if we should move her." Aidan adjusts the blanket covering my body.

You don't have to move me. I want to scream. The

frustration builds until I feel like I might explode. Still, nothing happens.

Stay calm. The voice whispers again.

At least I know I'm not imagining things. Who are you? What do you want, and how can you tell me to stay calm? The questions run through my mind, and I pray that whatever is in my head is friendly and will answer me.

The rock beneath my back shifts.

Aidan gasps. "Did you see that? I think she moved. Ciara? Ciara, can you hear me?"

I don't know what to do. I can't answer him, and it breaks my heart to cause him so much worry. A warm tear trickles down the side of my face.

"Look, she's crying." Zoe's voice is hushed but excited. "Is she waking up?"

"Ciara?" Aidan strokes my cheek.

Let me go, I think at the voice in my head. Please, tell me what's happening. Silence. Who are you?

I am the earth, she whispers in my head. My heart leaps. Can you help me?

Lie still. It's almost over.

My breath catches in my throat. Over? How? I'm not ready to die.

Not death, child. The voice is calm, and it helps to soothe my nerves.

Why can't I move? I try to stretch my arms, but my body still resists.

"What's going on?" Zoe asks.

"I don't know." Aidan places each hand on either side of my face and I feel a cool, soothing energy flow through me. "I think I can feel her in there, but she's not responding to my magic."

You don't belong here, child. Something hunts you. It wants your magic, the earth whispers.

Cold fear trickles down my spine. What's hunting me?

The rock beneath me shifts again. It is not natural even for this realm. *Be still and let the healing finish.*

I force my mind to be still, fighting every instinct to panic, and I relax into the thought that the earth will help me.

My body vibrates, humming with a warm energy that surges through my entire core. Every part of me tingles and my heart beats faster.

Aidan gasps above my head. "She's glowing."

"What?" Zoe's voice is sharp, followed by her own gasp. "What is that green light?"

I fight the urge to ask the earth what's happening to me and concentrate on the energy rushing through my body. My breathing feels easier, with each inhalation reaching deeper into my lungs.

"Is that her magic?" Zoe asks, hope in her voice.

"It has to be earth magic, but I don't want to disturb it." I feel Aidan's hands slip from my face.

Breathe, child, the earth whispers in my mind.

I take in a deep breath, filling my lungs, and let it out slowly. My hand involuntarily jerks.

"She moved." Aidan's voice is hushed.

The tingling energy intensifies, buzzing in my ears, until the sound is all I can hear. My body tenses, the muscles twitching on their own.

You must be careful. It isn't safe for you here. Go back home. The voice in my head is stronger, rising above the buzzing in my ears.

I can't go back home yet. I struggle to form the thought in my mind. I have to help Aries.

The energy shifts, running cold through my veins. What are you doing now? My body shivers, shaking me to the core.

Your magic will be stronger now and I have given you some protection, but you must still be careful. Every creature, every element, knows you will stop the unnatural magic.

The weight of her words weighs heavy on my heart. Everyone expects so much from me, and I'm not sure I can do what they need me to do.

You are a child of the earth, and you share my qualities. You are strong. Unbreakable. Open your eyes.

My eyes fly open and I suck in a breath sharp enough to send me into a coughing fit.

Aidan's hands are on me in a flash, supporting me behind my back as I struggle to breathe. "Are you all right?"

Zoe takes my hand in hers, the heat of her grasp almost too much to bear against my freezing skin. "What happened?"

I get my coughing under control and lean against Aidan. I try to speak but end up doubling over and hacking again. My throat feels raw, like I took a drink made of acid. I hold up my finger, waiting on the tingling to subside, and I squeeze my eyes shut, pushing the tears down my cheeks.

Are you still there?

I'm always with you, child. The earth's words are still strong in my mind, and I breathe a little easier.

Thank you for whatever you did. The ground shifts beneath me again and I imagine her to be rolling over, now that her job is done. She doesn't answer me, but I take comfort in the fact that she's with me.

Aidan rubs my back, holding me close against him. "Ciara? Are you okay?"

My body feels more alive than it ever has before, even

more than using magic or when I went through my ritual. I can feel every stone, every speck of dirt.

"I'm fine," I finally say, even though my voice is raspy.

"Can you tell us what happened?" Zoe asks quietly.

I sit up, stretching my arms carefully, and look at the small cave as Zoe's fire crackles happily between us. My body is stiff from lying on the hard floor, but the movement feels good. "The earth healed me. While she was helping me, she said that something was hunting me and trying to steal my magic."

Aidan sucks in a sharp breath. "The earth spoke to you?"

"Yeah, she said she's always with me." As the words come out of my mouth, I know they're true, and I think some part of me has always known that.

Zoe squeezes my hand so hard that I have to pull it free. "Something's hunting you? Does that mean it's hunting all of us? And what do you mean, steal your magic?" Her eyes are wide as the color drains from her face.

I glance at Aidan, but he only holds my gaze. "It has to be something to do with the mages. Think about it. They stole Delia's magic and used it to break Leo's stone, and they tried to do the same to Morgan. It's what they want to do to all of us to make their tethers."

"We're not even safe here on Polaris," Zoe says softly, speaking more to herself.

I glance out the opening of the cave, but it's still nighttime, and all I can see is solid darkness. "We're not safe anywhere."

"If you're feeling all right, we should get some sleep and leave at first light." Aidan pulls me back into his arms.

I relax into the warmth and comfort of his body, placing my palm flat on the rock. Please watch over us.

I didn't expect an answer, but the earth whispers in my mind once more. *You will be safe this night.*

Zoe stretches out next to the fire, using her bag as a pillow. "Should we take turns watching the cave?"

"The earth says we'll be fine tonight." I snuggle against Aidan and he wraps his arms tightly around me.

"Okay." Zoe yawns, falling instantly asleep.

Aidan leans close to my ear to keep from waking Zoe. "I was so scared that something awful had happened to you."

"When I first woke up, I could hear you guys talking, and I tried to speak and move but I was completely frozen. I was scared too, but I'm sorry to put you through that." I tilt my head back to look at him and he kisses my forehead.

"I'm not sure what I'd do without you now." Tears pool in his eyes, but he quickly blinks them away.

I smile at him, my heart full. "Let's hope we never find out."

"Let's hope." Aidan kisses my lips and I shift closer to him. "Get some sleep," he whispers, his mouth still on mine.

I sigh, leaning against his chest, with my forehead against the curve of his neck. "Fine."

He chuckles, squeezing me tight, and in the safety and warmth of his arms, I fall into a deep sleep.

I sit at the mouth of the cave, my knees pulled up to my chest with my arms holding them tight. The sun rises, splashing pinks, reds, and purples across the sky, shades of colors I never even dreamed of, so bright and vivid that they don't look real. Polaris is as beautiful as it is deadly.

I'm not exactly sure where we are, or how far they walked after I passed out last night, but I know this cave is still on the side of the mountain that faces the Zodiac compound because I can see it in the distance from this height. My shoulders droop at the thought of how much farther we might have to travel.

Absently, I toy with the silver goat that hangs around my neck, wondering if the magic inside will be enough to keep me alive in this realm as I listen to the soft breathing of Aidan and Zoe behind me. What else are we going to see out there? What exactly is after us if even the creatures here know it isn't natural?

My eyes scan the horizon, but everything appears to be perfectly still. It all seems so quiet and peaceful in the early morning hours, but I know that isn't even a little true.

The beautiful vision in front of me is deceptive, and that weighs heavy on my heart. The mages are out there somewhere and they're making their plans, even in this realm, but I still question whether I can stop them. I need to know what they're up to. What do they really want?

Footsteps shuffle across the floor, coming in my direction, but I know it's Aidan and I don't turn around. He adjusts the blanket around my shoulders before sitting down beside me with a soft smile. "You're up early. Did you get enough rest?"

"I actually feel great. I'm not tired, and my body doesn't hurt." I glance at him before turning my attention back to the sunrise.

Aidan snorts. "Shouldn't you be happy about that?"

"I am happy," I say with a frown.

"Then you should tell your face." He raises his eyebrows, mischief sparkling in his blue eyes.

I laugh, swatting him playfully on the arm, then quickly sober. "I was sitting here thinking about what evil is hiding out there in such a beautiful scene."

"Those are heavy thoughts for so early in the morning," he says softly.

I pause, trying to figure out how to tell him that my body feels different, finally deciding blunt is best. "I feel different."

"Different how?" One eyebrow arches high on his forehead as he studies my face.

"I'm not really sure how to explain it." I chew on my bottom lip to give myself time to make sense of my thoughts.

"I don't know what's following us or what exactly made me pass out yesterday. I just thought I was getting dizzy from the altitude or the cold or the fact that we'd been walking all day. But then I woke up and I couldn't move. I was terrified until suddenly the earth was talking to me in my head."

I shift my position on the ground, turning to face Aidan, and I tuck my legs beneath me as he waits patiently for me to continue. "The earth saved me. It's her magic that made me wake up, and it was her light that healed me."

Aidan sits up a little straighter. "How do you know about the light?"

"I heard you guys talking even though I couldn't answer you." My tone is more bitter than I mean for it to sound.

"What else did you hear?" Aidan's eyes widen as he watches me.

I hold his gaze for a couple of heartbeats. "A lot, but maybe not everything."

Aidan lets a slow breath out, puffing his cheeks. "So, how do you feel different?"

I refrain from shaking my head. "She told me when everything was done, my magic would be stronger and that she gave me some protection."

He lets out a low whistle.

"The earth strengthened your magic?" His tone holds a note of awe.

My heart beats a little faster at his reaction. "That's what she said. It scares me, though, because I still can't control the magic I have. Why? Is that unusual?"

"Unusual?" Aidan shakes his head. "Try that never happens. The elements allow us to work with them, those of us that are born with a stronger affinity to a certain element. We have a stronger connection, and that's how we can create the magic. I've never heard of any element giving magic to a person or even talking to a person."

My chin trembles slightly, and I take a deep, shaky breath. "Then why would she do that for me?"

Aidan reaches over, rubbing my cold fingers between his warm hands. "I don't know why she did that."

I pull my hands away. "And don't you dare say it's because I'm special."

Aidan tries to give me a stern look, but a warm smile wins, spreading across his face. He reaches for my hands again, holding them tightly but gently. "But you are special, and one of these days you'll understand that."

A tear slips down my cheek. "Sometimes being special has consequences."

He holds my gaze, his clear blue eyes unblinking. "Ciara, I..."

My breath catches in my throat.

"What are you guys doing? Is it time to go?" Zoe's voice cuts through the tension between us, shattering the moment.

I sigh, looking at her across the cave where she's propped up on her elbow.

"We were just chatting while you were getting a little more sleep, but yeah, we should get going soon." As I stand up and brush off my pants, I look down at Aidan, his face looking as disappointed as I feel.

Aidan hops to his feet and walks over to his backpack, glaring at Zoe as he sits down.

"What?" Zoe looks from Aidan to me, her eyes wide. "Why did he look at me like that? What did I do?"

I chuckle to myself as I shrug my shoulders at her, walking over to sit beside Aidan.

Zoe rolls her blanket, stuffing it in her bag as she mutters words I can't understand. When she's finished, Aidan passes around sandwiches to everyone, all made of soft bread, piled high with ham and cheese. The three of us eat in silence, each of us left to our own thoughts.

As soon as we finish breakfast, we slip into our backpacks and hesitate, none of us wanting to leave the safety of the cave.

"Do you think we'll find the fire today?" Zoe asks, her voice small.

My stomach twists at the thought that it could be anywhere on this mountain and we've barely searched anywhere. "We're going to have to find it soon. The magic in our necklaces will only let us stay here for a couple more days, and not only do we have to find it, but we have to get back."

"We have a lot of ground to cover, and it's not going to be easy. Let's go." Aidan leads the way out of the cave. Zoe and I sigh in unison as we fall in line, heading to who knows where.

A thin coat of ice covers the path, and the steep slope makes the walking treacherous. We move slowly, each step deliberate to keep from falling down or falling off the mountain. A quick glance up at least shows that we aren't far from crossing to the other side of the mountain.

"How did you guys find that cave last night?" I don't really care, but I'm hoping the small talk will take my mind off the climb.

"Aidan was carrying you and I saw it," Zoe says around pants of breath.

I snort. "That's exciting. Anything unusual about it?"

"Just a cave." Zoe's voice is flat, and I'm pretty sure that's all I'm going to get out of her.

An image of a different cave opening floats through my mind, and as I look up, I recognize the rocks up ahead.

"Speaking of caves, there's one coming up on the right." I stop short when they both turn to stare at me. "What?"

"How do you know that?" Zoe narrows her eyes at me.

"This is going to sound stupid, but it just floated into my mind." I shrug as her mouth drops open before turning my gaze to Aidan.

He nods at me, trusting me more than anyone has in my entire life. "Then let's go check it out."

The path, barely wide enough for us to walk in single file, grows steeper as we finally reach the crest that will lead to the other side of the mountain. It takes a slight turn to the right, and there, on the side of the mountain is the small cave, looking just like it did in my mind.

Aidan smiles at me, but Zoe still looks confused as she frowns at the cave.

The path widens enough for us to squeeze together in front of the opening, all of us reaching out to see if anything feels off.

The only energy I can sense is from the earth, so I turn to Zoe. "Can you feel any fire in there?"

Her eyes are still closed as she gives a small shake of her head. "There's nothing in there."

"I don't feel anything either, but we should still check it

out," Aidan says, walking straight into the shadow with Zoe and I right on his heels.

We stop in the center of the small space, no more than five feet across with a ceiling rounded to a perfect dome. The walls are perfectly smooth, as if they'd been sanded. There isn't a visible crack or dent in the entire cave. The only thing that seems out of place is a large, jagged boulder.

"Does this place seem weird to you?" Zoe stares at the walls. "Do you think it's another trap?"

I shake my head, chewing on my bottom lip. "It's not a trap. It doesn't feel like the first one, but I think you're right. This place is weird."

Aidan steps over to the side, running his finger lightly down the wall. "It's like someone polished it."

"Did someone polish it?" I ask, joining him near the wall.

"I don't know what would live out here and I don't know of any creatures that can do this." He glances at me, and the look on his face says that he's not quite sure of himself.

"Is it mages?" Zoe's voice is high and tight.

I lay my palms flat on the wall, closing my eyes. There's energy that runs through this rock, but I'm almost overwhelmed by a complete sense of love. I open my eyes, blinking back the tears. "No. There's love in this, and no mage I've seen can put that kind of feeling into something. This cave has been lovingly taken care of."

"It doesn't look like we're going to find anything in here, and I'm not sure I want to be here when whoever did this comes back." Aidan heads toward the opening.

"Hang on. Since we're in here out of the cold, let's have a quick rest and water break. It's going to be just as hard going down the other side of the mountain." I fold my arms over my chest, and after glancing at a nodding Zoe, Aidan pulls some water out of his pack.

"Thank you," I say as I pull water out of my pack and wander over to the large boulder, finding a place that looks flat enough to sit on, and take a few sips.

The rock lurches, tossing me with a shriek to the hard floor. I get my hands down to break my fall as pain shoots through my arms. A rough hand digs into my leg to the point it might break and I scream again, twisting around to see my attacker.

Looming above me is the rock, standing six feet tall in the shape of a man, with his head grazing the ceiling. His eyes, which are merely holes in his face, are fixed directly on me.

"Why are you in my home?" the rock creature bellows loud enough to shake the ground and make me slam my hands over my ears.

10

A fireball whizzes over my head, slamming against the rock creature and causing as much damage as if it were a fly.

I tilt my head back far enough to get an upside-down view of Zoe, her arms outstretched and gathering more fire around her fingertips.

The creature roars, stomping one heavy foot so that the ground shakes beneath me.

Aidan darts forward and grabs my wrists, straining to pull me out of the creature's grasp.

The rock golem tightens his grip around my leg and I shriek in pain, waiting on the bones in my leg to break. With his free hand, he swats at Aidan, sending him crashing against the wall, and yanks me closer to his feet.

I struggle in the golem's grasp, kicking my free foot with no luck. I throw my arms up as the creature looks down at me, the holes that act as his eyes narrow, and I swear he looks annoyed.

Another ball of fire races over my head, close enough that I feel the heat on my face, and it explodes against the creature's chest, leaving a small black smudge.

"That was really close," I shout at Zoe.

Zoe doesn't say a word, instead she shoots a steady stream of fire into the creature.

The creature howls, letting go of my leg as he rumbles toward Zoe. She stands her ground, her face pale and sweaty.

I jump to my feet, stumbling a little on my sore and bruised leg, and turn around to get a look at Aidan. He lies motionless against the wall, and a cold shiver runs down my spine. I race across the cave but only take a few steps before a thick stone arm swings down and shoves me behind his body.

Zoe pulls in her fire, wheezing from the effort of the constant magic, and she bends over with her hands on her knees, looking ready to fall over.

Aidan groans, shifting around until he stands on unsteady legs. His eyes meet mine as I peek around the golem and he sets his jaw, raising his hands.

The creature growls, again smashing his foot into the ground, and he sends a large crack shooting across the cave floor directly toward Aidan.

"Look out!" I race from behind the creature but only make it a few steps before he pushes me behind his body.

The creature turns to look at me, the sound of scraping rocks filling the air as he moves. "Stay."

He turns his attention back to Aidan, grumbling as Aidan deftly jumps out of the way of the crack.

Aidan lands in front of Zoe, putting himself between her and the creature, and raises his hands. Water seeps out of the ground, swirling around our feet.

Zoe straightens and moves beside Aidan, fire flaming around her fingers.

The rock golem shifts, keeping his eyes glued on Aidan and Zoe, and puts himself directly in front of me.

I lean around the creature, hoping for a chance to run, when he nudges me again, this time more gentle than before.

"Please, stay." The golem's voice rumbles deep within him like an earthquake shaking the ground.

The tone of his voice catches me off guard and I hesitate, one foot raised in the air and ready to run. "Stop using your magic."

"What?" Aidan lowers his hands, but the water continues to swirl over the floor.

I lean forward, pressing against the leg of the creature but careful to stay behind him. "I said stop using your magic."

"Are you crazy?" Zoe raises her arms, the fire blazing up her arms and almost to her elbows.

The creature raises his foot again, slamming it down and sending a spiderweb of cracks across the ground like shattering ice.

Zoe stumbles but stays upright as she forms the fire into a sphere.

"Damn it, Zoe, stop it. If he cracks this ground anymore, we're all going to fall through." I step around the creature's leg, moving out of the way of his arm as he tries to hold me back. I turn to face the golem, folding my arms over my chest. "And you stop it too."

The rock golem stares at me, unmoving.

I turn back around to face Zoe, who still has fire crackling between her hands. "Aidan, please."

Aidan raises one eyebrow, hesitating for a second before flicking his hand in an upward motion. The water from the floor shoots up, drenching Zoe and reducing her fire to a hissing cloud of steam.

"What the hell?" Zoe's voice is shrill. "What's going on?"

I take a cautious step forward, waiting for the creature to stop me, but he doesn't. "I think he's protecting me. He thinks you two are the danger."

I spin around to face the golem. "Is that right? You're trying to keep me safe?"

The creature stands so still as he looks at me that for a moment, that I think he turned back into stone. "I protect all things that are one with the earth."

"Thank you, but I don't need protection. These are my friends, and they aren't going to hurt you." I look over my shoulder, locking eyes with Zoe. "Right?"

Zoe glances up at the creature, her eyes wide, before returning to my gaze. "I won't do anything else unless he starts it."

I sigh. "That's very helpful."

Aidan crosses the cave to stand behind me, slipping his hand in mine as he stares up at the creature. "I've never seen a rock golem before, not in person anyway. The Zodiacs have books with pictures, of course."

The golem raises his arm, poking Aidan in the shoulder, and it sends him stumbling backward, but I squeeze his hand to keep him upright.

"I don't see many humans," the creature rumbles.

Aidan sputters and I bend over laughing, feeling some of the stress of this journey melt away. After a moment, Aidan joins me, and even Zoe chuckles.

I take a deep breath, settling myself, and look up at the creature. "I'm sorry we just barged into your home. The smoothness of the walls is really beautiful."

"It is not safe for you here." The golem lowers himself to

the floor, sitting down with enough force to add a few more cracks in the stone.

I grit my teeth, waiting for the crackling to stop, and when it does, I carefully lower myself beside the creature. "I know it's not safe, but we're on a very important journey. Someone depends on us."

Zoe grunts, giving a slight shake of her head as I glance at her.

"We should probably go," she says as she fidgets with her fingers.

I start to get up but I hesitate, then sit back down.

There's a feeling in the pit of my stomach and tingling on the back of my neck that tells me we're not done here yet. "We'll go soon, but sit down for a minute."

Aidan reaches a hand down toward me. "Maybe she's right."

Ignoring his hand, I glance over at the creature, who waits patiently. "Trust me. You both look like you're about to fall over."

Aidan sits close to me, and after taking the time to frown at me, Zoe completes the circle, sitting between Aidan and the golem.

I nod at both of them, sending them a silent thanks. "Why do you say it's not safe here?"

The creature drops his hands to the ground, rock scraping against rock. "It is not safe for any of us here. Not like before."

"Are you talking about the mages?" Zoe asks softly.

"The men that work their dark magic. It sickens this entire realm. They steal what is not theirs and they hurt the creatures that make this world home." The golem pushes his hands into the ground.

I reach over and gently hold his arm, hoping that my

gesture is okay, and I take his lack of movement as confirmation. "Do you know if the mages are here now? Are they close?"

The rock golem rumbles deep within his chest, and I imagine it to be a sigh. "The men come and go, but they always leave their things behind."

My heart skips a beat and I suddenly feel ice cold, more from the golem's words than the chilly cave. I shiver as I glance between Aidan and Zoe. "What things are you talking about?"

"Shadow things. Unnatural things with unnatural magic. They hurt the creatures here." More cracks splinter across the ground.

I close my eyes, taking a deep breath, and send my magic into the earth, quickly sewing the stone floor back together before anything bad happens.

Aidan clears his throat, staring up at the giant creature. "What's unnatural about the shadow things? Are they not from Polaris?"

The golem stares at him. "They are not from anywhere."

"What the hell does that mean?" Zoe quickly closes her mouth, shrugging as all three of us turn to stare at her. "Well? What does it mean?"

I gasp, struck by a sudden thought. "Do you mean the mages created the shadow things?"

"Yes," the golem rumbles.

My stomach twists in knots, and I feel a little sick. "That means we have no idea how to deal with them or if we can kill them."

Zoe groans, her face a few shades paler.

"Do you know if we can kill them?" Aidan asks.

The golem shakes his head, the sound of scraping rocks filling the air.

Aidan frowns. "No, you don't know, or no you can't kill them?"

"Others have tried and failed." The golem stands up, shaking the ground. "Come. I will take you to safety."

I stand up, stretching my legs as I brush the dirt off my pants. "Thanks, but we can't go back. We have a journey to complete, and the Zodiacs are counting on us."

"You will go to safety. I am to protect you." He reaches out one large stone arm, but I step out of the way.

"You can't make me go back." I fold my arms across my chest.

"You wouldn't even know I'm here if we hadn't come into your home looking for that fire." I press my lips together, wondering if I just said too much.

"Fire?" The golem scoops me up, raising me to his eye level, squeezing me so tight it's hard to breathe.

"The fire we need to help Aries. It's supposed to be in a cave on this mountain." My words come out more of a grunt as I bang on his hand. "You're squishing me. Can you put me down?"

The golem sets me down, and I stumble away from his hand, taking deep breaths. "I know this fire."

I almost choke on my air. "You know where we can find it?"

"At the base of the mountain on the other side. Pass through a field, then a forest, and then you will find the cave. You cannot take the fire." The golem steps carefully back to the end of the cave where he was resting when we came in.

"We have to," Zoe says, her voice tight.

He sits down, curling himself into the shape of a large boulder. "I cannot go to the cave. Tread lightly and watch the shadows."

His voice echoes through the cave as his body solidifies, looking exactly like a regular rock.

"That's just great." Zoe grabs her backpack from the ground where she dumped it.

I head for the mouth of the cave, stopping to wait for the other two. "At least we know where the cave is."

"Yeah, but why can't we take the fire?" Zoe asks, walking past me and into the silver afternoon light.

"I guess we'll find out." Aidan grabs my hand and pulls me out onto the path.

I squeeze his fingers tightly, trying not to think about what might be ahead. Or what waits for us in the shadows.

We stand on the edge of the mountain, huddled together to brace ourselves against the wind, staring at the steep path leading down the back of the mountain. From this vantage point, it looks like a vertical drop, weaving between jagged rocks.

"Of course we're going down there. Why wouldn't we go down there?" Zoe folds her arms across her chest, frowning down the side of the mountain.

"At least we didn't have to climb all the way to the top of the mountain." I snicker at her glare.

Aidan sighs. "I don't know what you two are complaining about. At least you both come from houses with rock-climbing animals."

"But you have those catlike reflexes." I bite my bottom lip to keep from laughing.

"Don't scorpions climb rocks?" Zoe asks, her eyes twinkling with mischief.

I can't hide it. The laughter bubbles over. "Yeah, don't scorpions climb rocks?"

Zoe and I share a laugh as he puts one foot on the path, testing his footing to make sure he doesn't fall. "Let's get this over with."

My laughter quickly fades as I step onto the path behind him, close enough to touch him but not so close that I bump into him, and lean way back as I walk to keep my balance.

We've barely trekked a mile down the path before we're all out of breath. My calves burn, and every muscle is tense and sore from keeping my body locked at a weird angle. The back of my neck tingles and I swat at it like a fly, wiping the sweat from my forehead with the back of my hand while it's near my face.

"What's your problem?" Zoe's question comes out more of a pant.

I shoot a quick glare over my shoulder, my legs wobbling with the sudden movement, and I throw my arms up to catch my balance. "I don't have a problem. The back of my neck was tingling. Shouldn't you be watching where you're walking instead of looking at me?"

Zoe snorts. "I am watching where I'm walking. You happen to be down there in front of me."

I roll my eyes even though I know she can't see me. "Well, enjoy the view."

Aidan stops walking, adjusting his footing as he slowly turns around to face me. "Did you say the back of your neck was tingling?"

"Yeah." I tilt my head, studying his face, but it's carefully blank. "Why?"

"What's making your neck tingle?" Aidan inches his way closer to me.

I reach back, placing my hand on my neck. "I'm not sure.

Probably because I'm sweating from all this walking. Why are you asking?"

"Are you sure it's not a warning?" Aidan scans the area around us, causing Zoe and me to look with him.

My heart beats faster. "I'm not sure. Do you see anything?"

Aidan shakes his head, a slight frown creasing his brow. "Not yet."

"Yet?" Zoe groans.

"I think we're too exposed out here like this. Let's pick up the pace and get down to that meadow." Aidan glances up at the sky. "Besides, it's almost night, and we don't want to be walking down this mountain in the dark."

I glance up at the sky and scrunch my nose. Other than the gray deepening in the clouds, I'm still not sure how he can tell it's getting dark. "Lead the way."

Without a word, Aidan continues down the trail, moving as fast as he can while still being safe. I pant as I work to keep up with him, my legs and hips putting up a full protest. The farther down we climb, the stiffer my body gets and the more my muscles scream.

"Finally," Zoe says, sounding like she's close to tears.

I glance up from the rocky path that I've been staring at for hours and see that we've reached the base of the mountain. Not far in front of us, the rocks gently even out into flat land that fades into a golden meadow. As soon as my eyes meet the grass, my stomach flips and the tingle returns. I absently rub my neck as I try to figure out why I suddenly feel so weird.

"More bugs?" Zoe scoots up beside me, looking at me out of the corner of her eye.

"I don't have bugs." I roll my eyes, blowing off her

comment. But something isn't right. The tingling in my neck increases, working its way into my shoulders.

"Aidan," I whisper, and he spins around. "Something is off. I don't think we're alone anymore."

Without a word, he grabs my hand, dragging me down the last of the path with the sound of Zoe's boots pounding the rock behind us.

"We'll search the area when we reach that tall grass," he shouts over his shoulder.

I grit my teeth, pushing my body to the limit as I struggle to breathe, and race to keep up with him. Just as we reach the edge of the grass, everything around us turns to night with a moon high in the sky, like someone just flipped a switch. "What the hell?"

We slam to a halt once we enter the meadow, and Zoe bends over with her hands on her knees.

"That's so weird how night happens here," she says between ragged breaths.

I'm too busy trying to get my breathing under control to agree with her.

Aidan works his way back to the edge of the meadow, desperately scanning the mountain and sky for any sign of a creature that might be here with us.

I look around, running my hand through the waist-high grass that's tinted gray in the light of the moon. My stomach tightens and I gasp.

Aidan and Zoe whirl around, rushing over to me, but Aidan reaches me first, his brows knitted tightly together. "What is it? Did you see something?"

"I've been here before," I say, breathless.

His eyebrows shoot high on his forehead. "That's impossible."

"I thought this was important." Zoe's shoulders slump.

I look at her out of the corner of my eye before turning back to Aidan. "Do you remember the dream I had the other night? I was dreaming about this place. I was alone, but I know this is the field."

Aidan squeezes my hand, leaning close. "And what happened in your dream?"

I hesitate, my blood running cold. "I was running from something I couldn't see. Something dark and shadowy. It caught me in the forest."

"That's easy. We don't go in the forest," Zoe says very matter-of-fact.

Aidan tears his eyes away from my face to look at her. "That forest stretches for miles, and there's nowhere else to go but back up the mountain."

"And we can't do that because the golem said the cave we need is through that forest." Pressure suddenly squeezes my head, and I put my hands up to my face as Zoe and Aidan do the same. "I think it's here."

Aidan's eyes widen, his gaze fixed on something over my shoulder. "Run."

He pushes Zoe and me in front of him and we take off full speed through the meadow, ignoring the grass that whips around us.

We run without looking back until I'm afraid that my legs won't carry me any further. The grass snaps with each step we take, but I can barely hear it over our pants. My chest heaves and burns with every breath.

Finally, we burst through the edge of the meadow and Zoe stumbles, crashing to her knees as she struggles for air. I bend over with my hands on my knees, panting as I struggle to get my breathing under control.

The moon slips behind the clouds, throwing the forest that stretches out in front of us into darkness. I blink, trying to get my eyes to adjust. The shadows beneath the leaves are deep, and a cold shiver runs down my spine, my pounding heart refusing to slow.

I turn around, searching the dark field behind us, and even though I can't see it, I know the thing that's following us is close. The energy is thick in the air, pressing against me and making my head throb. "We need to keep going."

Zoe looks up at the forest. "I don't want to go in there."

"No one does," I say, my eyes locked on the meadow. I strain to listen for anything moving in the grass, but the silence of the night weighs heavy on my shoulders, my mind spinning in wild circles. There are no sounds of birds, frogs, or even crickets. It's like the entire world holds its breath with us.

Zoe struggles to her feet. "Come on, before I change my mind."

The gray of the grass shifts into silver as the moon reappears, and the world around me changes from one thick shadow to several inky pools. The tall blades shiver and my breath catches in my throat.

The grass splits as a deep line moves quickly through the field, heading straight for us. The movement is so fast that it's hard to follow. My mouth instantly turns dry as I force my legs to step backward. It's almost here.

I turn on my heel and we race toward the trees as our feet pound against the ground. We're almost to the forest and I chance a quick look over my shoulder. There's nothing in the darkness behind us, but I know it's out there.

Tiny dots of light explode before my eyes and the air burns in my throat as we finally break through the tree line. The ancient trunks are thick and tower so high that the tops of the branches are lost in the dark. We slam to a halt, each of us ducking behind a tree, and I press my body tight against the rough bark. The wood snags at my clothes as my chest heaves with gasping breaths. I take a deep gulp of air and hold it, listening as my heart pounds in my chest.

Silence.

A cool breeze brushes against my sweaty face and makes me shiver. I swallow the lump of fear rising in my throat and carefully shift to see around the trunk without exposing too much of myself. Movement catches my eye and I gasp, quickly clamping a hand over my mouth. I squeeze my eyes shut as I slide back behind the tree, praying that it didn't see me too.

Floating through the forest is a large creature, at least six feet tall if it were touching the ground. Shadows float around it like smoke from a fire. I hear whispers behind me, like a thousand voices all talking at once, but I can't quite make out the words. They sound as if they're all coming from the same place. Inside the creature. And beneath the whispering is the soft crackling of flames.

My feet freeze to the ground, planted like I'm a part of this forest as my heart beats so fast it might explode in my chest. The voices grow louder. It's almost here. I can feel it searching for us.

I look to my left and lock eyes with Aidan, his face pale even in the darkness of the forest. Smoky tendrils weave around the trunk of his tree, brushing against his arm, and he grimaces to keep from crying out.

The icy grip of fear squeezes my chest, and I know I have to do something. I step out from my hiding place, making sure to step on a branch. The loud snap rips through the air, turning all eyes on me, except that the creature doesn't actually have any eyes.

Aidan hisses at me, but I give him a slight shake of my

head. Besides, this thing wants me, and I don't want anything to happen to Aidan.

My breath catches in my throat as I get a good look at the creature that's been stalking us. It's made completely out of shifting smoke in the vague shape of a human, and as it moves, I can see glimpses of blue fire within its body. In the center of its chest is a sickly yellow light that sends tingles racing up my arms.

Suddenly, the creature is hovering above me; it moved so fast that I didn't even see it happen. I stumble backward, catching my foot on that same branch, and crash to the ground.

The creature moves with me, pressure building in my skull as a clicking sound fills my head. It hovers almost horizontally as it peers down at me. All I can see are two black holes where the eyes should be, but they aren't empty. They're filled with darkness. Cold waves roll off it, despite the fire that burns in its body, and it makes my teeth chatter.

I try to push myself back and away from this thing, but my arms no longer work.

It floats down closer, just inches above me.

Fire flares over my head, hitting the creature square in the abdomen, but the creature absorbs the magic, causing the fire within it to glow brighter.

"No more fire. It's made of fire," I shout as I hear Zoe curse behind me.

Cold water rises out of the ground, soaking me through and causing me to shiver uncontrollably. It shoots up around me, splashing against the creature, but it still doesn't react.

The shadow moves, extending one long, bony arm, a skeleton without the skin but covered in a yellow jelly substance. It reaches for my hand.

"No," I whimper, but I can't seem to move my body.

The creature touches my skin and a scream rips through me as the jelly burns my hand like acid. It closes its grip on my hand and it burns with blinding pain as I struggle to remain conscious.

A crackling sound rips through the air as the water that Aidan splashed over us begins to harden into ice.

Hands grab me from behind, sliding me from beneath the creature. I look up, grateful to see Zoe dragging me across the ground as Aidan concentrates on his magic.

The creature straightens, floating in the air as the ice completely disappears in the rolling smoke.

Aidan steps over in front of us, his eyes narrowed. "It doesn't look like magic works on that thing."

"What do we do?" I ask as I climb to my knees, grimacing as I take a breath that feels like I have needles in my lungs.

Suddenly, the creature vanishes and the pressure lifts from my head.

Aidan whirls around, his eyes flashing with anger. "What the hell were you thinking? Why did you step out there like that?"

"It knew we were there and it was hurting you. I couldn't let that happen." A tear escapes, trickling down the side of my face.

Aidan drops to the ground in front of me, gently wiping away the tear. "I'm not worth your life."

I sniffle. "You are to me."

He gently kisses my lips. "I won't lose you. I—"

"You guys are gross." Zoe's voice cuts off his words, ruining another moment for us. "What was that yellow thing in its chest? It didn't look like it belonged there."

Aidan's shoulders slump, but he climbs to his feet and helps me up.

I lean against him, my legs feeling like jello. "It didn't belong there. That yellow light was a piece of Leo's birthstone, and we need to go get it."

11

"What do you mean, we need to go get it? We don't even know where that thing went!" Zoe's voice is loud and shrill in the silent forest.

I push myself away from Aidan, feeling bolder because of her frustration. "I'm sure we can figure out where it went."

Zoe folds her arms over her chest, leaning roughly against a thick tree trunk. "We don't have time to go chasing after some ghost."

"I don't care about the creature. We need to get that piece of the birthstone. Who knows where it'll disappear if we don't get it now." I pace in the small space between the trees.

"We need to get to the fire and get back to Aries. We're on a time limit, you know." She glares at me, the pink flush of anger staining her cheeks.

I glance at Aidan, who immediately drops his eyes to the ground, causing me to sigh. "I know we need to help Aries, but Leo needs us, too. His stone was broken, and he's very sick. The more pieces they have, the easier it'll be for the mages to build their tether."

Zoe pushes herself away from the tree, stopping close to me as she watches me pace. "Will that give you all the pieces of the stone?"

"No." Aidan's voice is almost a whisper.

I stop and stare at him, frowning, but then I remember where we'll have to go to find the final piece. "Leo's birthstone was broken into four pieces. One for the earth realm, one for this realm, one for the mage realm, and the final piece for Kyrell to control the tether. If we can get the stone from that creature, we'll only be missing the piece that Kyrell has with him."

Zoe pinches the bridge of her nose, squeezing her eyes shut. "Maybe we should just get the fire and then tell the Zodiacs that it's out here. It doesn't sound so important if it doesn't complete the stone."

My shoulders slump, a dull ache building in the back of my head. She has a point, but I can't shake the nagging feeling that we need to go after the stone. "We're wasting time standing here talking about this. Let's just go look for the stone so we can get back to the cave."

Her eyes narrow again, and she purses her lips. "We are wasting time, but we should go get the fire."

Feeling helpless, I turn to Aidan for backup. "You're the third vote. What do you think?"

Aidan sighs, looking at each of us before speaking. "I think both of you are right. We need to get to the fire as quick as we can, but we also can't lose the stone. We have no idea if the mages can take those two pieces and break them again to create the four. Not even the Zodiacs know this magic."

Zoe and I gasp in unison, and it's obvious neither of us thought of that possibility.

"I say we go after the stone, but if it takes too long or we get too far away from the cave, then we abandon the stone and get the fire. We also don't know how much longer your necklaces will let you stay in this realm." Aidan looks first at Zoe before turning to hold my gaze. "Are we all agreed on that?"

I really want to argue with him and say that we get the stone no matter what, but we also can't go back without the fire, and I don't want to die out here. "I agree."

We both turn to face Zoe as she closes her eyes for a second. "Fine."

Aidan nods, a hint of a smile that holds no joy playing across his lips. "Now, does anyone know where we are?"

Zoe groans as I look around the forest, paying attention to the details that I didn't have time to notice when we first ran in here. Each tree is so thick that it would take at least three people to get their arms around the trunks. The branches are high above us, twisted and hanging down like bony fingers slipping out of the darkness. Misty shadows hover above the ground, making it difficult to see very far.

This place looks like it's straight from the pages of a dark fairy tale.

"How are we supposed to tell where we are when everything in this forest looks exactly the same?" I turn in circles, my stomach sinking lower with each spin.

"It's actually pretty creepy in here," Zoe says softly, hugging her arms around her body.

I roll my eyes. "You think?"

"We came in from that direction." Aidan points behind us before turning toward his left. "So, the cave should be that way."

"Are you sure?" Zoe asks.

"Yes." Aidan drops his arm, turning back to us. "Maybe."

I snort but quickly sober. "That doesn't tell us where the creature went."

"Always with the obvious." Zoe walks in the direction of the cave.

"Where are you going?" I clench my jaw to keep from saying something that I shouldn't.

"If you don't know where that thing went, then we should start walking toward the cave." Zoe answers without bothering to turn around.

I open my mouth but I don't have time to speak before the pressure builds in my head with a clicking noise filling my mind. I slam my hands on the side of my head, bending over as I struggle to focus.

Zoe drops to her knees with her hands over both ears and Aidan grabs a fistful of his hair, his face turning pale.

Somewhere in the misty shadows, deeper in the forest, I catch the flicker of blue fire out of the corner of my eye. I turn toward the movement, desperately trying to clear my head.

The pressure stops just as suddenly as it started, leaving all three of us gasping for air.

"Did you guys see that?" I choke on my words, my throat raw like sandpaper.

"See what?" Zoe leans closer to the ground, groaning. "I think I'm going to throw up."

"I saw blue fire through the trees. We need to go deeper into the forest." My excitement helps to dull some of the throbbing in my head.

Aidan swallows hard, holding a hand out to steady himself. "I saw it too."

"Zoe, get up. Let's go before we lose it again." I head between the trees, moving deeper into the shadows.

"Screw you," Zoe shouts after me.

I glance over my shoulder to see Aidan helping her to her feet and chase after me. I scan the forest for any sign of movement, any flicker of flame in the darkness.

The deeper we walk into the trees, the colder the air grows, and it doesn't take long before I can see my breath, puffing out in steaming white clouds.

There. Several feet in front of us, I catch a flash of yellow light.

I pick up my pace, motioning for Aidan and Zoe to keep up as I weave between the trunks, concentrating on placing my feet down as soft as possible to keep my movements silent.

A high-pitched giggle echoes from somewhere above us, and I freeze mid-step. I search the branches but I can't see anything up there. I turn to my companions, careful to keep my voice low. "Why does everything in this realm have a giggling problem? It's creepy."

Zoe rolls her eyes. "Everything in this realm is creepy."

"There it is again." Aidan points behind me and I turn just in time to see a flash of blue flame.

I rush forward, keeping my eyes glued to the place where I just saw the creature, and swallow back the frustration as it stays just out of our reach.

"How much farther are we going?" Zoe hisses from behind me.

I stop to gather my bearings, but I can't tell how far we've walked or even what direction we're going. "We have to be getting close."

"We should probably turn around before we get lost," Aidan says softly.

I chew on my bottom lip, searching the forest. "It has to be here."

"We'll come back for it, I promise, but we should go." Aidan's head snaps up, his eyes scanning the forest.

I frown at him, but I suddenly understand what has his attention when a tingling energy crawls up my arms.

Zoe sucks in a sharp breath as she joins in, searching the trees.

"I feel the stone." I close my eyes as I hold my arms up, turning slowly in every direction to determine which way the energy is strongest. When I open my eyes, I find Aidan and Zoe staring in the same direction I want to go. "Let's do this."

The three of us squeeze close together, weaving through the forest as we slip from shadow to shadow, staying behind the large trunks. The tingling magic of Leo's birthstone grows stronger with each step we take.

My heart beats wildly in my chest, and I force myself to take steady breaths. I can't believe we're about to catch a break and get another piece of his stone back.

Up ahead, I catch the flash of yellow light and my stomach ties in knots. It's the closest we've been to the creature since we started following it through the forest.

I grab Aidan's and Zoe's jackets and pull them with me to duck behind a tree.

"It's not far in front of us," I whisper.

"What do we do when we catch up to it? Attack it with magic?" Zoe drops her voice low.

"Because that worked out so well the last time," Aidan grumbles.

I frown at him. "We'll try everything we can think of. Something will have to work on that creature. If anyone gets a chance to get the stone, grab it and we'll run like hell."

They both nod and we slip out of the shadows, zigzagging for the next tree as we follow the path of the energy.

Aidan stops so suddenly, Zoe and I bump into him from behind before he pushes us behind a tree.

"What is it?" I barely speak as a cold shiver races down my spine.

Aidan leans in close, his voice almost too low to hear. "It's right there around this tree. It's just floating there."

"Do you think it knows we're here?" Zoe asks, her eyes wide.

I glance at Aidan, then take a deep, slow breath. My mouth is dry, like I've been chewing on cotton balls, and it's hard to swallow. "I'm sure it knows where we are. After all, that thing has been following us for at least a day."

"So, what do we do now?" Zoe whispers.

"We go at it with anything we can think of and get that stone." My heart beats wildly in my chest, and I'm not sure my voice sounds as confident as I want.

Zoe sighs. "That's a great plan."

"Just don't let it touch you with its hands." I shiver at the painful memory of the creature's acid touch.

Aidan looks at me long and hard. "I'm going first this time."

He closes his eyes and takes a deep breath, standing so still that he could be a statue. The smell of moisture fills the air, and before long a cold rain starts, pattering against the limbs as it falls in fat drops.

I shiver as the water seeps into my clothes and pull the hood of my jacket over my head to protect me from getting completely soaked. I glance over at Zoe and she does the same, a scowl planted firmly on her face.

Aidan opens his eyes, his gaze fixed far away, and I stifle

a gasp as they glow with an electric blue light. He raises his hands and the rain pounds the forest.

I slip to the edge of the tree, careful not to disturb Aidan's magic, and peek around the trunk, frowning as I see the creature. It hovers in the same spot, the smokey shadows floating around it, oblivious to the rain.

As I watch, water runs toward the creature, collecting beneath its body and swirling until it creates a miniature whirlpool. The liquid shoots straight up, encasing the creature in a cone of spinning water that swells with the rain.

Suddenly, the water splashes to the ground, and Aidan gasps, stumbling against the tree.

I whip around, reaching out a hand to help steady him, and Zoe grabs his other arm.

"What happened?" I whisper.

"I don't know." Aidan looks pale, and his eyes are back to their normal blue. "It's like that thing just blocked my magic."

I look around the trunk to find the creature still floating there, unfazed by the magic. "It's just hovering there like it's waiting for us."

"Maybe this isn't such a good idea," Zoe says as she scrunches her face.

"I think we have to at least try. Something has to work against that thing." I turn to Aidan, leaning close as I place my hand on his chest. "If you're okay, we should try."

Aidan nods, straightening himself as he squares his shoulders. "Let's get this over with."

I move my hands to the tree, placing my palms flat against the rough bark that scratches my fingers. My eyes close, but my heightened connection thanks to the earth saving me allows me to still see the forest in every detail in my mind's eye.

Tiny orbs of green light sparkle in the air, like lightning bugs on a summer night. But there's something different about this energy. It's green like the earth essence I've seen before, but it's darker, tainted, and it immediately makes my stomach turn.

I swallow down the bile rising in my throat and focus on the plant life in the forest. I push my magic, reaching for the tree directly behind the creature as it floats, waiting as if it knows nothing of fear. I feel the strength of the ancient tree and become one with it, but it's cold and unforgiving, and I shiver.

My breathing quickens as I strengthen the magic, pushing into the branches so I can move them, like extensions of my fingers. I reach for the creature, the wood crackling in protest as I push the gnarled limbs down. They slice through it, a stick passing through smoke, leaving the creature unharmed.

I pull back, letting the branches whip back into their natural position, and I shift my magic to the wet ground beneath the creature. As I connect with the mud, I mold it upward, attempting to encase the thing in dirt, but again it passes right through it.

I let out a soft growl as I open my eyes and pull my hands away from the tree. "That thing is a ghost. Nothing works."

"Maybe instead of taking turns, we should go out, guns blazing, and hit it with everything we have," Zoe says softly.

I stare at her for a moment then shift my gaze to Aidan, who shrugs. A quick glance around the trunk shows the creature still floating there. I wonder why it's waiting when it knows we're here. Is this a good idea? My gut tells me it isn't, but I know in my heart that we need to get that piece of the birthstone.

Without wasting another second, I rush out of the safety of our hiding spot and lift my hands high in the air. The mud climbs high over the head of the creature, mimicking the cone that Aidan created with his water.

Aidan steps in behind me, drawing the water out of the earth so that it hardens into a structure. Zoe blasts it with fire, creating a type of homemade oven. For a moment, nothing happens and I lower my arms, thinking it can't possibly be that easy.

An explosion rocks the forest and the three of us hit the ground as sharp chunks of the shattered structure fly toward us, sticking in the ground all around our bodies.

I lift my head to stare at the creature and it turns its head in my direction, meeting my eyes with the black holes in its face. The pressure builds in my head and I cry out, digging my fingers into the soft ground, and I end up with a ball of mud in my hand from squeezing. I drag myself to my knees, slamming together the dirt from both hands to create one large ball of earth, and heave it with all my strength as I fall back to the ground.

The ball of mud hits the creature, slamming into the center of its chest and knocking it back toward the tree. My heart leaps. Did I just find a weakness?

I grab Aidan and shout, "Hit it in the chest," before I turn to Zoe and relay the same message.

I grab another handful of dirt, using my magic to increase the mud to the size of a volleyball, and pass it to Zoe. She lights it on fire as it hisses in the cold rain and sends it hurtling toward the creature, hitting her mark.

The creature hisses, the noise echoing through the

forest, a haunted sound that isn't natural in this world. Or any world. I grit my teeth as it makes my blood run cold.

Aidan holds his hand level with the ground and a foot above it, drawing out a stream of water from a puddle. The liquid hardens into a frozen stake and he throws it at the creature. It lands squarely in its chest, just above the stone, crackling and melting as it sinks into the flames inside its body.

Zoe blasts the creature with a steady stream of fire, creating a blowtorch that rages from the tips of her fingers. The heat of the fire instantly warms the air but doesn't do any damage.

"I don't think anything is working," she yells to me without taking her eyes off her target.

I stagger to my feet, thinking that maybe if I move a little closer, my magic might have more of an impact. I nearly fall as I dodge a ball of fire that the creature redirects at my head.

Suddenly, the pressure in my head disappears and I can think clearly again. I reach my magic back into the essence of the tree, commanding the branches to grab the creature around the chest, but the tree pushes back, sending me sprawling to the ground with my head spinning.

Aidan reaches for me, but I wave him off.

The creature hovers closer, drawing one arm out of the shadows and reaching for me with its skeletal hand, the yellow gel oozing from its bones.

I kick hard at the ground, scooting away as fast as I can, and leaping to my feet when I've put enough distance between us. I send my magic deep beneath the surface, reaching far into the cold ground, and finally see what I'm looking for. I coax the thick, white roots out of the ground and they whip around the creature, pulling it toward the ground by a hole in its chest.

The creature struggles against the bindings with minimal movements that match its blank face.

Zoe forms a ball of fire between her hands, throwing it at the creature, catching the roots in the crossfire.

Blazing pain rips through my body and I gasp, crashing to my knees.

"Watch the roots," Aidan shouts at Zoe. "Ciara is connected to them."

"I didn't know," Zoe yells back, forming another ball of fire, but this time giving her target a little more space.

Without moving, the creature suddenly tugs on the roots sticking out of its body, pulling them deep into his chest and the fire that burns within.

It feels like my body is on fire and the world around me tilts. I'm forced to pull back the roots and free the creature. I take quick, heavy breaths, trying to collect myself, and an idea pops into my head. Crazy, but an idea, and I'm done messing around.

I climb to my feet, my legs wobbly and still burning. I reach into the inside pocket of my jacket, my fingers curling around the handle of the turquoise dagger as I pull it into view.

The creature's head whips around and a grim smile spreads across my face, even as my heart pounds out of control in my chest. At least I have its attention.

"Hit it with everything you have, but don't kill me." I don't even bother to keep my voice down, not caring if it can understand me.

Aidan locks eyes with me, and love in his gaze screams at me to be careful.

I wink at him to let him know I understand before

rushing toward the creature with my dagger firmly in my grip and the deadly point aimed at the creature. To my surprise, it moves out of the way as if it's finally afraid of something, but not before I have the chance to stab at it with the blade. The dagger rips through the shadowy smoke beneath the birthstone and fire shoots out of the wound, filling the air with the smell of sulfur.

Burning pain rips through my arm as a jet of water shoots past me, hitting the creature in the same place I stabbed it. The water hisses, instantly forming a dark cloud of steam.

The creature howls, and the sound shakes me to the core. I rush forward again, swinging my dagger, but before I can reach the creature, I'm thrown backward, landing hard on the ground and nearly stabbing myself.

Fireballs whiz over my head, pounding against the creature as I roll out of the way to get up without getting burned.

Aidan adds water to the fray, and the creature is swallowed in a cloud of steam and boiling water.

I move around the side, the fingers of my free hand brushing a tree as I gauge the room I have around me, timing out my next attack. The bark shifts beneath my hand, stretching up to lock my hand in place. "What the hell?"

I yank on my arm, pulling to the point that I'm afraid I'll injure my shoulder, but it doesn't let me go. I reach into my magic until I touch the core of the tree, and I can feel a struggle inside myself that I know isn't mine. The tree is being forced against its will.

Pushing my energy farther, I search for the source of the other magic that's controlling the tree and finally find it near the top of the branches. As my energy mixes with the foreign magic, it puts a sour taste in my mouth, and my throat burns as I swallow. What is this?

Zoe and Aidan both shout behind me, and I turn as far as I can, just in time to see them flying through the air to crash at my feet. I stuff the dagger back into my jacket and reach down for Aidan, pulling against the grip of the tree.

"That thing is too strong." Aidan climbs to his feet, his eyes widening at the sight of my hand stuck in the bark. He grabs my arm, helping me pull until I cry out in pain. "What's happening?"

"I don't know," I whimper. "Something else is controlling it, and the tree is fighting my magic."

"I'll make it let you go." Zoe lays her palms on the tree, and a bright light erupts beneath her hands as she sends fire straight into the wood.

The tree screams in my head and I scream out loud. Snapping sounds rip through the air as the crooked branches race toward the ground, headed straight for us. I duck my head as the limbs slam into the ground, trapping us in a wooden cage as the creature floats off into the forest.

12

I let out a growl, yanking on my arm and not counting on the tree to release me. It does, and my growl turns into a yelp as I'm thrown off by the force of my pull and crash to the ground. I lie there on my back, trying not to explode with anger as I raise my feet and kick against the branches.

"I don't think that's helping." Aidan suppresses a snicker as he reaches down and pulls me to my feet.

I glare at him, unable to see the humor in the situation.

Zoe paces around the back of the cage. "I told you we should've just gone to the cave."

"Don't start. We'll find a way to do both, but we can't leave here without that stone. We can't risk leaving it in their hands any longer." I wrap my hands tightly around the branches, tugging to test the strength, but they're solid and don't budge.

"You're one with the earth. Why don't you just tell the tree to move?" Zoe raises one eyebrow high on her forehead and folds her arms across her chest.

I take a deep breath, trying to get my mouth under

control before I open it. "Right now, it's not exactly working that way."

"Why not?" Zoe taps her toe, her boot squishing in the mud.

My head bangs softly against the cold, hard branch. "I don't know. You're so smart, you figure it out."

"We'll figure it out together," Aidan says softly, rubbing my back.

I press my face against the branches as hot tears well up in my eyes, slipping one by one down my cold cheeks. "We need to figure it out quick. I think this was a trap."

"Always with the obvious." Zoe's statement makes me grit my teeth.

"Whatever. It was obvious. The mages know we're here in this realm, and that's why the creature wasn't doing anything. It just floated there, waiting for the cage to spring. I bet the mages are on their way here right now." I swipe at my tears with the back of my hand.

"Then we shouldn't waste any time." Zoe walks over to the wooden bars, gripping them tightly in her hands as flames erupt from her fingers.

I grit my teeth, my knees buckling under me and I fall to the ground, gasping for air. Aidan immediately drops to my side, cradling my head to keep it out of the mud. My stomach burns like I just ate the hottest pepper on the planet.

"Stop, please." I barely get the words out.

Zoe quickly pulls in the fire, releasing the branches. "I'm sorry, but fire is all I know."

"Is it doing anything?" Tiny dots of multi-colored lights flash in front of my eyes.

She glances back at the tree, and there isn't a mark on it. "Nope."

"Then stop." I put my hand on my forehead as I swallow down the nausea.

"I have an idea." Aidan lowers himself to a sitting position, tucking his legs beneath him. He places his hands flat on the ground, focusing on the water deep in the earth as he guides it to the branches buried in the dirt. I can hear the water rushing in my head as he pushes it up to wash out the branches, but it doesn't work.

"Never mind." I groan as I use the branches to pull myself from the ground, leaning against the side of the cage as I peer out into the forest. I see a flicker of blue fire in the distance, like a candle in the dark. "The creature is still there. I can see it."

Something brushes against the top of my head, and I swat at it without looking. I press my face against the bark as I close my eyes, my desperate mind racing to come up with any idea to get us out of here. What do I have to do to make my magic work with this tree?

I feel another tickle near the side of my face. Since when did this realm have bugs? I open my eyes and suck in a sharp breath as a fairy clings to the branches directly in front of my eyes.

I stand up straight, staring at the tiny creature. "Where did you come from?"

"Who are you talking to?" Zoe steps up beside me, her eyes landing on the fairy. "Oh."

The fairy flutters off the branch, beating her translucent wings to keep her just inches from my nose. She's three inches tall, her blue leather dress stops just below her knees, and her platinum hair hangs in thick braids down her back. Her almond-shaped eyes are as green as the summer grass, and they're fixed on me.

"I live here and I've been following you." Her voice is musical, like the ringing of a silver bell.

"You live here?" Zoe doesn't bother to hide the disgust from her voice.

The fairy straightens her shoulders, holding her head high. "Not here in this forest, but this realm."

I shoot a quick glare at Zoe, giving her a slight shake of my head before turning back to the fairy. "What's your name, and why have you been following us?"

"I am called Hazel, and I've been following you to keep you safe, of course." Her smile spreads across her face, and I can't help but smile with her.

"Great job so far." Zoe rolls her eyes.

Hazel's tiny shoulders slump, and she drops a little in the air.

"Don't listen to her." I glare at Zoe until she sighs. "Thank you for watching over us."

The radiant smile returns to Hazel's face.

I watch the fairy, and something nags at the back of my mind. "You look familiar to me."

"We've never met before, but I know all about you." Hazel claps her hands.

I chuckle at her enthusiasm despite my confusion. "How do you know about me?"

"Silly." Hazel floats up, landing softly on my shoulder. "My brother met you and he told me."

"Your brother? Pippig is your brother?" I look at her more closely, and now that I've made the connection, they could be twins.

"Yup." She shifts her position, pulling her tiny legs beneath her.

I instantly relax, if only for a moment. Pippig already saved my life once, and maybe his sister will be just as helpful. "Hazel, do you know what those shadow creatures are?"

The fairy shivers, tickling my shoulder. "No one knows what they are. Evil magic created by evil men. They don't exist in any one realm." She sniffles in my ear. "The evil men tried to capture my brother. They capture lots of things, trying to strip their magic."

Aidan stiffens beside me, his hands balled in tight fists at his sides.

"We're going to put a stop to that." His voice is tight, almost mechanical.

I glance down at the fairy, her hair blowing in the breath of my sigh. "It's not just creatures. They're hunting Guardians too, but I didn't know that about Pippig."

Hazel stands up, pacing up and down my shoulder, and I fight the urge to scratch the line of her leather-bound feet. "It's true. A lot of my people are missing. He probably would've died if Capricorn didn't find him."

"Capricorn?" I frown at her, but she doesn't seem to notice.

Hazel nods, her braids swinging in front of her body. "That's how he gets to work for Capricorn. He owes him for saving his life. It's a big honor, and that's why I'm helping too."

The smile is back and she puffs out her chest, her chin held high.

I look through the branches that make the bars of the cage, searching the shadows of the forest. The back of my neck tingles, and I feel like something is coming. "You said a lot of your people are missing?"

The smile slips from Hazel's face, and the sniffles are back. "Yes. Beings all over this realm."

I hold out my hand and she flies to it, tickling me as she

walks across my palm. "We'll do what we can to find them. But for now, can you help us get out of this trap? We've tried to use our magic."

Hazel's eyes grow wide. "Oh, no, magic won't work on this cage."

"Thank you, we know that," Zoe pipes up behind me.

I keep my eyes on the fairy even though I want to glare at Zoe. "No, it didn't work, but there has to be a way out of here. We can't be stuck when the mages come to get us."

Hazel fidgets with the sleeve of her dress. "You can't let them catch you. You need to get the fire."

"We're trying to get the fire. How do we get out?" Aidan asks softly, leaning in close.

Hazel smiles and winks at him.

"Hey." My frown earns me a giggle from the fairy. "Please, we have to hurry. We're also chasing a piece of a birthstone, and we can't let the creature get too far ahead of us."

"You don't want to follow the creature. Nothing good will happen from that." Tears form in the corner of her almond eyes, and I swear they're tinted green.

"We don't have a choice." I whip my head around at the sound of a twig snapping in the distance, but I don't know what direction it's from. "Hurry, Hazel, they're coming. Can you help us or not?"

Her sheer wings flutter, lifting her off my palm to hover in front of my nose. She places her hands on her pale cheeks. "The tree, this forest, have been poisoned. The evil men left dark spells that activate with certain kinds of magic. That's the only way." She slips through the branches, holding her hand up to wave.

"Wait. Where are you going?" I grab the branches,

squeezing them tight, and they might as well be cold metal in my grip.

"To get help." Hazel flies into the trees, and as she disappears, she calls over her shoulder. "Remove the poison."

"Remove the poison? What does that even mean?" Zoe picks up her pacing again.

"You know what that means." Aidan locks eyes with me, and I know he's not asking me a question.

I nod, rushing to the back of the cage and shooing Zoe out of the way. "Keep watch and be ready to fight anything that comes through those shadows. I don't think we'll be alone for much longer."

I place my palms flat against the bark, sinking deep into the essence of the tree. Deep down, I can feel the struggle of the tree. It's suffering, and that gives me the anger I need to fuel my magic.

I grit my teeth, sending my energy deep within the tree, starting from the bottom and working my way toward the branches, where I know something is wrong. I watch carefully along the way to make sure I don't miss anything. High in the tree, the limbs are turning black, like they've been burned. In my mind, they feel brittle, hanging on for every ounce of life. I move my magic slowly for fear of breaking the limbs.

Another snap of a tree limb rips through the air, closer this time, and I fight to keep my racing heart from beating through my chest. I push harder, searching the charred limbs for anything that could be the poisonous spell. I'm about to shift my magic when a mark on a branch catches my eye.

It would look like scratches to any normal person, but I've seen markings like that before. Even though I have no idea what they mean, I know it's the mages' work because I've seen symbols like it in their marble city.

I push for the marks, my magic recoiling as I get too close. My stomach twists and I nearly vomit on the ground. I swallow hard, focusing everything I have on healing the tree. Energy builds in my body, humming with magic as I push the earth back into the tree. The branches glow with a soft green light as it swirls around the symbols.

Zoe gasps behind me, but I keep my focus on the magic. My palms heat and my skin burns as a thin film of sweat covers my forehead. The heat moves down my arms, at war with the earth energy coursing through me. I swallow hard, my throat feeling like I haven't had a drink in days.

The tree bark shifts beneath my hands, and I can feel a renewed energy within its trunk. The only problem is I can feel the poison sinking into my body. The green light flares up above and I feel the branch that held the marks snap, freeing the tree from the spell. Inside my mind, I hear it sigh.

I collapse to the ground, struggling to breathe as the poison burns up my arm, and choke back a sob as the branches lift, freeing us from the cage.

Aidan drops to the ground beside me, holding me close. "What happened?"

"I pulled the poison out of the tree, but now it's in me." I gasp as fresh pain stabs my arms, leaving me barely able to move them as a tear trickles down my face.

Aidan presses his hand over mine and a cool energy flows up my arm, soothing the burning poison.

I begin to relax in his arms as his magic rushes through me. The tears flow beyond my control and I reach up to wipe them, but Aidan stops me with a gentle hand. After another minute, the tears stop flowing and I can breathe easier.

"How did you do that?" I ask, struggling to sit up.

He smiles at me. "The body is mostly water, and I flushed the poison from your system, pushing it out through your tears."

I plant a grateful kiss on his lips and let him help me stand.

"I think the mages are here," Zoe whispers.

Aidan grips my hand as the three of us race through the forest, heading for the last place we saw the creature.

We weave between the trees to keep from running a straight path, ignoring the low-hanging branches that whip our faces and pull at our clothes. I desperately cling to Aidan's hand as I push myself to keep up with his pace. The pounding of Zoe's boots is the only thing that lets me know she's behind us, because I'm too afraid to look over my shoulder.

I cry out as a ball of fire whizzes by my head, so close that I can feel the heat as it explodes against a tree to my right.

Aidan pulls my hand hard, veering to the left and slowing just enough to duck beneath a low and nasty-looking branch.

Zoe's scream rips through the forest, followed by a lively string of curse words.

I throw a quick glance over my shoulder in time to see a larger ball of fire heading straight for us. "Aidan, get down!"

Aidan dives to the ground, dragging me with him, and I land hard on top of him, grunting with the impact.

The ball of fire crashes against the tree in front of us, throwing sparks in all directions that ignite as they land. I cover my head with my hands as the fire rains down on us, catching my jacket on fire.

I scream, rolling off Aidan and thrashing around in the dirt to put out the flames, but it doesn't do any good. Hands grab my legs, and instinctively I kick my feet.

"It's me, be still," Zoe says, her voice low. She closes her eyes and her palms heat against my legs as she pulls the fire from my clothes.

I'm able to take a deep breath even as my heart pounds in my chest. My eyes catch movement behind Zoe, and I gasp as two mages slip out of the mist that hovers above the ground.

I leap to my feet, turning to run, but stop cold at the sight of two more mages dressed in the same black robes closing in behind us. We're outnumbered.

My body freezes, and the panic rises into my throat. I'm facing the second pair of mages, with two others that I can't see. Zoe and Aidan are out of my field of vision, but I'm guessing they're just as stuck as I am.

The mage on the left walks slowly up to me, studying my face with eyes so dark the pupils are hidden.

"They say this one can get out of our freezing spell." His nasal voice is high and dripping with disgust.

"She's the Capricorn Guardian?" a baritone voice says behind me, so close that I feel his breath on the back of my neck.

My body wants to cringe, but the spell holds me tight. The mage in front of me picks up a strand of my hair, sniffing it as he sneers at me. "It sure looks like her."

Everything inside me wants to scream at him and punch him in the face. I struggle against the spell and my muscles protest in their frozen state.

"You better be right, Layre. If we take her to the master

and it's not her, then you're as good as dead," says the voice behind me.

Layre twists the strand of my hair gently around his finger. "No, Olin, I am the master's favorite. It would be your life." A flash of fire burns deep within his black eyes, disappearing as quickly as it started.

"Draven is the master's favorite," says the mage to my right.

Layre lashes out with his free hand, gripping the mage's throat. "How dare you speak to me like that, Avanth? I am his favorite because I made the creatures."

Avanth sputters, turning an alarming shade of purple. His eyes begin to close, but Layre suddenly releases him, sending him into a coughing fit.

"Leave him alone," says a shaky voice behind me, which must be the fourth mage.

"Hush, Dario," Olin hisses.

Layre brings the strand of my hair back to his nose, his eyes locked on mine. "Such a pretty treasure. Maybe I should keep you for myself instead."

My scream starts deep in my chest, out of anger, not fear, but no sound comes out. I don't know who this guy thinks he is, but I'm going to kick his ass.

Olin and Dario slowly circle our trio, stopping just behind Avanth, who rubs the bright red marks on the front of his throat.

Dario stares at his feet. "What do we do with the other two?"

Layre finally drops my hair, moving in front of Zoe, like a snake toying with its prey. He picks up a fistful of her hair, sniffing deep. "This one smells like fire. It looks like we have two Guardians."

I can see Dario looking at me as I struggle to see what's

happening with Zoe. His eyes widen ever so slightly, and I get the feeling he's trying to tell me something. His face goes carefully blank when Layre moves again, stopping in front of Aidan.

"Water," Layre hisses, drawing out the word until it trails into nothing.

There's a flicker of yellow light in the shadows through the trees, and my heart skips a beat. The creature is still out there. If we can get away from these mages, we can still catch it. I sink my energy into the earth beneath my feet, remembering how I used my element to release myself from this spell when I faced Draven.

I reach down into the cold, damp earth, feeling the magic of the dirt, the rocks, and the roots. My muscles ache from being locked in one position, but the deeper I reach into the earth, the more I relax. My body tingles with the magic I draw from the ground. My toe moves.

I pull the energy into myself, soaking it in like the roots of a plant, and giddy laughter bubbles up inside me as the spell holding me frozen begins to weaken. I focus my concentration, pushing the energy around my body like a current of electricity to the point I think I might explode. Suddenly I stumble forward, to the shock of the mages standing in front of me.

Layre raises his hands. But the magic of the earth still courses deep in my veins. With a flick of my wrist the dirt rises, wrapping Layre in a thick cocoon as his scream rips through the trees.

I turn my attention to the other three as Avanth and Dario slip behind nearby trees. My fingers curl with my palm facing the sky and dirt climbs up Olin's legs, covering him up to his shoulders.

I rush over to Aidan with the sound of Layre thumping

behind me and lay my hands on the sides of his face, pushing my magic into his body.

Aidan gasps as the spell breaks free and he stumbles forward, leaning against my body.

"How did you do that?" he asks between pants.

A hole breaks in the cocoon holding Layre, sending dirt chunks flying.

"Don't know. Watch them." I rush over to Zoe, placing my hands on her face, and send my magic deep into her body.

Zoe sucks in a sharp breath as she regains movement in her body. "What the hell was that?"

"No time." I turn around just as Layre breaks out of his dirt prison.

Layre's face is red, and fire burns in his eyes as he raises his hands, a ball of fire forming in each palm. In a flash, he throws them in our direction and rushes over to Olin, placing his hands on the earth and melting it away.

I dodge out of the way, narrowly missing another burn spot on my jacket.

Zoe catches the fire flying in her direction, holding it between her hands as it doubles to the size of a bowling ball. She lifts it over her head, smashing it on the ground at Olin's feet.

Olin howls as the flames surge up his body, igniting his robes and burning his skin.

Layre reaches into the fire, soaking it into his hand and leaving Olin's smoking body to crumple to the ground in a motionless heap. Layre turns his gaze on me.

Aidan lifts his arms in the air, water soaking out of the ground and rising to create a twisting vortex of liquid. He pushes his hands in front of him, wrapping the water around Layre's body and lifting him off the ground in a liquid sphere.

The sphere explodes, splashing all of us with cold water as Zoe shoots a steady stream of fire toward the mage, his wet robes hissing but refusing to catch fire.

I reach for the trees, commanding the limbs to bend forward and reach for the ground. They creak as they move, twisting around Layre's body and pinning his arms to his sides.

Fire blazes on his fingertips, and he twists his hands to burn the branches. They scream in pain inside my head, and I sway on my feet.

Zoe holds up her hands, drawing the fire to her, and I'm able to breathe a little easier.

Aidan raises his arms, pulling more water from the ground, spraying it straight up beneath the mage. The water spins tightly around Layre, and through the liquid I can see him struggling against the limbs.

"I think you're going to drown him, and we should probably ask him some questions first." I loosen the branches around Layre, but not so much that he can get free.

Aidan focuses on his tornado of water. "Do you actually think he'll talk?"

Zoe snorts. "No."

"Well, we won't know for sure if you drown him." I fold my arms across my chest. "He said he made those creatures, and we need to know more about them."

"Fine." Aidan lowers his arms, the water splashing in a pool on the ground.

All three of us stand there, staring at the limbs that used to hold the mage.

I spin in circles, searching the forest, but I don't see any movement. "Where did he go? You guys could see him in the water, right?"

"I saw him." Zoe still stares at the branches, her mouth hanging open.

I release the branches and let them relax into their natural position before jogging over to one of the trees where the other two mages were hiding. There's no sign of them either. "Did you guys see what happened to the other two?"

Aidan walks over to Olin's body, nudging it with his toe, and wrinkles his nose as steam hisses around it. He points to the tree where I'm standing. "I just saw them running that way."

"That's helpful." I roll my eyes at him but finish with a wink and a smile.

Zoe watches Aidan inspect Olin, her face draining of color. "I can't believe they ran away like that. Quit touching him. Is he dead?"

Aidan stands, shrugging as he backs away from Olin. "It seems like it."

"The mages have a history of disappearing when it looks like they won't win the battle." I look one more time through the trees before joining the others.

Zoe looks from me to Aidan. "What do you mean it seems like he's dead?"

Aidan raises one eyebrow at her. "Why don't you check him?"

Zoe's eyes grow wide, and I'm afraid for a moment that she's going to throw up. I give Aidan a long look before grabbing her arm and pulling her away from Olin. "I saw that creature with the birthstone go this way."

We walk through the trees, stopping every few steps to

check our surroundings and make sure we're still alone. There's nothing around us but mist and giant trees.

A clicking noise fills the air and the three of us smash together, squatting behind a thick trunk. We exchange glances, but no one knows where it is and none of us want to speak.

Aidan slips out of our hiding spot, staying low to the ground. Zoe and I mimic his every move, taking care to stay out of sight. He slips behind another trunk and points in front of us, sweat beading on his forehead.

I inch forward with Zoe right behind me, and I slap a hand over her mouth as she lets out a gasp that's way too loud. A cold shiver runs down my spine, and I can't take my eyes off the scene in front of us.

Several feet deeper into the trees is the creature with the birthstone in its chest, surrounded by at least twenty more creatures, all floating in a cloud of swirling shadows.

13

___

Staying in a crouched position, I work my way back to Aidan with my hand still firmly clamped over Zoe's mouth. Once we're tucked safely behind the tree trunk, I slowly lower my hand.

"What the hell are we supposed to do now?" Zoe squeaks, keeping her voice low.

"We have to figure out a way to get that birthstone away from those creatures," I say with a sigh. In my head, it sounds so easy, but as bad as I want to get my hands on that stone, even I know it's a ridiculous task.

Zoe lowers herself into a sitting position, tucking her legs beneath her. "There's no way we can get the stone. We couldn't figure out how to take down one, never mind a whole army of them."

Aidan runs his hands through his shaggy dark hair. "She has a point. There are at least twenty of them gathered."

I chew on my bottom lip, pushing my brain to come up with any kind of plan. "Maybe they're just meeting really quick and they'll fly away."

Zoe rolls her eyes. "You can't possibly think we'll get that lucky."

I frown at her, my anger instantly flaring. "I suppose you have a better idea."

"Yeah." Zoe puts her head in her hands. "We leave before they realize we're here. We get the fire and get the hell out of this realm."

Aidan sighs, sitting down beside Zoe. "We don't have time to wait them out. It could take all night. We don't know how much magic is left in your necklaces, and we don't want to get stuck out here."

I join the other two on the ground, sitting down harder than I mean to given my frustration, and wince as a sharp pain shoots up my tailbone.

"I can't shake the feeling that we need to get that stone." I pick up a fallen branch, tossing it against the tree.

"Why? What's so important about it?" Zoe asks.

"Besides the fact that it's Leo's birthstone?" I scowl, her questions grating on my nerves.

She scoots herself across the ground, pressing in closer to Aidan and me. "I know it's the birthstone. I just want to know why we can't come back for it."

I stare at her while I pick up another branch beneath my fingers. Why can't we come back for it? We're on a time limit being in this realm, and we don't have the power to fight those creatures. But there's something nagging in the back of my mind that says I shouldn't leave without it. "I just don't think we should risk it."

The three of us sit without talking for a moment, listening to the clicking noise the creatures are making.

I turn to Aidan. "Do you know of any magic the mages have that makes those creatures? How did they do it?"

Aidan drags his finger through the dirt, and for a moment I think he's going to ignore my question, but he finally looks up at me. "I don't know of any specific spells that can create something like that. We aren't allowed access to magic that dark. It's possible the Zodiacs know of those spells, but I don't think they'd talk about it. That kind of magic is unnatural and always comes with a price."

"What kind of price?" Zoe asks softly.

Aidan's eyes narrow before he turns his attention back to drawing in the dirt. "Sickness. Madness. Death. It's nasty stuff."

"Is a creature like that something that can be conjured, or do you think they need something to make it out of?" I grab Aidan's hand from the ground, forcing him to look at me.

He shakes his head. "I don't know anything else."

The force of his tone makes it clear that he's done with this conversation. I gently release his hand, studying his face, but he won't meet my eyes. It's pretty clear that there's something else he knows, but I decide it's better not to push it anymore.

"So, we need to come up with some kind of plan to get the stone." Zoe sighs.

"Don't sigh at me. We get the stone and we get out. It's that simple," I say, forcing myself to drop my voice and keep my frustration under control.

Zoe's shoulders slump. "You're not going to let that go, are you?"

I glare at her. "No, so you might as well get on board and help me come up with some kind of plan."

She meets my gaze with the hint of tears forming in her eyes. "I don't know what to do. This is all new to me."

A sigh escapes my lips, the look on her face deflating some of my anger. "It's still new to me too, but we've recovered two pieces of that stone already, and we need to get the third."

"We should create a distraction and see if we can split up the group. If they're not all together, we might have a better chance." Aidan looks up from his drawing in the dirt.

I take a deep breath, holding it for a second before letting it out slowly. "That's a great idea. Any ideas on the distraction?"

Aidan points to the ground, and I gasp. The whole time we've been talking, he's drawn a small map in the dirt. "Zoe and I can go around each side and use our magic to draw them into the trees. You can go in here."

He draws a line on the ground leading into the center of the group. "You take on the creature with the stone using your dagger, since we know they're vulnerable to it. Cut the stone out of its chest and we'll make a run for it."

I stare at him, my mouth hanging open. "You want me to get the stone?"

A wry smile tugs at one side of his mouth. "I don't like it, but I don't think you'll have it any other way."

I chuckle softly. We haven't really known each other very long, but he already knows me so well. "You're right. I won't risk either of you getting hurt."

The smile slips from his face.

"We'll help you if we get the chance. Right?" Aidan shifts his eyes to Zoe.

"I'll help." Zoe's voice is soft, and I wonder for a second if she means it.

I slip a water bottle out of my backpack, taking a few sips before putting it back. Aidan and Zoe do the same. I slide my feet beneath me, raising into a crouched position, and pull the turquoise dagger out of the inside pocket in my jacket.

The clicking noise from the creatures grows louder and faster, making me wonder if they can somehow communicate using the sound.

Carefully I rise, half standing, and peer at the creatures. They shift their position, rearranging themselves into a circle surrounding the one with the stone in its chest. I turn back to my friends, taking care to keep my voice a whisper. "Something is happening. I think they know we're out here."

Zoe stands up, brushing the dirt off her pants. "Then what are we waiting for?"

Aidan climbs to his feet, slipping off behind a tree to the right. "Zoe, you take the left. Ciara, wait for the best moment before you go in there."

I hold his eyes for a long moment, so many unspoken words hanging between us I want to say. Finally, I settle on the most obvious. "Be careful."

Aidan nods, disappearing into the shadows and mist.

Taking a deep breath, I turn to Zoe. "And you be careful."

"You too," she whispers as she hesitates.

"We need you." With that, she takes off through the trees.

I turn to face the creatures standing guard over the birthstone, my fear an icy stone settling in my stomach, and I swallow down a bit of nausea. My shoulders are tight, but I force them straight and stand tall.

As I wait for the diversions to begin, I send a silent prayer to the earth to protect us. A peaceful energy flows through me, and I know she's with us. I just hope that I'm making the right decision and not sending all three of us to our deaths.

An explosion rocks the forest to my left, and out of instinct I drop to the ground. Angry black smoke spirals into the sky as flames lick around the tree branches.

I quickly jump to my feet to check on the reaction of the creatures. Several of them float into the forest toward the fire while the remaining creatures tighten their circle around the one carrying the birthstone. They're protecting it, and I don't know if I'm going to get the chance to face the creature one-on-one.

Rain falls in heavy, cold drops, pattering against the hard ground. I hear a rumbling noise from the trees on my right and I squint through the rain, trying to figure out what is making the sound. It doesn't take long before I have my answer.

A brilliant blue wave, ten feet in height, crashes through the trees, breaking limbs as it tumbles over itself. The water spills over the creatures, but it mostly passes straight through their shadowy forms.

I grimace at how little Aidan's magic disturbs the creatures standing guard over the stone, shifting my weight back and forth as I wait for any opportunity I have to get the birthstone.

The rain picks up, soaking into my jacket and hair, and I shiver against the cold I feel inside and out. The water collects in large pools across the forest floor, the fat drops plopping on the surface. As the puddles race toward each other, they form a river rushing straight toward the creatures, who silently wait as if nothing is happening.

Another giant wave splashes through the trees, with a third one directly behind it, as if there's an ocean hiding somewhere in the forest. The river swirls beneath the creatures, and each fresh wave of water raises it higher, binding the creatures in a five-foot whirlpool.

Fireballs fly between the trees, hissing into smoke as they strike the water. Zoe shouts as her footsteps crunch over fallen branches. Another explosion rips through the forest, and I can feel the heat from where I'm standing.

I pace in my small area, my fists balled tightly by my sides. Standing here watching everything happen is killing me. I should be in the fight, and I know I can help, but I'm afraid if I act too quick, it could get us all killed.

There are still too many creatures around the birthstone. But why aren't they leaving? Why are they just letting us attack them with magic? Is there something holding them here? Unsure of what else to do, I kick at the ground with the toe of my boot.

A steady stream of fire blazes, lighting up the shadows of the forest, causing the creatures that went after Zoe to click loudly. The others in the water click in answer, and it confirms my idea that they communicate with the noise.

The water swirls faster and higher, reaching the heads of the creatures in a violent whirlpool, spinning so quick that it doesn't make any sound. The cone of water caves in on itself as another large wave covers it from the top. As the water splashes across the ground, all but two of the creatures fly off in Aidan's direction.

That leaves two in front of me. The one carrying the birthstone and one creature left protecting it. My odds are as good as they're going to get, and it's now or never.

I wipe the rain from my face, then reach inside my jacket, finding a dry patch on my shirt and wipe my hand to help me keep my grip on my dagger. I flex my fingers around the handle, the weight of the turquoise comforting in my palm, and take a deep breath, racing toward the two creatures as the water splashes around my shins.

Neither being moves, even when I raise my dagger to shoulder height, the razor point leading the way. I swipe at the first creature, bringing my blade diagonally across its chest. Smoke and fire seep out of the cut, and a white-hot pain burns up my arm.

I veer to the right of the creatures, grabbing my arm with my free hand, my breath coming in short gasps. What the hell just happened? There wasn't any pain when I cut the stone creature earlier.

I grit my teeth and stand tall, checking the strength of my grip on the dagger. Everything seems to still be working. I fix my eyes on the back of the birthstone creature, ready to charge again when suddenly they're facing me without ever moving. I stare into the black holes that pass for eyes, a chill running down my spine.

Flames flash out of the corner of my eye, but I keep my gaze fixed on the creatures in front of me. Zoe's high-pitched scream rips through the air and I hesitate, fighting with my instinct to go help my friend. Fire shoots high into the air, flying past the tops of the trees, and I hear Zoe laugh. I guess she's okay, after all.

A smirk slips across my face and I wipe away the strands of hair that are plastered to my face by the rain. I charge the creatures again as they stand there motionless and plunge my dagger into the guardian creature. Pain rips through my arm and I pull out my weapon, staggering backward. The world tilts in front of me and I drop to my knees as I struggle to breathe.

My fingers involuntarily open and the dagger falls from my hand, landing in the water with a soft splash. My arm burns like there's liquid fire in my veins and tears spill down my cheeks, mixing with the rain. I pull up the sleeve of my jacket to examine my arm and gasp. Black lines weave from my fingers to my forearm, leaving jagged marks that look like lightning.

Movement in the trees catches my eye, and I blink through my tears to see Aidan standing in the shadows. I shake my head and drag myself to my feet. He glances over his shoulder, distracted by something I can't see, and disappears into the mist.

I sway on my feet as my stomach turns, and I feel like I might pass out or vomit. My foggy brain struggles to make sense of what is happening. Why does it hurt me now to use the dagger on the creatures? Does it have something to do with this spot in the forest? Is that why they didn't leave even though they knew we were here?

I force my feet to move forward, but stagger around until I lose my balance and fall on the ground, water splashing high in the air. My hands shoot down to break my fall and a fresh wave of pain rolls through my arm. It's then I realize I don't have the dagger in my hand.

My heart skips a beat as I scan the water, but I can't see any sign of it as I roll over onto my hands and knees, crawling across the ground. I search with both hands, my fingers sifting through the mud. Fresh tears fill my eyes as my heart races faster with each swipe of my hand.

My fingertip brushes something sharp, and I cry out as a bright red cloud of blood fills the water, but I don't care that my finger is bleeding because I found my dagger. I wrap my fingers around the handle and lift it out of the water, my injured hand shaking with the weight.

I climb to my feet and close my eyes against a fresh wave of dizziness and slip the dagger back into my jacket. I squat down and grab a fistful of mud in each hand, smashing them together, and mold it into a rope, using my magic to stretch it out and harden the dirt. Shifting it into one hand like a whip, I lash out at the creatures, letting the rope fly. My heart sinks as I watch it pass right through both of their smoky bodies.

The rain stops as suddenly as it began, and the water that's nearly up to my knees suddenly runs into the forest, headed in the direction that I last saw Aidan.

A large fire bursts to life, sending brilliant yellow sparks through the air. I watch them float around me, desperately searching for any idea to take on the creatures without losing my arm.

My shoes squish into the soggy ground and I push my feet deeper to make sure I don't fall and raise my hands with my palms facing the ground. Mud lifts from the ground, sliding over itself as it builds a cone beneath the creatures, rising high enough to cover their heads. I seal the top, staring at my handiwork, and take a step closer, freezing as soon as I see the creatures hovering in front of it.

What the hell is going on? Nothing seems to work on these things. They aren't fighting back and they aren't running away. What am I missing? How am I supposed to get the birthstone when my dagger does more harm to me? What do I do now?

I feel safe enough to close my eyes, since they aren't retaliating with their own magic. Wind blows across my face, chilling my rain-soaked skin. My only hope of getting help is to contact the Zodiacs and hope they can send reinforcements, but nothing happens. I scrunch my face, putting all my concentration into the whisper speak, but all I can hear is the wind, like static in a bad connection.

My eyes open in time to see a large ball of fire headed straight for my face. I throw myself to the ground, catching the heat full force but luckily not the flames. I roll to my feet, ready to yell at Zoe and tell her to be careful where she throws her fire, but my words die on my lips.

My eyes land on Avanth and Layre, and Avanth holds another very large fireball.

14

My heart drops to my toes and my mouth goes instantly dry. I swallow hard, my throat feeling like sandpaper as I stare at the flaming mass hovering an inch above Avanth's palm.

Layre clasps his hands behind his back, strolling in front of Avanth like he's on a Sunday walk. His eyes scan the area, moving from burned tree limbs to the mud beneath our feet. He stares a second at my hand before turning his gaze to the creatures, his expression carefully blank.

I tuck my hands into my jacket pockets, squaring my shoulders.

"Did you come back to get your ass kicked again?" I put all my strength in my voice to keep it from shaking. There's no reason to let them think they have an advantage.

Layre meets my gaze, a sneer pulling at one corner of his mouth. "I've heard all about you and how you think you're so much better than you are. You're famous, really."

He glides closer to the creatures. "You have power, though, and I can see why Kyrell wants you for his magic, but I think," he pauses, looking me up and down, "that you can be put to much better use."

My blood runs cold as a flicker of fire burns in his eyes. "You wouldn't know what to do with a power like mine. Your secret is out that you mages are stealing power wherever you can get it. What's the matter? You don't have your own magic?"

Layre is in front of me in a flash, and I barely see him move. His face stops inches from mine, and the waxy quality of his skin makes my stomach turn. I'm not even sure he looks like he's human. I also want to know how he moved so fast.

Layre darts forward, sniffing the side of my face, and I fight the urge to pull away.

"I have more magic than you could dream of. We're not afraid to use it, unlike the Zodiacs and their pets." He spits on the ground, swiping at his mouth as if he's getting rid of a bad taste.

I take a deep breath, trying to clear my nose of his rancid breath. "You're one to talk about being a pet, out here doing Kyrell's dirty work while he sits in his cozy marble city."

Layre slaps me hard across the face, my cheek stinging as I swallow down the metallic taste of blood. "Don't you speak his name. You are not worthy."

I blink to keep my eyes from watering and chuckle. "I'm not afraid of any of you. Your time will come and I'll be there in the end, standing over you."

"Brave words for a stupid girl," Layre hisses. "But we'll see."

"I guess we will." I stand perfectly still, watching the mage glide across the ground in front of me, the hem of his black robes dragging through the mud. "What are you doing here? If you didn't notice, I'm a little busy."

"Yes, wasting your magic on my precious babies. Did you

notice it doesn't work on them?" His voice drips with venom as he stops in front of the two creatures.

Precious babies? I almost throw up in my mouth to hear him talk about those things that way. "Did you really just call them babies?"

Layre looks at me over his shoulder.

"I created them. Born of fire and dark magic. They're too strong for you mere humans. I'd tell you to ask your friends in the woods if it weren't too late." He tilts his head back, his cackle echoing through the air.

My heart skips a beat. What does he mean, too late? I look to both sides of the trees, but I don't see any sign of Aidan and Zoe or their magic. I refuse to believe anything happened to them. "Your things might be strong, but they aren't invincible."

Layre narrows his eyes at me, turning back to inspect the shadow figures hovering in front of him. He leans in close, his eyes fixed on one of the slash marks across the guardian creature with smoke still spilling out of the wound and mixing with the shadows floating around it. Layre whips around, a scowl on his face. "How did you do that?"

I shrug my shoulders, keeping my face carefully blank. "I don't know. Maybe I'm as good as I think I am."

Layre's in my face again in a flash, his hand raised to lay another blow across my cheek. I grit my teeth, steeling my nerves for the slap, but he lowers his hand. "Give it to me."

"I don't know what you're talking about. I don't have anything." I do my best to keep my expression blank, but inside, my heart hammers against my ribs.

"You carry the Capricorn dagger. Give it to me or I'll take it from you." Layre takes a step back, holding out his hand as if I'd just give it over.

I snort. "Capricorn would never give me his dagger to carry."

The fire is back in his eyes, and watching the tiny flames dance in his pupils turns my stomach.

"You have a Zodiac weapon. Nothing else could do that. Give it to me." His voice tightens with each word.

I stare at him, my mind racing over what he just said. Zodiac weapons can hurt those creatures, but what other weapons are out there? The only one I've ever seen is the dagger. "I think you just underestimate me."

Layre's hand snaps out, wrapping tightly around my throat as he crushes my windpipe. "Have it your way," he hisses.

Tiny lights explode around the edges of my vision, and I struggle to find enough air to keep from passing out. I reach up and grab his hand, trying to pull it away from my throat.

His gaze flicks down to the dark lines running up my arm. He chuckles, releasing his grip on my throat. "I see the dark magic is in you now."

I bend over, gasping for breath. Dark magic? What's he talking about?

"There's no dark magic in me. I'm nothing like you," I say between pants.

"Not yet." Layre glides over to stand beside Avanth, who still holds the fire in his hand, and speaks to the mage even though his eyes are locked on me. "Light her up. We'll pull the weapon from her ashes."

Avanth locks eyes with me and for a moment I don't think he's going to throw it, but he rears back and launches the fireball straight at me. Just before it reaches me, a wave of water splashes up from the ground, blocking the fire.

I look to the trees to see Aidan racing out of the shadows, water streaming from his fingertips.

Fire blazes from the other side, a jet stream aimed directly at Avanth, and I choke back a sob, grateful to see them both alive.

Avanth throws up his hands, sending Zoe's fire splitting around him.

Zoe holds the stream steady with one hand, and with her free hand she conjures more fire that she tosses at Avanth's feet like a tiny bomb.

Avanth is too busy shielding himself from the onslaught of fire to do anything else. The flames erupt at his feet, instantly catching his robes on fire. He screams as they work their way up his body.

Zoe raises her hand and the fire rages higher, consuming Avanth in the blaze. As he crumples to the ground, she turns her attention to Layre, who flicks his wrist and sends her flying off her feet, screaming as she hits the ground.

Aidan places himself between Layre and me and raises his hands, lifting a sphere of water from the ground and wrapping it around the mage. He flips his hands and Layre rises higher, turning somersaults in the water.

Layre opens his arms and the sphere starts to splash apart, but Aidan quickly slams the water back together.

Aidan shouts over his shoulder, "Get ready to trap him in the earth."

I take a deep breath, quickly reaching into the ground while forcing myself to stay as calm and focused as I can. My magic mixes with the earth and my body hums with power. A wide fissure rips through the dirt, racing past Aidan's feet until it opens beneath the mage.

Aidan releases the water, and the mage screams as he disappears in the crack.

I slam the earth back together, and all at once the forest falls silent.

"Well, that was cool." Zoe smiles bitterly as she walks up beside me.

I wrap my arms around Aidan, hugging him tight. "Are you all right?"

Aidan pulls me close, holding me against him. "I'm fine. You?"

I nod, pulling gently away after kissing him softly.

Zoe rolls her eyes. "Yeah, and I'm fine too, thanks."

Smiling, I hug her lightly. "I'm glad, but now what do we do about them?" I point to the two creatures still hovering near the trees.

"They didn't die with the mage?" Zoe asks.

"Doesn't look like it." Aidan takes a few steps closer to the creatures.

"Layre said that only Zodiac weapons will work on these things," I say, inching up behind Aidan.

"We only have your dagger, and I don't think that's enough for them." Zoe's voice is small as she points toward the trees.

Aidan and I follow her pointing finger and my heart skips a beat. The army of creatures float out of the shadows, their arms outstretched as the sickly yellow gel oozes from their bony fingers.

I rush past Aidan, heading straight for the creature with the birthstone embedded in its chest, ripping the dagger out of my coat pocket. I grit my teeth, steeling my nerves against the burning pain I know will come, but I sink my dagger into the chest of the creature.

Pain blazes through my arm, more black lines spreading across my hand as the creature struggles beneath my blade. I twist the knife and pull, popping the piece of birthstone loose from its chest.

The creature writhes, the shadows twisting along its

body as flames erupt from the cavity that held the stone. It grabs my free arm, and the skin on my hand bubbles into angry red blisters.

I scream, yanking my hand out of its grasp as the flames burn brighter. I drop to the ground and grab the piece of Leo's birthstone as an electric shock rips through my body. I scream again, tossing the stone toward Aidan and Zoe.

Zoe scoops up the stone without a problem and shoves it in her pocket.

The creatures swarm around us in a tight circle, leaving no room for escape.

I grab the dagger in both hands and raise it high above my head, slamming the blade deep into the ground. Bright green light flares from the hole, shooting straight into the sky. The light weaves around the creatures as a clicking noise erupts around their circle.

The green light twists around, forming a cage made of pure earth energy.

"Run for it!" I race right through the bars, the magic tingling my body as I pass through it with Aidan and Zoe hot on my heels.

We put some distance between us and the creatures and I stop to see what they're doing. The shadow things bump against the cage but can't break through the magic.

"Maybe that will hold them for a while, but I don't think we should stick around and find out. Let's get the fire and get back to the compound." I race through the trees without waiting for an answer.

We speed through the forest without looking back and without any real idea if we're heading in the right direction to find the cave. Before long, the panting of our breath drowns out the pounding of our feet.

"Wait for a minute." I slow down to a stop, leaning

against a tree with my hands on my knees. The air burns through my lungs, and I wince at the stitch in my side.

Aidan stops beside me, his hand on my back. "Is everything all right?"

"You mean besides the fact that I can't breathe?" I stand up straight, slowing my breaths, but my chest is still tight.

"I can run all day," Zoe wheezes. Her face is flushed, and sweat covers her forehead.

I snort. "Yeah, you look like it."

Zoe frowns at me but doesn't argue.

I stretch my arms in front of me, working out the kinks in my aching muscles, when Aidan suddenly grabs my wrist. I pull my hand free, frowning at him. "What was that for?"

"Let me see your hand." Aidan holds out his hand, staring at me until I give him my arm. "What happened? What are these black lines?"

The black lines have darkened, covering my hand like a web of veins. I pull the sleeve of my jacket up to show the rest of the marks that spread almost to my elbow.

Aidan gently runs his finger up my arm, following the web, and his featherlight touch makes me shiver. "Tell me what happened. I've never seen anything like it."

"I attacked the two creatures left after your diversions started, and since my dagger worked to wound the one earlier, I started with that. When I stabbed at the first one, burning pain shot through my arm and the lines appeared." I stare down at my arm, wondering if it will ever look the same.

"Then what?" Aidan asks softly.

I blink back the tears starting to form in my eyes. "I wasn't sure what was happening, so I tried to stab it again and it just made everything worse."

"That didn't happen earlier when you stabbed the creature with the birthstone?" Zoe asks, pacing beside us.

I shake my head, afraid I won't be able to speak.

"Do you think there was a difference in the creatures and that's why it happened this time?" Zoe stops pacing and stares at me hard enough to make me squirm.

I swallow hard, hoping my voice doesn't shake. "No, because when I cut the birthstone loose, it spread faster up my arm. I think it had something to do with the place they were gathered. Maybe that's why they didn't move even though we were attacking."

Aidan gently pulls my sleeve down, squeezing my hand in his. "That would make sense. I thought it was weird that they didn't disappear or fight back. There are places around Polaris that have different energies that can be used for certain magic. Some of it can be rogue."

"That's great." I let out my air in a huff and open my mouth to say something else but hesitate and close it.

"Out with it. Whatever you were about to say. Secrets can put us all in trouble." Zoe puts her hands on her hips, one eyebrow arched high as she waits for an answer.

I sigh, not sure that I want to say it, but I also know that she has a point. "Layre saw my arm too, and he said it was dark magic in me."

Aidan sucks in a sharp breath as he runs a hand through his hair. "That's not good."

I roll my eyes to play off the fact that my heart is pounding in my chest. "You think? What's going to happen to me?"

He avoids my eyes. "Nothing if we can get it taken care of."

"And if we don't?" My voice squeaks out and I scrunch my face, the high pitch hurting even my own ears.

Aidan slowly lifts his eyes.

"It's different for everyone. Some people think that magic like that started the order of the mages. But we won't let it happen. Not to you." He leans in, kissing my forehead.

"So, there's a cure?" Zoe steals the question I'm about to ask.

"Let's hope." Aidan grips my hand and pulls me through the trees, all of us understanding the unspoken need to hurry.

We weave through the trees at a quick pace just shy of running as Aidan swats at the bony limbs to keep them out of the way.

I reach into the trees, bending the branches up to give us more room. My arm burns with the use of my magic, and a whimper escapes even though I try to keep it quiet.

Aidan glances at me over his shoulder, his eyes crinkled with concern. "Don't use your magic if you don't have to."

"What am I supposed to do if I can't use my magic? I can't run around and be useless all the time," I grumble.

Aidan's shoulders slump, and his face softens. "You won't be useless, and it's only for a while. Using your magic might make it spread faster."

I scowl at him, but in truth, I'm not upset with Aidan. I'm just scared about what's happening with the dark magic. I've come too far to have it all taken away from me now. "Hey, can't you use your magic to flush it out like you did with the poison?"

He shakes his head, surging forward and twisting through the trees. "It doesn't work that way."

"Well, how does it work?" I snap at him and quickly hang my head as he stops to stare at me. "I'm sorry. I didn't mean it to sound that way."

"I know. You're scared and I'm scared for you, but I

promise we'll figure it out." Aidan wraps his arms around me, hugging me close.

I lean into the warmth of his body to stop my own from shaking. "You can't promise that. We don't know what will happen."

I lay my head against his chest and don't even bother to wipe the tears that stream down my face and onto his jacket.

Aidan tightens his grip, pressing his face into my hair and holding me while I cry.

"I hate to break up the party, but does anyone know if we're going in the right direction?" Zoe's voice cuts through the moment and it makes me cringe. Why does she always do that?

I hesitate, then push myself gently away from Aidan, turning to face her as she twists something absently in her hand. "What are you holding?"

"What?" Zoe looks down at her hand. "Oh yeah, it's that piece of Leo's birthstone."

My mouth hangs open as I watch her play with it as if it were a marble. "How can you touch it? That thing basically electrocuted me. I thought only Jocelyn could touch the broken birthstone."

Zoe shrugs. "I don't know. After you popped it loose and tossed it, I figured since we went through so much trouble to get it, I'd put it in my pocket."

"Aries and Leo both rule the element of fire, so that's probably why she can touch it when it burns you," Aidan says, watching Zoe play with the stone with his eyebrows knitted. "You should probably put that away before you lose it or draw any unnecessary attention to it."

"Fine." She slips the stone into her pocket and zips it closed. "Now, are we headed in the right direction? All I see are trees that look the same."

She's right. All I can see in any direction are gnarled trees, deep black shadows and a gray mist that floats above the ground. I don't see any sign of the mountain or any hint of daylight breaking through the trees. "Are we going in the right direction?"

"We have to be." Aidan grabs my hand and pulls me along.

"That doesn't mean we are." Zoe rushes to catch up, trotting beside us.

Aidan picks up his pace, and I rush to keep up as I nearly trip several times over fallen tree branches. "This is the way we came from, and this is the way to the mountain. The rock golem said that the cave is at the base of the mountain."

"Are you sure?" Zoe asks as she ducks beneath a low branch.

Aidan growls as he grits his teeth. "I'm sure. I live here, don't I?"

"Then you should tell your face." Zoe snickers when Aidan glares at her.

"Your face doesn't look like it's so sure." I chuckle softly, which earns me a glare of my own.

Suddenly, I break out into a sweat, and my whole body feels warm as I wipe my face with the back of my free hand.

"Are you okay? You look pale," Zoe says.

I give Zoe a slight shake of my head, but it's too late.

Aidan glances over his shoulder at me.

"I'm fine."

"You don't really look fine," he says, studying my face. "Do you need to rest?"

"We don't have time to rest. I'll be fine once I get out of these trees." I shoo him forward and we walk for a while in silence with dark thoughts twisting in my mind.

What will happen to me if we can't find a cure for the dark magic? What if I don't get it in time? What if it doesn't even exist? Will I turn into one of the mages? Are they even human still? Will I turn into something else and attack my friends? Will I still be me? Will I even live?

There are so many questions tumbling around in my head that it makes me want to lie down on the ground and just forget everything. My body is tired and my arm burns and I don't want to think about anything anymore.

Finally, the air gets lighter, making it easier to breathe, and the shadows begin to get brighter. Silver light shines through the branches, and for the first time in a while, my heart lifts. I choke back a sob of relief and rush toward the edge of the forest, stopping to take a deep breath as soon as I'm free of the trees.

The forests back on Earth make me feel alive in a way I never thought possible, but there's something sick and twisted about that forest.

"I told you we were going the right way." Aidan arches his eyebrows but quickly smiles.

Zoe takes a deep breath, letting it out in a sigh. "We're back at the base of the mountain, so now where's the cave?"

"I think it's that way." He points directly in front of us.

"Do you live here or not?" Zoe snickers as Aidan sputters, turning a healthy shade of red.

Not wanting to be caught in the middle of that, I walk toward the mountain. The hard dirt fades into gray spotted stones, ranging from the size of peas to boulders that someone could carve into a house. I find a rock that's the same size as me, and I lean against it.

"*Be strong, child,*" the earth whispers into my mind.

I want to collapse on the ground but I steady my feet,

hugging the rock. "I'm not sure I know how. I feel sick, and I'm afraid of what will happen to me."

"Do not fear." Her voice is soothing as it caresses my mind, and I relax into the stone.

"Can you help us find the cave we're searching for?" I'm sure it's a long shot, but it doesn't hurt to ask.

"The cave is near. You'll know it when you get there. It'll all be over soon." The earth slips out of my mind and suddenly I feel alone.

"Ciara?" Aidan's hand on my back makes me jump. "Are you okay?"

"Just having a little conversation with the earth. She said the cave is near." I push myself away from the rock, ignoring the fact that they stare at me with their mouths hanging open, and climb over the next rock.

"Did she say where the cave is?" Zoe climbs up onto the rock next to me.

I shake my head, slipping from one boulder to the next.

At least the dark magic isn't killing my Capricorn connection. Yet. "She said I'll know it when I get there."

Zoe sighs, keeping pace with me. "Of course she did."

As I slide over the next rock, something tugs at the corner of my mind. I step cautiously to the side, slipping between two larger stones. My scalp tingles with the energy in this spot. "I think this is it."

"Looks like two rocks to me," Zoe says.

Aidan finally catches up, a deep scowl on his face at being left behind. "I don't see anything either."

"Trust me, this is the cave." I stare at the two stones and notice that they stand upright like a gate, and flying on pure instinct, I head for the space between them.

Energy crackles around my body as I walk through the

magical barrier and find myself standing in the center of a dark cave.

The rock walls have an inner light that casts a soft glow through the cave, providing just enough light to see.

Aidan and Zoe pop into the cave as if appearing out of nowhere.

The three of us stand in a line, staring at the scorch marks on the floor where the fire used to burn.

15

"There's no fire here," Zoe says, staring at the floor.

I roll my eyes, the thought of finally finding the cave and no fire settles heavy in my stomach. "Talk about being obvious."

Zoe huffs, puffing her air out through her cheeks. "What are we supposed to do now? Are you sure this is the right cave?"

Aidan squats down, running his fingers lightly across the scorch marks on the stone floor. "This is the right cave. I can feel the magic from the fire that was here."

"Maybe it's still in here somewhere and we just can't see it," I say softly, walking along the walls of the cave.

"I have a closet at home bigger than this cave. I think we would see fire if it were here." Zoe leans against the wall, letting her head bang softly against the rock.

I stop beside Aidan, my eyes on the floor. "What do you think happened to it? Do you think it went out somehow?"

He shakes his head. "That fire burns forever. There's no way to put it out. Something else happened to it."

"What could've happened to fire that's magic?" Zoe

slides against the wall, her feet pushing out until she's sitting on the floor.

My mind races over the possibilities as I examine the stone. Fire was obviously here, because the rocks have black smudges burned deep into the rock. The cave is completely hidden, and there's no chance that enough air got in here to put out the flames. It had to be magic. "Do you think the mages found it?"

Aidan slowly shakes his head, but the frown on his face makes it plain that he isn't totally sure. "I don't know how they could've found it. I can feel the magic in this place, and it's a secret that would be protected at all costs."

"How is the fire a secret? The Zodiacs know about it, you know about it, and that rock told us where to find the cave," Zoe grumbles.

"She has a point." I circle around the marks on the ground. What am I missing? There has to be some clue here about what happened to the fire. "Do you think someone or something moved it?"

Again Aidan shakes his head, running a hand through his hair. "According to the lore I know, there's only one cave on Polaris where this fire is known to exist."

"That's great." Zoe slumps even farther, nearly laying down. "I don't want to be the one to go back and tell Capricorn that we failed." Her face falls as she hangs her head. "What's going to happen to Aries? What's going to happen to me?"

"Nothing is going to happen to either of you. The fire can't be gone. We just have to find it." I make another pass around the cave, scanning the floor.

"Sounds super," Zoe says, hiding her face behind her hair.

I sigh, watching her basically give up, but I understand

how she feels. Standing here in the middle of an empty cave, I feel like a failure. The Zodiacs are immortal, but will Aries ever recover if we can't find it? And where else are we supposed to look? I don't even know how much time we have left in this realm. It has to be getting short.

My mind mulls over one dreary thought after another, my mood sinking lower with each passing second. As I stare at the scorch marks, I'm suddenly struck by a crazy inspiration, and I lower myself to a sitting position on top of the blackened stone.

Aidan watches me, one eyebrow arched high on his forehead. "What are you doing?"

I take a deep breath and settle myself, my legs tucked beneath me and my hands resting lightly on the ground. "I'm going to see if I can figure out what happened to the fire."

Zoe sits up a little straighter. "You think you can do that?"

I shrug my shoulders, closing my eyes. "It's worth a shot."

Aidan lightly lays his hand on my arm. "I don't think it's a good idea for you to use your magic," he says softly.

"I'm not." I peek one eye open to look at him as he kneels in front of me. "I'm going to chat with the earth. Quit talking to me. I want to see if this works."

Aidan narrows his eyes at me but backs up, giving me space to work.

I close my eyes and relax into the energy humming through the cave. The magic running through this place is old, maybe as old as the realm itself. A burning sensation runs up my arm and I grit my teeth, doing my best to ignore it.

My breath catches in my throat as images flash through

my mind like watching a slideshow. Polaris is in its infancy, a realm with nothing more than a couple of wild forests. The earth rumbles, two sides warring against each other as the Beinn Dorcha Mountains shoot high into the sky, their jagged peaks stabbing at the clouds.

Magical sparkles float in the air like fireflies on a summer night. Blue. Green. Yellow. Red. All the raw essence of the four elements, dancing in a stunning swirl of light and power.

Cold rain falls, pattering against the trees and coating the mountains in a thick layer of pure white snow. Water rushes across the ground, forming the frigid river between the mountains and forest.

Winds blow, stripping the leaves from the forest behind the mountains, exposing the gnarled branches that create a skeletal forest, but it's still bright and airy. Not the dark, mist-shrouded forest that now houses the shadow creatures.

Green grass ripples across the plains, growing high in places and forming soft fields in others. The golden meadow at the base of the mountain rustles softly, a whisper in the wind.

A field of stone grows from the ground, forming the boulders we crossed to get to this cave. The red essence of fire congregates around the stone, floating like sparks from a fire, then disappears.

A flat stretch of ground, some place I haven't seen since we've been in this realm, is black and hardened like coal. Patches of fire burn across the area, flickering in shades of pink like the fire we seek, blazing red, neon green, the soft blue of the portal fire and the lavender fire I've seen in the compound and in the tunnels of the mages.

A small fairy floats over the field of fire, carried lightly by translucent wings, landing softly next to the pink fire. His platinum hair, tied in a tight ponytail, blows in the wind, brushing against his brown leather tunic. His face is pale and smooth, but his almond eyes hold a wisdom that belie his young appearance. He whispers under his breath, words I don't understand, and reaches a tiny hand straight into the flame. As he removes his hand, pink flames cling to his fingertips, and he tucks them quickly into a small satchel hanging across his body.

A black hooded figure weaves between the twisted trees.

He stops, raising his hands above his head, chanting in an arcane language. Darkness and mist fills the forest, and the trees bend over as dark magic sickens them. He glances over his shoulder as his gray eyes, so light they're almost white, scan the forest. My heart skips a beat. I'd know those eyes anywhere. Kyrell.

Back against the mountain, two boulders shift, standing tall and forming the gateway to the cave. A flicker of movement and the same fairy appears. He reminds me of Pippig and his sister Hazel. He flutters between the rocks, reaching into his pocket and pulling out a small handful of glittering dust. Whispering soft words, he blows the dust, and energy flickers between the rocks.

Inside the cave, the fairy reaches into his satchel, pulling out the fire and cradling it lovingly. He sets it on the ground, waving his hands in series of swirls. The fire spreads across the floor of the cave, forming a small pink line of flames.

Kyrell hunches over in the middle of the gnarled forest.

He holds the squirming fairy tightly in his fist. A muddy yellow jelly drips from Kyrell's free hand.

A figure stands over the fire, his black robes barely missing the flame. He kneels next to the flames, wiggling his fingers as the brightness of the pink fades. He scoops his hand against the rock, lifting the flame from the rock. He turns around, taking care with the fire, and a primal hunger fills his black eyes. Layre slips out of the cave, leaving nothing more than a scorch mark on the stone floor.

Layre crouches on the ground in the same spot where we found the nest of creatures, the pink flame burning in front of his feet. He whispers ancient words and black smoke curls around the flame. The pink hue of the flame fades to gray, then flashes blue. Layre reaches into his pocket and pulls out a handful of small yellow orbs, made of the same gel substance.

Inside the orbs are tiny creatures. Fairies, nymphs, and others I don't recognize. He takes his hand and carefully peels the flame into strips of fire. Layre pushes some of the orbs into the flames as sparks shoot into the air. The black smoke twists and stretches high into the air, forming the shadow creatures. He buries the remaining orbs, waving his hand over the spot. Yellow light sparks and disappears just as quick.

The fairy is back inside the cave. He stares at the ground, tears streaming down his pale cheeks. With his arms hanging by his sides, his wings flutter and lift him off the ground, carrying him slowly to the back of the cave. He reaches inside his satchel, pulling out fingers coated with pink flame, and lays a tiny hand on the rock wall. A crack opens in the stone and he disappears inside.

My eyes fly open, and I fall back, violent coughs shaking my body.

Aidan is with me in an instant, leaning me forward and supporting me as I struggle to breathe. "What happened? Did you see something?"

I nod, swallowing hard and wincing at the dryness in my throat.

Zoe crosses the cave and hands me a bottle of water, and I take a grateful sip.

I look from Zoe to Aidan. "I know what happened to the fire and I know where to find more."

"Did you really see something? Tell us what happened." Zoe drops to her knees beside me, bouncing lightly as she waits.

I close my eyes against a wave of dizziness as I replay the images in my mind. What exactly did I see? How could I have possibly seen the beginning of Polaris?

"You're killing me," Zoe whines.

"She looks a little pale. Maybe we should let her rest," Aidan says softly as he strokes my hair back from my face.

"I'm fine." My words are a little slurred.

"I know she's pale, but she has to tell us what she saw. We are running out of time in this realm. We have no idea how long we have." Zoe's shoes scrape against the stone as she scoots closer to me.

I try to open my eyes, but they seem to be stuck. "I said I'm fine. I just need to open my eyes."

"No one knows where this cave is. I think we're safe enough here to let her rest," Aidan says.

I struggle to sit up, peeling my eyes apart and rubbing them with the backs of my hands.

"Why isn't anyone listening to me? I'm fine. I'm just trying to figure out what I saw." I lean forward the rest of the way, dropping my face into my hands.

They let me sit in silence until the dizziness passes. "That's not true," I mumble into my hands.

"What's not true?" Zoe asks.

"The mages know where this cave is." I feel the need to stand up and stretch my legs that grew stiff from sitting on the stone floor. Everything tilts around me, but it feels good to get up and move.

Aidan follows behind me, keeping close in case I fall over, which is a good possibility. "How is that possible? And how do you know that?"

"When I sat down and connected with the rock, I saw the history of Polaris flash through my mind. From the very beginning, when the magic came and formed the mountains, forests, the river, and the field of fire."

"That must've been amazing to see." Zoe props her chin on her hand as she stares up at me.

I muster what I can of a smile and nod my head. "It was."

Aidan cuts me off as I open my mouth to continue the story. "There's no such thing as a field of fire."

"Even if it doesn't exist anymore, there was a field of fire." I stop walking for a second as the ground tilts. "It was a flat stretch of ground and it was burned like coal. Flames of all colors were lined up like a row of crops. The lavender fire in the compound. The blue fire from the portal. The pink fire we're looking for. I saw it all."

"You've never seen it before?" Zoe asks Aidan.

He shakes his head, brushing his dark hair out of his eyes. "I didn't know anything like that existed."

"Wait a minute. Where is this field of fire? Is that where we have to go now to get the flame we're looking for?" Zoe's eyes widen as she slowly rises to her feet.

"I'm not sure exactly where it is, just that it's somewhere on Polaris that I haven't been." I frown, trying to force myself to remember.

"That could be almost anywhere." Aidan leans against the wall.

I shake my head. "It doesn't really matter. There's more fire in this cave."

"Umm, where?" Zoe turns in an extravagant circle to prove her point that there's no fire visible in the small cave.

I roll my eyes, pointing to the back of the cave. "It's on the other side of that wall."

"So, we walk through it?" The corner of her mouth tilts up in a half-smile, but I don't appreciate her humor.

Aidan must've sensed my mood shift, because he reaches out and softly grabs my hand, pulling me closer to him. "Tell us the rest of your story. What else did you see?"

I relax against him but keep my eyes glued to Zoe. "There was a fairy that reminds me of Pippig and his sister that took some of the pink fire and brought it to this cave. I saw Kyrell show up on Polaris, and he cast some kind of spell that made that forest creepy and bony."

Aidan draws in a sharp breath. "The forest where the creatures are living. If you can call it living."

"That's the one." I squeeze his hand, taking comfort in the warm tingle of touching him. "Kyrell somehow caught the fairy, and it looked like he was torturing him for information. I'm assuming he told him the location of this cave, because Layre came here and stole the fire from this chamber. He tainted the flames with his magic and used it to create the creatures."

Zoe gasps. "Is that why our magic doesn't work on them?"

I shrug my shoulders, shifting my eyes to the ground. Tears form, but I quickly blink them away. All I want to do is lie down and sleep for a while, but I know that's not an option. "It could be one of the reasons."

Aidan wraps his arms tight around me, and even if it's only for a moment, I feel safe. "Did you see more fire in another chamber of the cave?"

I shake my head, wiping my tired eyes with the sleeve of

my jacket. "That fairy got away from Kyrell. I don't know how, but he did. He was so sad when he saw the fire missing. But he brought more to the cave and hid the flames behind the back wall."

"Great. How do we get through it?" Zoe walks to the back of the cave, inspecting the wall.

"You're not going to find a doorway if that's what you're looking for." I feel like I should untangle myself from Aidan, but I decide to stay in his arms a little longer.

Zoe glares at me over her shoulder. "How did the fairy get through?"

I sigh, blowing my air out through puffed cheeks. "He cast some kind of magic and the rock split enough to let him pass through."

"I don't suppose you know any fairy magic," Zoe says.

Aidan follows behind me as I cross the cave, running his hand lightly on the bumpy surface. "No one but the fairies have access to their spells. They're the only ones that could perform them anyway," he says absently.

Zoe and I stare at him until he looks up from the wall. "What?"

The confusion on his face makes me chuckle.

"That's great, but how do we get through the wall?" Zoe places both hands on the wall and grunts as she pushes, her boots sliding across the floor.

I gently pull her hands from the wall. "That isn't going to work. I think it's going to have to be my magic."

"No," Aidan says sharply, the force of his tone catching me off guard.

"Why not? How else are we going to get through?" I raise my arms to fold them in front of me when I'm suddenly struck with the reason for his tone. The veins of dark magic spreading up my arm have grown wider and darker.

"I'm sorry." Aidan gently grasps both hands. "It's not a good idea for you to use your magic."

I know that he's right, no matter how much I hate to hear the words, but I hate even more feeling useless. I also know that my connection to the earth is the only thing that's going to get us through that wall. Our time on Polaris is growing short. I understand that even if I don't know how short. The fire we need is on the other side of that wall, and we need to get to it now.

I lift my eyes to meet his worried gaze. We stand there for a moment in silence, and I see his look shift from fear to frustration to caring resignation. "I have to try. My magic is the only thing that's going to get us through that wall."

"Yeah, but I don't have to like it." Aidan squeezes me tight before turning me to face the wall.

"If anything happens, we'll make sure we get the fire back to Aries," Zoe says.

I shoot a quick glare over my shoulder. "Gee, thanks."

She winks at me, but I can see her jaw muscles twitch beneath her halfhearted smile.

I lay my palms flat against the stone, energy immediately racing through my hands. A searing pain races through my right arm and I'm blinded by a white flash. I cry out as I stumble backward into Aidan's arms.

He scoops me up, pulling me close. "Are you all right?"

I press my head against his chest, breathing deep until the tears stop streaming down my cheeks. My arm burns, and I know without looking that the dark magic is spreading.

"I have to try again." I push against Aidan, but he holds me tight.

"I don't think that's a good idea," he mumbles, his face pressed against my hair.

It's definitely not a good idea, but my gut tells me it's the only way to get through. "I have to try again."

Reluctantly, he lets me go.

I move back to the wall, but this time I drop to the floor, choosing a place where I think the fairy cast his spell. My fingers brush against the wall, feeling for any trace of magic that doesn't belong to the earth.

About three inches up from the floor, magic tingles against my fingertips. A warmth spreads through me like sunshine on a summer day. The smell of fresh cut grass reaches my nose, and I can taste the sweetness of honey in my mouth. A smile spreads across my lips.

There's magic here that I've never felt before, and it's safe and warm, but there's also a wildness to the energy. It's mysterious, and it has to belong to the fairy.

I focus on the magic and press both hands against the stone. Warm energy tingles up both arms, but none of the burning pain, and I breathe a sigh of relief. But before I can relax too much, the magic pushes back. I brace myself for the worst before I realize that the magic is testing me. It wants to know if I'm friend or foe.

I reach into the earth, pulling its energy into my body and pushing it out through my hands. My body relaxes as a steady stream runs through me, mixing with the fairy magic. I focus my mind on going through the wall, getting some fire and taking it to heal Aries. My thoughts stay light to show that we mean no harm.

Beneath my hands the rocks shift, and a loud crack rips through the air. My eyes fly open as the stones split, creating a doorway large enough for us to squeeze through. I keep one hand on the stone and motion for Aidan and Zoe. "Let's go. I don't know how long this is going to stay open."

Aidan slips through, with Zoe close behind him. Once

she's clear, I slip through the opening and the rocks scrape against each other as they slip back into place.

I stare at the new chamber with my mouth hanging open.

"I've never seen anything like this," Zoe says softly.

The chamber is large, bigger than my house, with a curved ceiling so high I can't gauge the distance. The walls and floor are smooth obsidian, so dark and polished that I can see our reflections like black mirrors. Several rows of flames spread across the center of the space, all the different colors glowing brightly and providing the only light to see.

Aidan turns to me, his eyes wide with excitement. "Is this the field of fire you were talking about?"

"No. That was out in an open field, but it's the same fire, and I bet it's where these flames came from." I walk up to the first row of fire and shiver as cold waves roll off the blue flames.

"What's it doing in here?" Zoe joins me, squatting near the fire and breathing deep, as if she's smelling a flower.

"I think it was brought here for protection." I move around the rows of fire, stopping in front of a line of pink flames. "Let's get it and get out of here."

"How do we move it?" Zoe asks, crossing the chamber to stand beside me.

"Layre just picked it up and left with it." I squat, pressing my hands together to form a scoop, and slip my hands beneath the pink flames. I scream, pulling my hands back so fast that I fall onto the floor, my skin turning angry and red.

"Let me try." Zoe scoots closer to the flames but tumbles on top of me as the ground of the chamber shakes.

"What is that?" I shout over the rumble that feels like an earthquake.

A crack zig-zags across the smooth obsidian, splitting

into a door that creaks as it opens. Through the opening appears a woman, and I can see right through her body.

The woman's skin is a dark gray against her white linen dress. Black hair floats around her head, and she stares at us with eyes that glow orange. Her shriek rips through the air, and we all slam our hands over our ears.

She floats toward me, hovering several inches above the ground, and smiles, revealing a mouth full of jagged black teeth. "Who dares to steal my fire?" she hisses, the smell of decay filling the air from her breath.

16

I turn my head away from the creature, swallowing down the bile as the stench turns my stomach.

The woman floats to the side so that she's in front of my face again, leaving a trail of black smoke behind her. "What are you doing here, human? How did you find this place?"

My eyes water and I swear the smell is burning my nose, but I don't think it'll help my cause if I vomit on the floor. I take a second to collect myself before meeting her pumpkin-colored eyes. "The earth showed me, but I swear we're not here to steal your fire."

"You lie," the creature hisses, following my movement as I turn my head again. She opens her hand and a black stream of mist shoots from her palm. "You've come to steal my fire to make more of those vile creatures."

"Wait a minute. Don't do that." I take a couple of hasty steps back, careful not to get too close to the rows of flame. "We aren't making more creatures. We've been trying to kill them."

The mist floats above her hand in a rolling cloud as she

tilts her head, her eyes glowing with an inner light. "Tell me why I shouldn't kill you all where you stand."

Zoe steps up beside me, her eyes fixed on the creature. "Because we're not here to steal your fire. The Zodiacs sent us to collect some of the pink flames."

"Yes." She lets the word trail off into a hiss. "I can feel their magic on all three of you."

Zoe squares her shoulders. "So you know we're telling the truth."

"Do I?" She locks eyes with Zoe, letting the mist dissipate above her hand. "Come here, child."

Zoe hesitates, glancing at me as I give her a slight shake of my head, but she takes a deep breath and steps forward. "What do you want?"

The creature sneers, floating a full circle around Zoe, and I get the feeling she's toying with us. She lays a gray finger on Zoe's forehead and her body stiffens.

I rush forward to help Zoe, but the creature flicks its free hand and I grunt as I slam into an invisible wall.

Zoe's eyes flutter, then fly open wide as she sucks in a sharp breath.

The creature removes her finger, nodding her head as her hair floats around her. "You are who you say you are."

She turns her attention to Aidan, waiting without a word. Aidan walks to the creature, stopping a foot from her, wrinkling his nose as she leans in close to inspect him.

"You are different, but of the same magic." Her voice is low, barely above a whisper.

Aidan nods, holding his body steady with his head held high. "I am the Aid of Scorpio."

"You smell of rain and water." The creature's eyes widen as she bares her teeth, and after a moment of hesitation, she lays a finger on his forehead.

I watch Aidan's body stiffen and I slam against the invisible barrier, still unable to get through.

The creature releases Aidan and he stumbles back, panting. "You are who you say you are."

My heart skips a beat as the creature turns her attention on me. "Come."

"How can I when you have me blocked by some spell?" I slam my mouth shut, thinking it's probably better to watch what I say.

"Come!" the creature shrieks, and we all cringe as her shrill voice bounces off the chamber walls.

I take a tentative step forward and find that the barrier is no longer in front of me. I'm not sure what she's doing with her finger, but something inside me says I don't want to find out, even if Aidan and Zoe seem to be fine. I force each step of my heavy legs to take me closer to the creature.

The woman floats in front of me, stopping at arm's length, and runs a bright blue tongue over her gray lips. I fight every instinct I have not to run as she lays her finger on my head.

Every muscle in my body locks, and it feels like I have an electrical current racing through my body. My jaw clenches so tight that I'm afraid my teeth will break as my eyelids flutter uncontrollably.

Images race through my mind, and I understand the creature is sifting through my memories. Only I'm not the one controlling what she sees. She is.

Kyrell stands on my front porch, his platinum hair blowing in the winter wind. I'm pulling Taurus's birthstone out of the tomb wall on Fannette Island. I'm throwing the spell beneath Taurus's feet to banish him back to Polaris. I'm standing in the forest, facing Layre and Olin.

My eyes fly open and I gasp, coughing as I breathe in the creature's stench, her face an inch from my own.

She raises a pointed fingernail, yellow and brittle with rot, and places it against my throat. "You are not who you say you are. Your life is forfeit."

I dive to the side, throwing myself roughly against the stone floor, her nail scraping me as I move, and a thin line of blood runs down my neck. I wipe the wound with the sleeve of my jacket and put more distance between us. "I am who I say I am. You're just guessing based on the memories you pulled up. I'm the Guardian of Capricorn."

"Capricorn would never allow a human that uses dark magic in his service. I feel it inside you." She flies toward me, both hands held up with her fingers forming claws.

"Hold up." I dodge out of the way of her attack and she shrieks. "I don't work dark magic. I can barely work my earth magic."

"Stop lying!" The creature's voice shreds the air.

"She's not lying." Zoe takes slow steps toward me as if she's afraid of spooking the woman.

She looks at Zoe, narrowing her eyes before turning her gaze on me. The orange light pulsing in her eyes like a flickering flame. "There is dark magic in her. It's running through her veins. I saw their faces in her evil mind."

I look from the creature to Zoe. Is the creature really listening to her? My heart skips a beat. Maybe Zoe can somehow get us out of this. I whip back around to stare at the creature as her words finally sink in. "I'm not evil, and there's no dark magic in my veins. That's crazy."

The creature lashes out, yanking my arm toward her before I have a chance to react. She traces a jagged nail over the black lines running up my arm. "Lies."

I yank my arm free, wincing as her nail breaks the skin

and more blood wells up. "That's not my fault. Something happened when I attacked one of those creatures in the woods. I'm not like the mages."

The creature hisses at me, spit dripping from her lips. "Those things are vile."

I take a slow step back, feeling like I'm standing in front of a snake that's coiled and ready to strike. "I agree with that." I soften my voice. "I know they stole some of this fire to make those things."

"Only someone who works with them would know that." She flies to me, raking her nails across my hand, leaving four long scratch marks on my skin with burning pain shooting up my arm.

"Damn it!" I pull my arm close to me, backing up so fast, I bump into Aidan. "I don't work with the mages. I'm trying to kill them before they end up killing me. I know that because the earth showed me. That's how we even found this stupid cave to start with."

Aidan quickly places himself between me and the creature.

"That's the truth," Zoe says, adding authority to her tone.

For a second, I'm afraid she's going to be attacked, but to my surprise, the creature backs up a little. What is going on with that woman and Zoe? Why is she responding to Zoe when all she does is accuse me of lying? Do they have some kind of connection?

"If that is the truth, then why are you in my cave, stealing from my garden?" The creature's eyes flare.

"Your garden?" The words slip out before I realize what I'm doing.

Zoe holds up her hand, shooting me a glare that says I better keep my mouth shut, and I know she's right. She turns to the creature, keeping her voice soft as if she's talking to a cornered animal. "We came into this chamber to take some of the pink flames from your garden. I'm sorry if you think we're stealing from you. We didn't even know that you were here."

Black smoke forms around the creature, twisting itself around her body like a snake.

"We were sent here by the Zodiacs, by Capricorn," Zoe continues in a rush. "Aries is sick because of a spell that the mages cast on him. I'm his Guardian. Capricorn sent us to get the fire because that's the only thing that can reverse the magic. We won't take any more than we need."

The creature stares at me as I peek around Aidan's shoulder. He lifts his arms, ready to call on his magic in case she attacks again. Her gaze flicks to his hands before returning to me. "If you are to leave this cave with the sacred healing flame, you must prove your worth."

"Great," I mutter. "And what exactly do we have to do?"

The woman floats high in the air, black smoke twirling around her body, growing thicker with each passing second. The smell of burnt wood and ash coat the air.

"The trials are for you alone." Her voice echoes through the chamber, filling the space with her command.

I grab Aidan's arm, hanging on to him as my blood runs cold. "Trials? What do you mean, trials? What do I have to do? Why me?" My questions tumble out of my mouth before I can stop them.

"Because you have the darkness within you. Three tests you must pass before you're worthy of keeping the flames. Fail and you die. Get help from your friends and you die. Pass and you may leave with the fire unharmed. Do you accept?"

All kinds of crazy ideas race through my mind. What kind of tests will this creature put me through? If the tests don't kill me, what if the woman still does? Who is she anyway, besides some protector of the fire garden? "What exactly do I have to do?"

"Do you accept?"

I sigh, stepping in front of Aidan even though he yanks on my arm to hold me back. "I accept."

"Then let us begin." The creature throws her head back, and her shrill cackle sends goosebumps down my arms.

The woman hovers in the air, her eyes locked on my face, and I squirm beneath the weight of her stare. My heart beats faster, and the longer I stand here, the more I think I've made a huge mistake.

"Can we just get on with this?" It's probably not a good idea to push her, but I can't stand her looking at me anymore.

She clicks her tongue, and the noise echoes off the obsidian walls as a sneer pulls at the corner of her mouth. "In a hurry to die?"

I fold my arms across my chest, ignoring the looks I feel coming from Aidan and Zoe. "Not so much, but I'm in a hurry to get back and help Aries. You know that by keeping us here, you're responsible for anything that happens to him. That would make you like the mages, not us."

Aidan groans beside me, and Zoe drops her head into her hands. I know I'm playing a dangerous game, but I'm quickly growing impatient.

The woman disappears in a puff of slate-colored smoke, reappearing an inch from my face as I stifle a scream. She smirks as I lay a hand over my chest as if I can still my pounding heart. "We can't have you passing easy tests, now, can we?"

I cough into my cheeks as the smell of decay burns my nose. "I can't stand around all day waiting for you, either."

The woman cackles, her jagged teeth shining in the light of the garden of fire. "I like you. You have a bit of fire within you. Too bad that won't save your life. But let us have some fun first. Tell me, child, do you have knowledge?"

Her question catches me off guard, and I frown at her. "Am I smart?" When she nods, I continue. "I'm smart enough, I think. Why?"

She floats up, returning to her place high above us. "The first is a test of knowledge. A philosophical question, if you will. Are you ready?"

My stomach twists. Philosophy? Is she kidding me? How am I supposed to answer a philosophical question to her satisfaction, especially when she's already so excited about killing me? "Let's get it over with."

The woman smiles at me, looking far happier than I'm comfortable with. "Considering you're here in my chamber, standing amidst the flames of my garden, tell me, what is the turning of fire?"

I stand there staring at the creature. What the hell is the turning of the fire? I've never heard of such a thing. My mind races through several ideas, each one dumber than the last. I refuse to look at Aidan or Zoe for fear she'll think I'm trying to get help.

"Are you stuck?" The woman practically sings her words as she drops a little lower in the air.

I pace in front of Aidan, hoping the movement will help kick my brain into gear. "I'm thinking."

She chuckles, and it makes the hair on my arms stand up. "You have sixty seconds."

I freeze, watching the creature with my mouth hanging open. "What do you mean, sixty seconds?"

"Tick, tock, tick, tock," the woman sings.

"You didn't say there was a time limit. That's cheating." I fight to keep myself under control even as my voice rises.

"My game, my rules," she snarls, and flicks her wrist.

I cry out as a deep cut slices the back of my hand, blood instantly dripping down my arm. "Damn it," I say through gritted teeth. The stinging pain clouds my already panicked brain, and I struggle to wrap my mind around her question.

"Oh dear, time is almost out." Again she drops, and she's almost even with me.

"Then let me think," I grumble.

The woman lifts a finger and another deep cut rips through my skin, forming a burning X on the back of my hand.

I cry out, tears springing into my eyes as I drop to my knees. The instant my legs hit the obsidian floor, images flash through my mind. I see a man in a toga from ancient Greece, standing beneath a star-filled sky. Next, a giant burning core filled with molten fire. The fire gives way to the sea. The water splits in half, forming the earth, and from half the earth comes air. My eyes fly open, leaving me gasping for breath.

The woman drops to the ground in front of me, tipping my chin up to look at her face. Her skin is unnaturally hot, and it burns my skin. "Time's up."

"Wait. I have an answer." I swallow hard, coughing as my dry throat sticks together. "The turning of fire is about each element feeding into the next. Transformation and how each element needs the other, but it all begins with fire."

The woman pulls her hand from my chin, scraping my face with her nail. She stands up and crosses the chamber, stopping near Zoe. "Clever girl. Or did you have help?"

I climb slowly to my feet. "You didn't see anyone help me, so I guess I'm clever."

The woman hisses, spit flying out of her mouth. She licks her lips with a long blue tongue. "Test number two will be a battle of magic."

Damn. I don't even know what this lady is, and I'm supposed to beat her with magic? "What are the rules this time? And no changing them in the middle of the test. If you want to beat me, then do it without cheating."

A smile slips across her face as the orange in her eyes flares, and I have the feeling that I added gasoline to the fire. "Yes, I do like you. These are the rules. Block three attacks in order and you pass. Miss one and you start again. Die and you lose."

"I guess that sounds simple enough." I barely get the words out of my mouth when a blast of fire shoots straight at my face. I dive to the side as a wave of heat tingles against my skin. "That's one."

"You moved like a coward. I said block my attacks," the lady cackles.

Neon-orange flames blast from the ground directly beneath me. I scream as I roll over, my clothes on fire, and desperately beat my hands on my body to put it out.

Aidan twitches in my direction but the lady holds him steady with a glare.

I finally put out the fire when another jet of the orange fire blazes out of the wall. I throw my hands up out of instinct, pain ripping through the black veins in my arm, and I'm relieved to see a small shield of gleaming obsidian shoots up from the floor, blocking the flames. "Now that's one."

The lady growls deep in her throat and flicks her hand. The large piece of obsidian melts into the floor as the flames ignite my sleeve. "Back to nothing," she cackles.

I smother the flames with my other arm, carefully

sidestepping away from the wall. How am I supposed to beat this woman with magic? My eyes never leave her face, hoping that she'll somehow give herself away. Her gaze flicks to my right, a movement so subtle I'm not sure it happened, but before I can question myself anymore, a fountain of bright blue flames erupts from the floor on my right.

I throw my hand up, pulling the obsidian floor with it, creating a wall between me and the cold fire. Ice crackles and coats the side of rock, spilling over the top, but I'm left untouched.

The woman shrieks, flying high into the air as she raises both arms above her head with her fingers pointing toward the ceiling. An explosion rocks the chamber as fire rains down in flaming chunks.

Aidan and Zoe rush for cover as I drop to the ground, placing my palms on the warm floor. A cloud of dust puffs up from my hands, sealing my body in a protective bubble, and I watch as the fire bounces off the barrier.

How did I do that? Where did the dust come from, considering I haven't seen a speck of dirt in this place? Why does my magic always seem to work best when I'm trying not to die? Burning pain floods through my arm, cutting my questions short. My breath comes in quick pants as it spreads nearly to my shoulder. Sweat covers my body as I slip to the ground and curl into a ball, my vision blurring as the shield dissolves.

"Get up and fight!" The woman screams, her voice coming from somewhere above my head.

I hear the crackling of fire, but the pain in my arm is so intense that I can't seem to drag myself from the floor. My eyes squeeze shut and I wait to be engulfed in flames.

When the fire doesn't come, I push myself onto my

back to see flames licking around the edges of an obsidian wall. Somehow, I block her attack without using any magic. I groan as I struggle to sit up. "I believe that's three."

The woman kneels in front of me and I struggle to focus on her face through the tears in my eyes. She trails a finger down the side of my cheek, careful to avoid the tears. "There's more to you than I thought, but you will not survive the final test."

My shoulders slump, and all I want to do is collapse to the floor. My body is tired and my mind is clogged with pain and fear that the dark magic is spreading. What will happen if it gets too far? Even if I survive the final test, I may not survive this poison in my veins.

She floats to her feet, holding her arm out toward Aidan, and he suddenly appears in her grasp. He struggles as her hand tightens around his throat, his face shifting shades of red.

I leap to my feet, my heart pounding against my chest. "What are you doing? Let him go. He has nothing to do with this. Please, you're hurting him."

The woman relaxes her grip, but only enough to let him breathe. "I can feel the fire of love burning between you two, but I wonder where is your truth. Where is your loyalty placed?"

"Let him go. Your game is with me." I muster all my strength to stand tall and straighten my shoulders even as I sway on my feet. "I'll kill you to save him. I tried to do it your way, but I'll leave with him and the fire when I'm done with you."

"This test is but a simple choice." The woman's skin glows, and Aidan's eyes widen as steam rises from his body. "You may take the pink flames and leave, if it's true that you wish to save the Zodiac and not destroy my garden. Walk out of here and I will kill the boy."

I snort. "That's not happening. Option number two?"

A sneer slides across her face. "You may have the boy, but you will not get the fire."

"Ciara." Aidan chokes out his words, barely able to speak. "Your duty is to the Zodiacs. Always."

I shake my head, more tears sliding down my face.

"No, I won't leave you here to die." I rush forward but the woman yanks him back, his eyes bulging with the movement, and I stop.

"Help Aries." Aidan's face shifts from red to purple, his eyes rolling back.

"Stop it! You're killing him!" I scream at the woman, but she merely watches me with a blank face. "Take me instead. Let them leave with the fire."

The lady's eyes flare, and she loosens her grip around Aidan.

He quickly grabs her wrist, keeping her hand locked firmly on his neck. "No."

She floats toward the ceiling with Aidan's legs kicking wildly.

I thrust my hand into the air, sending the obsidian spiraling toward Aidan, but his legs stop kicking as the black glass reaches him. My knees buckle and I hit the ground hard, sliding across the slick surface.

"Aidan!" I scream, but all I hear is the woman laughing.

"You are too late. I'm feeling generous, and even though you made no choice, you may leave with the flame." She lets go of Aidan as if he's a piece of trash and his body plummets toward the ground.

With tears in my eyes, I shift the obsidian to stop his fall, lowering him gently to the floor. I throw myself on the ground next to him, my fingers on his throat, looking for a pulse. Nothing.

I choke back the panic, placing my head on his chest, listening for the sound of breath or a heartbeat. Nothing.

I lay myself across his body, sobs shaking me to the core. He can't be dead. This can't be happening.

A hand gently pulls on my shoulder. "Ciara."

Shaking my head, I push Zoe away. "Go away."

"I'm sorry." Zoe kneels in front of me, her eyes filled with tears. "We should really go."

I bury my head into his chest, my tears flowing harder than I've ever cried in my life. "I'm not leaving him here."

"Ciara," Zoe sniffles.

"I said go!" I swat at her, but I'm too weak with grief to come close. I lie down beside him, feeling the heat fade from his body as I choke through my tears.

"I'm sorry, Aidan. Please don't leave me. I need you to protect me.I just need you." I run my fingers through his dark hair, brushing it out of his eyes like I've seen him do so many times before. "I'm in love with you. I'm sorry I didn't tell you that." My voice fades to a whisper.

The floor rumbles and a crack splits open next to Aidan. The edges smooth, inching closer to him, and he slides gently into the hole. The rock melts together and he's gone.

I throw myself onto the floor, banging my fists against it. "Give him back! Give him back!" My breath fogs the obsidian just as my tears drip to wash it away.

"Ciara, he's gone." Zoe reaches down, carefully pulling me up to my knees.

I lean against her, my body trembling. Across the chamber, a sliver of the pink flame flickers in the distance.

This can't be happening. My heart breaks into a thousand pieces, and even if I get out of here with my life, I can't imagine living without him. But I know he wouldn't want me to die in this chamber too, and the longer we stay here, the more that risk becomes a reality.

I leap to my feet, wiping the tears from my face and turning to look at the woman. "I'll take my fire and leave."

She drops to the ground. "Very well."

Her body shifts and stretches. The gray of her skin darkens to black as it turns smooth and shiny. The woman's arms and legs shorten as a long tail stretches from the back. Her face elongates, flat and long, with razor-sharp teeth. She lands on the floor on four legs, her long blue tongue flicking at the air as fire burns at the end of her tail.

I stumble back, trying to understand why I'm looking at a giant lizard.

Zoe backs up so fast she bumps into me. "That's a salamander. She's not some creature. She's a fire elemental."

"A what?" I can't take my eyes off the reptile.

Zoe screams as the blue tongue shoots across the chamber, wrapping around Zoe's body as it drags her toward the salamander. "Ciara!"

The fire elemental releases Zoe, pinning her with a clawed foot as she tries to crawl away. "She is fire. She is my price for the flame," the lizard hisses.

"Price? You didn't say there was a price." I dive for Zoe but miss her as the salamander scoops Zoe up in her mouth and darts up the wall.

17

The salamander scurries up the wall with lightning speed as Zoe kicks her legs in the lizard's mouth.

I run for the wall, my mind racing over any possibility of stopping the thing from disappearing with my friend. I crash into the obsidian, pressing my palms against the glassy surface. Closing my eyes, I shove energy into the wall and a flat shelf shoots out wide, high up the wall.

The salamander darts to the side, narrowly missing the ledge. She climbs onto the flat surface, aiming for the ceiling.

Zoe screams, her arms and legs flailing. She uses her fist to beat against the lizard's head, but it doesn't deter the salamander.

I chase after them, trying to keep them directly above me, but they're getting so high, it's hard to see them. My breath catches in my throat as I notice an opening between the wall and ceiling, and it's exactly where the salamander is heading. I can't let her get through that crack.

I slam my hands against the wall, directing my magic to the slit above me, and grit my teeth as I focus on closing it.

Pain rips through my arm and pins and needles shoot through my shoulder, causing my arm to go numb. My knees buckle, and by the time I hit the floor, my body is covered in sweat. My vision blurs as I put my hand down to keep from falling over.

A hiss echoes through the chamber and I look up, blinking my eyes to help me focus. The salamander flips around, her head pointing down, and stares at me with fire flashing in her bulging orange eyes. She looks pissed.

The hint of a smile tugs at the corner of my mouth with the satisfaction that I blocked her escape in time. "Now what?" I shout up at the lizard.

Flames leap from the floor, quickly closing around me as it traps me in the center of fire that rises above my head. I curse myself for running my mouth as the flames close in around me. Sweat beads on my face from the intense heat.

I leap to the side as more fire shoots up from the floor directly between my legs, and check myself to make sure my pants aren't burning. I look up to see that the salamander has crawled halfway down the wall and that Zoe is hanging limply from the creature's mouth.

Fire closes all around me, forcing me onto my tiptoes to keep from being burned. I take a deep breath, focusing on the obsidian beneath my feet, grateful to be in a chamber made of a natural rock. I reach into the rock, pushing it across the circle and snuffing enough of the flames to leap across.

My feet hit the ground and my tired legs give out as I slide headfirst across the floor. I shout, rolling to the side and onto my hands and knees as the lizard lands right in front of me.

She jerks her head to the side, tossing Zoe to the ground. Zoe's body slides to a stop and she doesn't move.

"Zoe, get up," I yell at her, keeping my eyes locked on the lizard.

"Don't worry about the girl." The salamander's blue tongue shoots out of her mouth, and I roll out of the way.

It's strange to see a giant lizard talking to me. My heart pounds against my ribs and my arm is still numb as I try to support myself and stay ready.

The salamander skitters toward me, and I scoot back. With her short legs, her stomach brushes the ground, but she's still taller than me while I'm in a crouched position.

I grit my teeth, pushing against the floor and connecting with the earth beneath the obsidian layer. The rocks are even hotter between the fire garden and a layer of molten earth flowing down deep. But there's more than just rock and dirt down here. Tickling on the back of my senses, I find traces of metal.

Reaching deeper, I push my magic into the earth and tap into the metal. Thick, cylindrical bars crash through the floor, shattering the rock as they trap the fire elemental inside an iron cage.

The salamander hisses at me, spit dripping from her mouth. She slams her body against her prison, but the bars hold.

I concentrate on melding them together, closing her in across the top of her cage.

She reaches a leg through the bars, swiping at me, but I'm well out of her reach.

I take the moment of distraction and crawl across the chamber to check on Zoe. Her breathing is shallow and her face is pale, but I'm glad to see that she's still alive. I grab her shoulder to shake her but immediately pull my hand back. Her body feels like it's on fire from the inside.

"It's against your laws to attack an elemental. I'm too

powerful for you. Let me out before you regret it." The salamander twists circles in her cage, climbing over her body as she moves.

I grab Zoe by both shoulders, ignoring the burning sensation in my hands, and give her a rough shake. "Zoe, you have to wake up. I need you."

Zoe moans but doesn't open her eyes.

"Last chance to let me out." The elemental's voice is low and vibrates with a power that sends chills down my spine.

I'm playing a dangerous game, but there's no way I'm letting her out of that cage. As I stand, I concentrate on thickening the bars, and grit my teeth as the pain from the dark magic spreads into my chest. I sway on my feet but stay upright. "I'm done with rules and laws. You started this. What have you done to Zoe?"

"You came to my home with dark magic to steal from me." The salamander coils into a ball, pressing her head flat against the ground.

I pull on Zoe but I don't have the strength to pick her up, and I grimace as she slips from my grip and thuds against the floor. "Zoe, please. You have to get up."

Zoe stirs her arms, her brows knitting into a frown. "What's happening?" she mumbles.

"You have to get up. I can't lift you. We need to get the fire and get out of here. That cage won't hold her much longer." Tears slip from my eyes, racing down my cheeks. My thoughts slip to Aidan, but the pain quickly overtakes my mind and I feel like I'm on the verge of passing out. "I can't do this without you."

"Cage? What cage?" Zoe peels her eyes apart, blinking as she tries to focus on my face.

A deafening explosion rips through the chamber, sending flames and shards of metal flying in all directions.

I throw myself across Zoe, wrapping the back of my head and neck with my hands. A few pieces of sharp metal scrape across my back and I cry out, burying my face into Zoe's shoulder as shrapnel clangs across the floor.

When it's safe to look, I tilt my head to the side and peek with one eye, gasping as I see the salamander race across the chamber, heading straight for us.

I roll off Zoe, dragging her with me. "We have to move." I use every ounce of strength I have to get to my feet and pull her up with me.

"Don't let her get me again." Zoe clings to my arm as she watches the elemental with wide eyes.

"Zoe, listen to me." I swallow hard as more tears fill my eyes. "I'm going to distract her. I need you to get some of the flame and get out of here. You should be able to get out the same way we came in. Take the flame back to the Zodiacs and tell them what happened."

Zoe shakes her head so hard her hair flies around her face. "I'm not going to leave you here with that thing."

"I don't have the strength left. I'll give you as long as I can." I turn my back on her, taking a deep breath as I pull energy into my body from the earth.

Zoe pulls on my arm. "I'm not leaving you."

"Go!" I feel her hesitate behind me, but my focus is on the lizard. "I'm going to kick your ass."

She hisses at me as I hear Zoe's shoes pound across the floor, heading for the garden of flames.

Zoe makes it halfway to the garden when she screams. I look over to see lavender flames twisting around her body, pinning her arms to her sides. She struggles, but it's useless.

While I'm looking at Zoe, a blue tongue wraps around my body, yanking me from my feet as it drags me closer to her. I pull on her tongue, but she's too strong.

The elemental opens her jaws wide, breathing a jet of fire in my direction. I twist my body but I have nowhere to go.

Cold water splashes in front of me, soaking my clothes and hair. The flames sizzle, engulfing me in a cloud of smoke. I search through the haze and my heart skips a beat. As he comes into view, I choke back a fresh sob. Aidan.

The fire elemental twists to the side to get a better look at Aidan, whipping me with her as she turns. "How are you still alive?" She takes a hesitant step back.

"How doesn't matter. Let her go." Aidan's voice sounds different, a little richer.

I can't take my eyes off him. I want to drink in every detail, since I thought I'd never see him again. My heart swells to the point of bursting, and I have a feeling that I have the earth to thank for him standing here. "Aidan."

His eyes meet mine for a brief second, the normally bright blue now glowing, before he turns his eyes back to the salamander. "I said let her go."

The salamander's tongue wraps tighter around my body, and I gasp as she cuts off most of my air. I dig my nails into her tongue, but she refuses to let me go. The elemental takes a deep breath, releasing it in a wave of fire.

I duck my head, bracing for the burning heat, but it doesn't reach me. Instead, it shoots high into the air like a blowtorch. I glance over at Zoe, still trapped by lavender flames, as she focuses on directing the fire.

I claw at the salamander's tongue, but she only squeezes me tighter. My lungs burn with what little air I'm able to draw in, and I know I have to get free before she suffocates me. I wanted to keep the turquoise dagger a secret if I could, but I no longer see any choice, and reach into my jacket, drawing out the blade.

With my hand wrapped firmly around the handle, I jam the razor-sharp tip straight into the tongue, and it slips through like butter.

The elemental shrieks, instantly dropping me to the floor. My knees fold as I hit the ground, and I nearly stab myself as I crumple into a heap.

Aidan is by my side in a flash, dragging me away from the lizard and pulling me to my feet.

I wrap my arms around his neck, never wanting to let him go, and more tears stream down my face as he pulls me close. "I thought I lost you."

"I'm not that easy to get rid of." He smiles, but it quickly slips from his face.

I squeal as he throws me to the ground, pressing his body over me. A flash of fire crackles over our heads and the heat singes my face.

Aidan pushes me out from under him, giving me a gentle shove in Zoe's direction. "Help her. I'll take care of the lizard."

"But..." I don't get to finish my argument as he rushes toward the salamander.

Rain falls directly over the salamander. It sizzles as it splashes across her back, as if the drops were made of acid. The elemental shrieks, writhing on the floor as the skin on her back bubbles and steam rises from her body. Lightning crackles near the ceiling, and I can feel the electricity on my arms.

I stand, transfixed with the storm. I've never seen him conjure anything like that before.

"Damn it, Ciara, come help me!" Zoe's shout shakes me out of my thoughts, and I rush to her.

Her body is covered in lavender flames, but they don't look like they're burning her skin. I reach for them but hesitate, my fingers hovering an inch above the fire. I don't feel any heat or cold coming from the flames. "What is this stuff? Is it hurting you?"

"It's the lavender fire, and other than my arms falling asleep, no, it isn't hurting me. Hurry up." Zoe stares over my shoulder, her eyes wide.

I glance over my shoulder as thunder booms through the chamber. The rain pounds the elemental that's now barely visible in a cloud of white steam.

"Ciara!" Zoe whines.

I whip back around, wishing I could just stand there and watch the storm. "Each of the colors does something different, right? What does this one do? Why can't you just use your magic and take it off?"

Zoe rolls her eyes, grimacing as she adjusts her shoulders. "You don't think I tried that?"

I take a deep breath and reach for the fire, afraid of what it's going to do to my hand. Nothing happens. My fingers pass through it, but I don't touch Zoe either. In fact, my fingers pass right through her too. "Um, that's not good."

Sparks fly into the air as lightning strikes the ground closer to us than I'm comfortable with. Thunder cracks overhead and orange light fills the chamber as a giant fireball explodes from the lizard. Aidan shouts as he dives out of the way, sliding across the rain-soaked floor.

"Will you pay attention to me, please?" Zoe's short tone pulls my focus back to her.

"Sorry. I don't know what to do about this stuff." I stick my hand all the way through her but feel only a slight tingle on my skin.

"Stop that. Get your hand out of me. How is that possible?" Her voice rises with each sentence as she struggles to break free.

I pull my hand out of her. It's like the lavender fire is turning her into a ghost. "This is so crazy."

Zoe growls at me. "What about that blade in your hand? Try that."

Somehow, I'd forgotten about the dagger in my hand. I bring it up to the fire and this time it feels solid. I saw through the flames and they slip from her body like a rope, coiling at her feet before dissolving into the ground. I slip the dagger back into my pocket.

Zoe slowly raises her arms, sucking in a sharp breath. "That really hurts."

The rain picks up, falling so thick, it's hard to see anything through the drops as they pound against the ground. I search the chamber but I don't see any sign of Aidan or the elemental. I motion to Zoe to follow me as I jog toward the storm.

Zoe groans, but her footsteps splash behind me. "Where did they go?"

"I don't know." I can barely hear my voice over the rain.

Zoe screams, and I whirl around in time to see the salamander's tongue wrap around her body, but she loses her footing on the slick floor before the elemental gets a good grip. Zoe crashes to the ground, rain splashing in her face as a tiny object falls out of her pocket, plunking into the swirling water.

My heart almost stops. I can see the glow of the birthstone from where I'm standing, but so can the elemental, and her eyes light up with primal greed.

"Zoe, get the stone!" I surge through the water, diving when I get close enough. I'm knocked to the side by the salamander's tongue as she crawls closer. The stone brushes my fingers, sending a shock through my arm, but I can't get a grip on it.

Zoe dives into the water beside me, her hands frantically searching the water. "Where is it?"

The salamander joins the search, thrashing her long face through the water, which begins to bubble.

My skin turns bright red and I realize what is happening. "Aidan! She's boiling the water!"

The water swirls, draining somewhere I can't see, but I'm glad it's gone. Aidan rushes up beside me, lifting me to my feet. "Where's the stone?"

"I'm not sure." I turn in circles, my eyes scanning the floor. My stomach twists the longer I look without seeing it. The only small comfort I have is that everyone else, including the salamander, is also still searching.

Fire erupts along the back of the salamander as her body shifts, stretching as she stands up on two legs. She's no longer the lizard or the woman, but a being in the shape of a human made of pure white fire.

I swallow hard, my mouth instantly dry, and I drop my eyes to shield them from the glare of the elemental. That's when I see it. Leo's birthstone lying on the ground, beneath the elemental's feet.

Zoe gasps to my right, and I'm sure she sees it too.

I glance at Aidan and he nods, neither one of us daring to look anywhere close to the stone.

"The stone will be mine." The elemental's voice drips with power as it fills the chamber.

"The water must've washed it away. We don't have it anymore." I stare up at the elemental and it takes my breath away. There's something beautiful about the pure flame, even if it is ten feet tall and trying to kill us.

A giant wave rises from across the chamber, and I understand now that the water didn't drain, Aidan just moved it. It arcs high above the elemental's head, crashing down on the being as it bellows.

Zoe and I both dive for the birthstone and she reaches it first, wrapping her hand around the stone as the water pours down, sweeping us across the floor. She stuffs the stone into her pocket, zipping it closed as the water carries us back toward Aidan.

Aidan stares at the elemental as wave after wave crashes against the being, causing it to stumble backward and fall into the garden of flames. As the elemental lands, the flames shoot high as if someone turned on the gas before returning to normal.

The elemental is gone.

I stand there, staring at the rows of flames. "Did you kill it?"

Aidan shakes his head. "I don't think you can kill an elemental."

"I say we don't stick around to find out." Zoe walks over to the row of pink flames.

I throw myself into Aidan's arms and he chuckles as he squeezes me tight, pressing his mouth against mine in a heated kiss. I pull away as a blush floods my cheeks. "I thought you were dead."

"I was." His eyes narrow, and I wonder what's passing through his mind.

I squeeze his hand, drawing him out of his memories. "I'm glad you aren't dead anymore. What happened?"

"You two can reunite later. How about helping me with this fire?" Zoe crouches near a flame, examining the bottom like she's going to uproot a plant.

I groan as Aidan pulls me over to join her. "How do we take that back?" Aidan asks.

They both look to me like I should know the answer. "Why are you looking at me?"

Aidan holds my gaze, and the light glowing in his eyes makes them even more breathtaking. "What did you see in your vision?"

I force my mind to work. "Right. The fairy picked it up from the bottom like a flower and carried it in a pouch. Layre used some kind of spell I didn't understand and carried it out in his hands."

Zoe takes a deep breath and reaches for the flame.

"Wait. Are you sure you want to touch that? It burned me, remember?" I squeeze Aidan's hand as I watch her.

"Why don't you let me try?" He walks toward her but hesitates when she holds up a hand.

"I'm taking the fire. It's my responsibility. I'm the Guardian of Aries." She shakes her head when I open my mouth to argue. "Think about it. You already tried to pick it up but it burned you. Fire has the power to destroy the earth. Aidan wields the power of water, which could destroy the flame, but I am fire. This is my element."

Her argument makes perfect sense. "Okay. But be careful."

Zoe turns back to the pink flame and scoops both hands beneath the small fire, picking it up without any trouble. A smile spreads across her face. "Let's go."

The ground rolls, sending all three of us crashing to the floor. Zoe hitting the hardest as she hangs on to the fire. She uses her elbows to push herself off the floor. "What is that?"

"Hurry up!" a tiny voice squeaks behind us.

I whirl around and my eyes land on Pippig, his iridescent wings beating a mile a minute as he hovers near the wall.

"Pippig. Where did you come from?" I'm amazed at how relieved I am to see the fairy.

Pippig's hands fly to his head, his tiny hands gripping his platinum hair. "Now! Run!"

I look over my shoulder and my heart drops.

The elemental is back, and she brought five more with her.

The three of us race into high gear, slipping and sliding on the floor that's still slick from the water.

Pippig flies to the wall, waving his hand in circles for us to run faster.

We all reach the wall at the same time and I frantically search for a way out. "Pippig, where's the door? Are we stuck in here?"

Pippig reaches into the brown leather pouch, the same chocolate color as his tunic, and pulls out something tucked in his fist. He slams the blue, glittering powder against the wall and a small door opens. He flies through and shouts from the other side. "Come on."

"We can't fit through there." I drop to my hands and knees and peer through the door, but it's too small.

"Come on." Pippig zooms across the cave.

Aidan shoves me from behind as a ball of fire smashes against the wall above our heads.

I slam my eyes shut, but instead of bumping into the wall, I roll out into the cave. There's no way I should've fit through that door. I scramble out of the way as Zoe dives into the cave, followed by Aidan.

Pippig slams his hand against the wall and the door seals shut. He floats to the ground, his wings relaxing against his back. "That was close."

"Why are you just standing there? It won't take them long to break through there." I head for the entrance of the cave but stop when no one follows me.

Pippig flies over to hover in front of my face. "Those particular elementals are bound to the inner chamber. They cannot leave unless they are set free from the spell that holds them."

I stare at the fairy, and his face triggers a thought. "Your people moved the fire here, didn't they? They're the ones that bound the elementals? Was it someone in your family?"

Pippig's almond eyes open wide. "How do you know that?"

I smile, finally able to relax a little. "The earth showed me when we were trying to figure out how to get into the chamber."

He puffs out his chest, holding his chin high. "It was my grandfather that built the garden and bound the elementals to protect it."

"How did you find us?" Zoe crosses the cave, her eyes locked on the fairy.

"Why is she staring at me?" Pippig squeaks.

Aidan chuckles. "I'm sure she's not used to seeing fairies."

"This would be a first." Zoe reaches up a hand and pokes him.

He grumbles, kicking at her finger.

I hold out my left hand and Pippig flies over to land on my palm, tickling me as he walks. "How did you find us?"

"Hazel told me I needed to come help you. She knows it is my duty to protect you." Pippig puffs out his chest again, his hands on his hips.

Aidan narrows his eyes at Pippig. "It's my job to keep her safe."

"I didn't see you getting her out of the cave." Pippig folds his arms across his chest, his eyebrows raised high, daring Aidan to argue with him.

Aidan scowls at the fairy, and it makes me laugh. I lift my hand and lightly kiss the fairy. "I'm honored to have you both protecting me. I wouldn't be alive if it wasn't for you two."

With a smile on his face, he flaps his wings, flying up to land softly on my shoulder. He traces a finger along one of the black veins in my neck. "What is this?"

Something in his touch triggers the dark magic, and pain burns through my arm as a sickly yellow light flashes in front of my eyes. Before I can stop myself, I tumble to the ground, barely conscious.

Zoe and Aidan immediately drop to the ground beside me, with Aidan carefully propping my head in his lap.

Pippig floats down to land softly on my stomach.

It's hard to breathe. Every ounce of air burns in my lungs. Sweat covers my body and my legs feel like lead. Shadows fill my mind, thoughts of death and sweet darkness. My body grows cold as I fight to stay awake.

Pippig runs up and stands on my chest. "Hold on."

I try to force a smile, but it's no use as a tear slips down my face. "I think it's too late."

I shift my eyes up to Aidan's face. "I'm glad I got to see you again."

Aidan nods, tears filling his eyes. "I came back for you. I..."

Every muscle in my body spasms, my back arching off the floor, nearly tossing the fairy to the ground.

Pippig climbs up my face, sitting cross-legged on my forehead. "Close your eyes but don't give in."

I do what he says, focusing on the feel of Aidan beneath my head and Zoe's hand on my arm as shadows swirl in my mind. Something tickles my face, and I fight the urge to brush it away.

Pippig begins to sing, his voice high and clear like a silver bell. No words fill his song, only the most beautiful tones I've ever heard. There's magic in his voice, and its ancient sound resonates deep in my bones.

My chest tingles, and I can feel the darkness pulling out of my body. Each breath is easier than the last, and I begin to have hope that I'll make it after all. The burning pain slowly flows out of my chest, through my shoulder and down my arm.

Pippig's song picks up in pace. The faster he sings, the faster the magic flows toward my fingers. The darkness gathers in my hand, and the heat is so intense, it feels like it might catch on fire. I whimper as Aidan strokes my hair, and I do my best to lie still.

Suddenly the cave is silent and Pippig flutters off my forehead. I open my eyes and watch the fairy land beside my hand, which is now completely black. He snaps his fingers and Aidan and Zoe freeze.

I look from one to the other then back to Pippig. "What did you do? Why are they frozen?"

Pippig inspects my hand, touching each finger. "I have to release the dark magic. I didn't want it to infect either of them." He nudges my hand with his foot. "Turn it over."

I flip my hand, resting it with the palm facing up. "What about you or me?"

"We'll be fine. Now, let me take care of this before it spreads again." Pippig reaches into the pocket of his tunic and pulls out a blade so small, I can barely see it. He drops to one knee and stabs the knife into the center of my palm, slicing it in one swift movement.

I suck in a sharp breath as the cut stings my hand. A dark cloud of smoke pours from the open wound, rolling around itself as it floats toward the ceiling of the cave.

Pippig reaches into his pouch, throwing a handful of the fairy dust into the air. The powder instantly forms a shimmering bubble over us, blocking the magic from coming back down. Pippig flicks his wrist and a pale blue light streams from his fingers, wrapping a glowing rope around the cloud. He guides it to the wall that leads to the inner chamber and shoves it through.

"What did you just do?" I look for any trace of the dark magic, but it's gone.

Pippig shrugs. "I sent it into the chamber. Nothing purifies like fire. The elementals will take care of it. How do you feel?" He purses his lips, blowing out a stream of air, and the bubble disappears.

I struggle to sit up, testing my body. "I'm a little weak, but I feel normal again. The pain is gone. That was amazing. Thank you."

"You're welcome. Now don't go getting any more of that dark magic in you again. It was almost too late this time, and it'll be worse next time." Pippig shakes a finger at me. "Capricorn will have my job if something happens to you, and I can't go back home without my job. None of my people have been so honored by the Zodiacs, and I'm a hero to them."

The pride in his voice makes me smile. "You're a hero to me, too."

Pippig flies up to sit on my shoulder, a broad grin across his face. "We should get going."

I snort. "Aren't you forgetting something?"

"Forgetting what?" Pippig grabs a strand of hair to hold on to as I slowly climb to my feet.

"Aren't you going to unfreeze them?" I test my arm, and it feels normal again.

Pippig snaps his fingers and Zoe and Aidan spring back to life.

Aidan leaps up, wrapping me in a tight hug, and almost knocks me over as Pippig pulls my hair to keep from falling off my shoulder. "Are you okay?"

"I'm fine, thanks to Pippig." I smile, returning the hug.

"Hey, don't squish me." Pippig flies over to the safety of Zoe's shoulder.

Aidan reluctantly steps back. "Where is the dark magic now?"

"Toasted by the elementals." I laugh as his mouth drops open.

"Speaking of elementals, they're not going to be happy that you got away from them with some of their fire." Pippig flies toward the mouth of the cave.

"I thought you said they're bound to that chamber." Zoe carefully shifts the pink flame in her hands as if it might break.

"They are, but they're not the only fire elementals in the realm, and the others will eventually look for you." Pippig's tone is very matter-of-fact.

I roll my eyes to play off the shiver running down my spine. "Thank you for that."

"No problem." Pippig beams at me. "Oh, and one more thing."

"I hope it's not more cheery news." My heart beats faster, afraid to hear what he's going to say.

Pippig frowns at me. "That fire was hidden by my family centuries ago. There's more than one thing out there that has searched for it. The flames will draw attention, so you'll have to move fast."

"I was afraid of that." I sigh, not looking forward to leaving the safety of the cave.

"Don't worry, I have a shortcut." Pippig flies near the ceiling before swooping back down.

"Are we ready?" I look from Zoe to Aidan, and when they both nod, I turn back to Pippig. "Lead the way."

Pippig zips through the air, his iridescent wings beating so fast that they blur as he flies higher up the back side of the mountain.

"Pippig, wait up," I say between pants as I scowl at the fairy. "None of us can fly, you know."

The fairy zooms by my face, landing softly on my shoulder. "We have to hurry. Time is running out."

"I know that," I grumble, and immediately soften as his face falls. "I don't mean to snap, but I still don't feel totally normal. Zoe is carrying that fire, and Aidan doesn't have any mountain animal in him." I shake my head, thinking about how crazy that sentence sounds.

"The creatures will come out and everything will be drawn to the fire." Pippig grips a fistful of my hair as I look behind me for Zoe and Aidan. "We also don't know how long those flames are going to last."

I tilt my head to stare at him, and he shrugs. "That's all great news. Thanks."

Aidan and Zoe catch up, both breathing hard and their faces flushed.

Pippig flies off my shoulder, hovering in the center of

our small circle. He points a tiny finger ahead of us, and I'm grateful it's in the opposite direction of the gnarled forest. "Continue across the mountain and climb down. Around a bend you'll see a small lake. You'll find the portal there that will take you back to the Zodiac compound."

I glance at Aidan and Zoe, and their eyes are just as wide as mine. "Wait. You're not going with us?"

Pippig shakes his head as he tucks his legs beneath him, reminding me of a genie floating in the air. "Nope. I have to go tell Capricorn that you're on your way with the fire. They have preparations to make."

Aidan steps forward. "What preparations?"

"They have to move Aries to the ritual chamber and get him ready for the healing." Pippig frowns at Aidan. "Didn't you know that?"

Aidan shakes his head. "A Zodiac has never been sick before."

Pippig loops around, twisting as he flies, and I'm taken aback at how graceful he is. "Sometimes I forget how young you humans are."

"The portal is in the lake?" Zoe's face is scrunched, and sweat lines her forehead.

"It's under it, actually." Pippig loops around, stopping in front of her nose. "You shouldn't handle that fire much longer."

I lay my fingers on Zoe's hand, careful to avoid the flame. Her skin burns my touch. "Can't you take the fire back for us?"

Pippig shakes his head, his platinum ponytail swinging against his back. "Nope."

I stare at the fairy, waiting for more of an answer. Instead, he just stares at me. "Why not?"

"She picked it up. The flames are hers now until she

chooses their purpose." Pippig flies around the three of us, heading toward the peak of the mountain. "Do hurry."

"Pippig?" Aidan waits for the fairy to stop and turn around. "You said the portal is under the lake? How will we find it?"

He tilts his head, staring at Aidan. "You'll know." With that, he flies away so fast, it seems like he just disappears.

Aidan kicks at a rock, muttering to himself.

I snort. "I take it you don't know where to find the portal."

He glares at me. "I didn't know there was a portal that can take us to the compound. How does he think I'll know how to find it?" He reaches into his backpack and pulls out a bag of chips, absently stuffing them into his mouth.

Taking his cue, I pull a small sandwich out of my bag and take a couple of bites. It feels like it's been years since I've had anything to eat. I rip off a piece of the sandwich and hand it to Zoe. "Probably because you work with water." I finish off my half of my sandwich and wash it down with a swig of water.

Aidan dumps the last of the chips in his mouth, crumpling the bag as he stuffs it into his backpack. "If you girls are ready, we should get this trip over with."

Zoe tilts a little and for a second, I'm afraid she's going to fall over, but she squeezes her eyes shut and shakes her head. "Are you sure we should go to that portal? It's in the opposite direction of the compound."

She has a point, but I know in my gut that we can trust the fairy. "Pippig said it was a shortcut, and I don't want to go back through that forest. Especially not with the birthstone and the fire. It seems dumb, but Pippig has saved my life twice, and I trust him."

"Do you trust him?" Zoe looks to Aidan, her eyebrows raised.

Aidan nods. "I didn't know there's a portal that goes straight to the compound, but I know there are portals all over this realm. I say we get there as quick as we can and get rid of that fire."

Zoe sighs, her eyes drooping. "I'll try to keep up."

We head for the portal, the three of us keeping to a single line with Aidan leading the way. I let Zoe walk in front of me so I can keep an eye on her unsteady footing, and she slips a few times, nearly falling down the rocks. "Are you feeling okay?"

Zoe shakes her head. "Not really. I feel like I have a fever."

We can't afford for anyone to get that sick, especially Zoe, since she has to take care of the flame. "Do you think it's from being out here in the cold?"

"I think it's the fire." Zoe lifts the hand, carrying the flame so I can see it over her shoulder.

I suck in a sharp breath. "Did the flame get smaller?"

Zoe glances at me, tucking the flame in close to her body. "I think so. Pippig said he wasn't sure how long the flame would last outside the garden."

"Yeah, but we haven't had it very long. If it disappears that quick, we'll never make it back to the Zodiacs." My stomach twists. What will happen if we don't make it back in time? It's not like we can just come back out here and get some more.

"That scares me too," Zoe says softly.

Without saying a word, Aidan picks up his pace as he winds between the jagged boulders, and we do our best to keep up with him.

A cold gust blows, whipping our clothes around us, and

I duck my head against the icy wind as Zoe struggles to keep the flame close.

"Do you feel that?" Aidan stops, turning around to face us.

"Yeah, it's freezing." I pull my coat tighter around my body, gritting my teeth to keep them from chattering.

Aidan stands still, his hair whipping wildly in the wind. "There's moisture in the air."

"Does that mean we're close to the lake?" Zoe doesn't look cold at all, despite the dropping temperature freezing the sweat in her hair.

Aidan smiles. "We are."

The wind whistles through the rocks, and I scoot in closer. "Has anyone noticed anything following us? I don't think it'll be a good idea to lead something to that portal."

Zoe shakes her head. "I haven't seen or felt anything."

"Me either, but you're right. The closer we get, the more we have to be on the lookout for anything around here." Aidan grabs my hand and pulls me toward the base of the mountain. I hook my other arm with Zoe's, making sure we all stay together. "The lake is this way. I can feel it pulling me."

We keep our arms linked as we weave between the rocks that grow steeper toward the base of the mountain. The blustery wind tugs us in every direction, each step getting harder than the last.

Finally, the ground flattens and we're off the mountain. The wind still gusts, but it's not as strong.

I look around and my heart sinks. There isn't a lake anywhere that I can see. There's only flat grassland with no rocks or even trees. Did we make a mistake coming this way? Did we go the wrong way on the mountain? I look over at Aidan. "Where's the lake?"

He frowns at the horizon. "It's here. I can feel it."

"Feel it where?" Zoe sits down on the ground, watching the pink flames flicker on her palm.

Aidan closes his eyes, turning in a slow circle. "We keep going straight."

"Straight into what? There's nothing for miles," Zoe grumbles.

I reach a hand down to her, and after a moment, she lets me pull her to her feet. "It's too late to turn back now. The flame is still shrinking, isn't it?"

Zoe nods, her eyes locked on the fire.

Aidan takes off at a jog, with Zoe and me following close behind him. I'm not sure where he's leading us. I only know that we're getting farther away from the mountain and more exposed the longer we run. I constantly glance over my shoulder, but so far, I haven't seen anything else.

I catch my toe on the ground, crying out as I land hard on my hands and knees. The instant my body connects with the earth, an image flashes through my mind. The flicker of blue fire in a swirl of black shadows. I gasp as my eyes fly open and the back of my neck tingles.

"Are you okay?"

I look up at Zoe, and I swear I see a flash of red in her eyes. "I'm fine. I saw an image of those shadow creatures when I fell." I climb to my feet, brushing off my pants.

"Come on, the lake is just ahead." Aidan waves us forward, excitement filling his voice.

I look past him, but I don't see anything. "Where?"

"What do you mean, where? It's right there." He points in front of us, his face falling into a frown. "Can't you see it?"

I shake my head as I strain to see anything that looks like a lake.

"Are you sure?" He jogs back to stand by me and get the same viewpoint. "It's right there."

"There's nothing there." I glance at Zoe. "Do you see it?"

Zoe narrows her eyes, searching the land. "No."

"The lake is huge. You really can't see it?" Aidan clenches his jaw, staring at me as if he can force me to see the water.

"Take us to it. Maybe we can see it when we're closer." I push him forward, grabbing Zoe's hand.

The moment I touch her skin, the flame in her hand flares, rising above her head. Zoe turns her head to avoid the heat as I take a step back. She stares at the fire, which is now barely larger than the flame of a candle.

I swallow hard, fighting the rising panic. We're losing the flame quick. "What the hell just happened?"

"I don't know," Zoe says softly as she brings her eyes up from the fire to meet mine. "But we're not alone."

19

I whip around, my eyes scanning the grassy plains and running up the side of the mountain. I'm sure the shadow creatures are near, but I can't see them. "Where are they? Are they close?"

Aidan pulls me closer and the three of us huddle with our backs together to keep an eye on all sides. "I don't see them either. Can you feel them coming?"

Zoe takes a shuddering breath. "Coming? No. They're already here. I can feel their connection with the pink flame."

I glance at Zoe over my shoulder. "You can feel them through the fire?"

"That's what they're made of, right? The flame is calling them and they're calling it. It's weird, kind of like babies searching for their mother." Zoe pulls the flame in close to her body, shielding it with her free hand.

Aidan presses against Zoe and me. "Get ready, because it's about to be nighttime. They need darkness and shadows."

I scan the sky, squinting against the silver light shining through the clouds. "It looks like early afternoon."

The moment the words come out of my mouth, the sky turns black and the full moon hangs high, its glow diffused by puffy clouds. It happens as fast as someone flipping a switch.

"I told you," Aidan whispers, making me groan.

Darkness closes in around us as soft voices filter through the air. I can't understand what they're saying. There are too many of them talking over each other. They weren't there the last time we faced the creatures, but I remember them all too well from my dream. I tap into the energy of the earth, scanning the night for the creatures I know are out there.

Zoe sucks in a sharp breath. "Do you hear them?"

"Yeah, but I don't know what they're saying." Movement catches my attention, and I whip around, but I still can't see anything in the darkness.

Zoe sniffles, and I can feel her body trembling. "There are so many of them."

Aidan grabs her arm. "How many creatures are out there?"

Zoe shakes her head, a sob shaking her body. "Not the shadow creatures. There are so many innocent beings trapped inside those things. They absorb fairies and other magic in order to survive, but they don't just steal their magic. The victims are trapped inside them as they use them."

A cold shiver races down my spine. The voices and the faces I saw in my dream are their victims? I squeeze my hands into fists as I fight to keep my anger under control. "How do you know that?"

Zoe turns toward the center of our trio, holding up the tiny flame in her hand. "I can see it in the fire."

I study the flame, but it only looks like pink candlelight to me. "I believe you. Can you tell how many of the shadow creatures are out there?"

She shakes her head, tears trickling down her cheeks. "It's not all of them. At least four or five."

I scan the darkness, listening to the voices that are even more chilling now that I know where they're coming from. What are the creatures waiting for? Why are they hiding out there in the darkness? They need to show themselves so we can get this over with and get back to the compound. I reach inside my jacket, pulling out the turquoise dagger, and adjust the hilt in my grip as I turn in slow circles, looking for any sign of the creatures.

Aidan plucks the dagger out of my grip and tucks it inside his jacket.

"Give that back," I hiss. "I need that to fight those things. Don't you remember that the only thing that can hurt them is a Zodiac weapon?"

Aidan places his hand on my neck, sweeping my jawline with his thumb. "And don't you remember that it's because of that dagger that you had dark magic in you? You might not survive it if that happens again. Your dagger was made by a Zodiac, but it isn't a true weapon."

I fold my arms over my chest, trying not to pout even though I know he's right. "But it did damage to them."

"And to you." Aidan shakes his head. "Get over it, because I'm hanging on to it until we get back to the compound."

I mutter under my breath.

Aidan looks sharply at me. "What was that?"

"Nothing," I grumble. "What are they waiting for? Why aren't they attacking us?"

"They're waiting on instructions." Zoe takes a step forward, her eyes unfocused in the distance.

I look around, trying to see what she's staring at. "Who's giving them instructions?"

"Their master." Zoe's voice is barely above a whisper.

The fire is giving Zoe a far better connection with the creatures than I'm comfortable with as I stare at her zoned-out face.

Aidan's eyes narrow as he looks at me, and his face tells me he's as unnerved by her reaction as I am. "But Layre was their master, and we dropped him into the earth and slammed the door."

"That you did."

My heart sinks at the cold voice behind us. I turn around slowly, and eventually my eyes find Layre in the darkness.

Obviously, we didn't slam the door hard enough. "How are you still alive?"

"You don't think you can kill me that easily, do you?" Layre slips his hands into the pockets of his robes, his shoulders relaxed like we're all casual friends.

"I saw you fall into the earth." My body stiffens as I try to track every move he makes in the dark.

He clicks his tongue. "Next time you want to bury someone alive, make sure they're still in the ground."

My face flushes with angry heat, and I'm grateful he can't see me. "Thanks for the tip. I'll make sure I do a better job this time."

Layre chuckles, but the sound is hollow as he strolls to his right. "We don't have to fight. Just give me back what you stole from me and we'll call it even. For now."

The three of us shift with him, but it's too late. His eyes light up as he glimpses the fire in Zoe's hand.

Layre freezes, his gaze locked on the flame as Zoe pulls it behind her. "Where did you get that? I thought all the fire was gone."

I shift my feet, keeping myself between Zoe and Layre. "See, you're not as smart as you think you are. You can't have it to make more of your creatures. That's ours."

Layre cuts his eyes up to mine as he tilts his head. "And how do you know that's what I used to make my babies?"

I cringe at the word babies. "That doesn't matter. All I know is that you're not going to get that flame."

A sneer spreads across Layre's face, and his eyes are cold enough to make me shiver. "Are you willing to die for it?"

I swallow hard, shifting my gaze to the grass at his feet. "Are you?"

Flames ignite on his fingertips. "Shall we dance?"

The blades of grass quiver and shoot up, twisting their way around his body. They pin his arms against his sides as he releases the fire in our direction.

The three of us dive in different directions as the fireballs fly harmlessly over our heads.

I concentrate on the grass, thickening their hold by adding more blades. They braid themselves into a thick rope, weaving all the way to his neck.

Layre growls as he struggles against his restraint.

"That's not going to hold him long. We need to get to the portal." I leap to my feet, dragging Zoe with me. We hesitate at the sound of snaps coming from the mage.

The grass pinning him in place hardens into what looks like plastic in the dark and explodes, sending sharp chunks flying in all directions. Layre stretches his arms. "You're not leaving so soon, are you?" With a flick of his wrist, he sends another fireball flying in our direction.

Zoe steps in front of me, the flames hitting her square in the chest and absorbing into her body. She doesn't even flinch.

"Are you okay?" I grab her arm, turning her to face me.

Zoe nods, meeting my gaze, and her normally amber eyes glow with a pink light. The sweat is gone from her face and a flush is back in her cheeks. She turns her attention on the mage, and her body glows.

Layre's eyes widen slightly as he takes a step back. Zoe takes a deep breath and opens her mouth wide, exhaling a stream of fire, aiming directly for Layre's head. But he jumps out of the way.

I stare at her with my mouth hanging open. "You're like a dragon. I didn't know you could do that."

Zoe chuckles, and it makes her cough. "Me either."

"He's gone." We both look at Aidan as he stares at the place where Layre was standing.

"Did I get him?" Zoe's voice is raspy and dry.

I shake my head. "He moved. I don't get it. The mages cause all this trouble and think they're so bad, but whenever we make a stand against them, they disappear into thin air. It's dumb. Why don't they leave us alone if they can't handle it?"

Aidan slips his hand into mine, grabbing Zoe's free hand with his other. "I'm sure he didn't go far. Let's see if we can get to the portal before he comes back."

"We better run."

I barely hear Zoe's words. I glance over my shoulder to see what she's staring at and gasp. Shadows swirl and one by one, the creatures come into view, with blue fire crackling in their chests and the faces of their victims melting and swirling together.

Aidan races across the grass toward a lake that only he can see, dragging Zoe and me behind him.

Something shoves me roughly from behind, making me stagger and eventually trip as my legs can't catch up with the rest of my body. I hit the ground hard, nearly dragging Aidan with me and forcing Zoe to jump over my body to keep from falling on top of me. I roll over in time to see one of the shadow creatures headed straight for me.

The creature raises its hand, the sickly yellow gel dripping from its bony fingers.

I scramble back to my feet, refusing to let that thing burn me with the gel.

It chases after me, swooping down fast as black shadows twist around its body with blue flames that flicker out of the gaping hole in its chest. It's the same creature that originally had the birthstone.

I throw my hand up in the air, the earth at my feet obeying my command as it rolls up to form a mud wall. My heart drops when it doesn't even slow the creature down.

"Ciara, stop!" Aidan shouts from my left.

I skid to a halt, whirling around to see why I can't keep running, but there's nothing around me. "What? Why?"

Aidan rushes to my side, pulling me closer to him. "You were about to run into the lake."

I frown at him, then search the area behind me. I don't see anything but miles of grassy field shining in the moonlight. "What lake?"

He runs his hand through his hair, shifting his weight. "You still can't see it?"

I shake my head as Zoe rushes up to us. "Why are you guys standing there? Are we making a plan?"

"Not exactly. Apparently, we made it to the lake." I glance at Aidan as she spins around, searching for the body of water.

"Are you sure?" Zoe scans the horizon. "I don't see it."

"Me either." I'm confused by the idea that Aidan can see a lake but it's hidden to Zoe and me, but he's trusted me from the moment we met, and I'll do the same for him. "I believe you, but we need to figure out why we can't see it."

Aidan nods, suddenly shoving Zoe and me to the ground before he dives on top of me.

One of the shadow creatures flies by, tossing the gel at us like a bomb. Some of the substance lands on my skin, smoking as it burns the back of my hand.

I cry out, wiping my hand on the ground, and the gel instantly kills the grass.

Aidan rolls off me, writhing on the ground as he groans.

I'm on my knees, pinning him to the ground. "Where is it? Do you have that stuff on you?"

"It's on the back of my neck." He barely chokes out the words.

I roll him over, using my sleeve to wipe off the gel, revealing an angry red blister on the back of his neck. When he stops squirming, I turn to Zoe. "Did any get on you?"

Zoe holds her arms out, checking for any of the gel. "I don't think so." Her eyes suddenly grow wide. "Look out!"

I duck down in time to avoid being grabbed by a creature as it swoops by, its bony hand held out like a claw. I grab Aidan, pulling us both to our feet. "Can you figure out the portal? We need to get out of here."

Aidan rubs at the back of his neck, wincing as his fingers cross the blister. "I need to help you fight."

Zoe climbs to her feet. "You need to get us the hell out of here."

I glance at her and do a double take. Her skin glows with a soft orange light that covers her entire body. "Are you doing okay? You're glowing."

"It's the pink flame. It feels like it's feeding into my magic, and I'm afraid we're about to lose it." Zoe holds up her hand, and the flame is little more than the flame on the end of a match.

"Aidan, go. I'll hold back the creatures as long as I can. Figure out the portal." I nudge him forward.

He hesitates but takes off in the direction of the lake. I watch him disappear into the darkness and I swear I hear him splashing in water.

"Are you ready?" Zoe takes a deep breath and her skin glows brighter.

I can feel the heat radiating from her body. "I hope you don't explode."

Zoe snorts. "Me too."

Voices whisper in the darkness behind me. I whirl around just as the creature reaches for me, and drop into a squat as Zoe throws flames over my head, hitting the thing square in the chest.

The creature howls, which fades into a series of clicking noises.

I scoot back out of his grasp. "I think it's communicating to the others."

"You think?" Zoe's eyes are focused behind me.

I twist around to see several more creatures forming in the darkness, and there are too many to count. I grab Zoe, pulling us back, but the shadows move in fast.

Zoe closes one hand around the pink flame and opens her free hand with her palm facing the creatures. Fire blazes from her palm, spreading out to form a fiery wall between us and them with flames tinted pink.

One of the shadow creatures flies into the blaze and instantly catches on fire. It twists, coiling around itself as the smoky shadows that make up its body ignite with pink flames. The creature disappears into a wisp of smoke and the others float back, looking for a way around the fire.

Zoe drops to her knees as the fire magic withdraws back into her body. She leans forward, panting. "Damn."

"Damn is right. That was amazing." I reach down to help her stand, but she shrugs me off. "We need more of that fire. You actually killed one of those things."

"I don't think I can do that again." Zoe pants. "Is Aidan back yet?"

I scan the darkness. "I don't see him."

The clicking noise starts again as the creatures quickly close in around us, forming a tight circle with no room for escape.

I pull Zoe to her feet, hanging on to her arm, as much to comfort myself as to help her stand. "Are you sure you can't do that again?"

A tear trickles down her cheek. "I'm sure."

An idea slips through the panic in my brain. A crazy thought that will either save our lives or kill us. Whatever happens, I can't let those creatures touch us with more of that gel. I won't let them have the birthstone or Zoe with the pink fire. "I need you to sit down on the ground, because this is probably going to be bad."

Zoe yanks her arm free and practically throws herself to the grass. "What are you going to do?"

"Whatever I can to keep them from grabbing us." As I lower myself to the ground, I look around at the creatures as they close the distance. There isn't much time left, and I hope this works.

I dig my fingers into the grass and instantly feel the rush

of the earth's energy. In my mind, I can see the roots of the grass. Deeper into the earth, the dirt turns cold and damp, and I can smell the mud in my nose and taste it in my throat. Just below the mud is a raging river of energy that I know to be the primal earth.

I take a quick breath and dip into the magic. My muscles lock and my jaw clenches so tight it feels like I might break my teeth. Energy courses through my body, and I can't let go of the magic even if I wanted to.

My body hums and every inch of my skin prickles as a green light shoots out of the ground. I focus on the light, shifting it into a barrier between us and the creatures. I'm happy to see that they can't move through the light.

The cone of green magic shoots so high that it disappears into the sky, and I know it's going to attract the attention of every magical being in this realm, but I don't care because for the moment we're safe.

The creatures bump against the light, but it might as well be glass between us. I can hear them clicking as they form a plan.

"How long is this going to hold?" Zoe asks, staring up at the light.

"I don't know." I focus on the energy to keep it from taking over me. Somewhere in the back of my mind I hear Aidan's voice telling me the primal elements have killed other Guardians.

My body vibrates, and I shift the magic into the ground outside the cone of light. The thought barely enters my mind and a dirt spike shoots up through one of the creatures, stabbing it in the chest as it disappears into a wisp of smoke.

I turn my focus on the next creature when they all turn their attention to something in the distance. Scanning the darkness, I can't see anything, but then I feel it through the ground. Aidan running in our direction.

I pull my magic back, but I can't unplug from the primal stream of energy. The harder I try to disconnect, the tighter it entwines with my energy.

"Ciara, you have to let it go. Those things are going after Aidan. We need to help him." Zoe tugs on my arm.

"I'm trying." I can barely force the words out. The magic pulls me closer to the ground as my heart pounds against my chest. I close my eyes, taking slow, steady breaths, and reach out to the earth herself.

Thank you for keeping us safe. Please, let me go. I have to help Aidan. I form the words carefully in my mind, praying that she's listening.

The earth doesn't respond, but I'm suddenly released, and I fall backward as the cone of light returns to the ground.

I leap to my feet, following Zoe through the darkness. My heart skips a beat as I hear Aidan shout. I can barely make out his outline in the dark, and I pick up my pace. I'm almost to him when the ground lurches, sending all of us crashing to the ground.

The creatures close in, and I dig my fingers back into the ground, but before I can work any magic, the ground rumbles.

"What are you doing now?" Zoe frowns at me, her face pale and covered in sweat.

"That wasn't me."

The ground rumbles again.

I look at Aidan, hanging on to the grass as it quivers around my fingers with the shaking earth. "Did you find the portal?"

Aidan nods. "It belongs to Scorpio. I think that's why I'm the only one that can see it. It's protected by his magic."

"Can you get us through it?" I grit my teeth as the ground shakes again, only this time it sounds closer.

Pressure builds in my head as the creatures push in so close that I can feel their shadows like a light breeze against my arm. "Zoe, can you give us any more of that fire?"

Zoe squeezes her eyes shut and a weak circle of flames ignites around us as she collapses to the ground.

The earth trembles again.

Green sparkles float through the air like embers from a fire. My heart leaps at the sight of the earth magic, only I don't know where it's coming from.

Another boom as the ground shakes.

"Look," Aidan whispers.

Out of the darkness I see a massive form take shape, and my breath catches in my throat. Heading straight for us is the rock golem.

The creatures shift into a swirl of shadows as the earth rumbles with each mighty step he takes.

I leap to my feet as Aidan scoops up Zoe, cradling her in his arms. "What are you doing here?"

"You summoned me. Now go." His voice cracks through the night.

"Thank you." I place my hand over my heart, hoping he understands the gesture.

The golem nods his head, rock scraping rock. He lifts his massive stone leg and kicks at the swirling shadows.

"Hurry." Aidan races toward the lake, holding Zoe close to him as he runs.

I chase after him, staying close, and before long I'm splashing through water that still looks like grass to me. It's cold and wet, rising higher with each step, but I can't see it. "How far out do we have to go?"

"We're almost there." Aidan grunts as he pushes through the water now up to our waist. He turns, passing Zoe to me. "Hang on to her. I need to open the portal."

I support her body, which mostly floats in the invisible water, hanging on tight to her arm. The water swirls into a whirlpool, tugging on my body as I struggle to stay on my feet.

I'm not sure she's conscious, but I lean down close to her face. "I don't know what's going to happen, but we're going into the portal. I need you to help me hold on."

I throw a quick glance over my shoulder to see that there are now three golems fighting with the shadow creatures.

"Ciara?"

I whip around at the sound of my name. "You still with me?"

"Sort of." Zoe coughs weakly as she holds up her empty hand. "I lost the fire."

The current sweeps me off my feet, carrying us around in circles until it washes us through the portal.

20

The rushing water tosses us around as we swirl through the portal. My lungs scream for air, and I pray we're not underwater much longer. I desperately cling to Zoe to keep her from floating too far away from me.

The water drops and we cascade down a miniature waterfall, riding the momentum until we splash on the orange marble floor. I land hard on my stomach, sliding across the wet floor as I lose my grip on Zoe.

I'm on my hands and knees in a flash, splashing water as I crawl across the floor. I get to her seconds before Aidan. He reaches down, pressing her neck for a pulse.

"Is she still alive?" I desperately watch her chest for movement, but her body lies still. The water right beside her body boils, and steam rises around her.

"She's alive, but barely." Aidan leans close to her face, feeling for breath, but pops up as he gets a look at her hands. "Where's the fire?"

"Right before we washed through the portal, she said she lost it. We did that for nothing. Everything we went through was for nothing." Tears stream down my face, and I don't even bother to hide them.

"You did not fail."

I whip around at the sound of Capricorn's voice as he stands behind us, looking calm with his hands tucked inside the sleeves of his robes. "How can you say that? We lost the fire that we almost died for. In fact, I lost count of how many times we almost died. Aidan did die."

Capricorn absently toys with his horn as he shoots a sideways glance at Aidan, a smirk playing across his lips.

"How can you just stand there like that? Zoe is dying. I don't even know where we are." I grab Zoe's hand, immediately letting it go as her skin burns my fingers. "Why is she so hot?"

"You are in Scorpio's suite. It makes sense that his portal controlled by his Aid would drop you off here." Capricorn levels his eyes at me, but I refuse to respond. "Zoe is not dying yet, but she could if we don't properly finish the healing. She didn't lose the fire—she absorbed it, which also happens to be why she's so hot to the touch. Did I miss anything?"

I turn my eyes to Zoe. That must've been why the flame was shrinking. Not because it was going out, but because it was going into her body. That also has to be how she worked some magic with the flame.

"Oh, yes, I did miss a question. I'm standing here like this because I'm waiting on you to finish your outburst, and because the fire has to be fully absorbed to be useful. Unfortunately, when it's fully absorbed, she'll be closest to death."

I look up at the Zodiac, a warm blush filling my cheeks. "I'm not having an outburst. Not really. If she had to absorb the fire, why didn't you tell us that before we left?"

"Because she may not have been so willing to take the fire." Capricorn keeps his face blank, but he shifts his weight in a slight fidget.

"I can't believe you're so willing to sacrifice her." Fresh tears sting my eyes.

The green and gold swirl in Capricorn's eyes as he holds my gaze. "Not sacrifice. I didn't want her to be afraid, and she doesn't have to die."

"Ciara?" Zoe's voice is weak and raspy.

"I'm right here. Everything is going to be fine." I slip my hand in hers, trying not to make a face as I struggle to hold on despite the heat. "How are you feeling?"

"Tired. Hot." She groans as she tries to move, and a tear slips down her face. "I'm sorry about the fire. Are the Zodiacs mad? Why is it so hot?"

I smile gently, using my free hand to pull a few wet strands of hair away from her face. "You didn't lose the fire."

Zoe raises her eyebrows, searching my face. "Seriously?"

I nod, my smile growing wider. "Seriously. You actually absorbed it, which is why you're so hot."

Her eyes widen. "It's in me? How's that going to help Aries?"

Capricorn walks over, his hooves softly clicking on the marble floor. "You will transfer the healing flames to your Zodiac. It must be you and it must be this way."

Zoe sniffles. "Am I going to die?"

"No." My answer is a little too quick, but it makes Zoe smile. I gasp as her skin takes on the same bright pink tint of the flame.

"What? What is it?" Zoe struggles to sit up, but Aidan and I push her back to the floor.

"It is time." Capricorn turns abruptly, his robes swishing

around his hooves as he heads down the hallway, pausing just long enough to look at us over his shoulder. "Come on."

"I don't think I can get up." Tears fill Zoe's eyes again.

Aidan silently bends over, scooping her gently into his arms as he follows Capricorn.

I trot behind them until I catch up, then grab Zoe's hand to give it a squeeze.

Zoe smiles weakly at my gesture, then glances at Aidan. "Are you sure you can carry me?"

Aidan keeps his eyes locked on the Zodiac, sweat already beading on his face from Zoe's heat. "Just be still and quiet."

We twist and turn through the halls of the compound, and even though we're in an area that I haven't been before, I pay little attention to the decor. My eyes are locked on Capricorn and my mind worries about Zoe.

We turn down one final hall with white floors, white walls, and a white ceiling. Every surface is perfectly smooth and sterile. The lavender fire flickering in pans hanging from the ceiling is the only splash of color in the entire hallway.

"What is this place?" There's something about this area that makes me uncomfortable.

"This is the healing wing. Fortunately, we don't usually have a need for it, but we keep it for the Aids and servants. There's a ritual room prepared." Capricorn pushes through a set of white double doors with no windows and into another white hallway.

"This place is creepy," I whisper to Zoe, but I'm not sure she can hear me.

Zoe groans, and pink flames ignite on the fingertips of her hand that dangles at her side.

"Um, she's on fire." I grab Zoe's wrist, holding her hand up for the others to see.

Capricorn glances at her hand, then races down the hallway, his hooves thundering against the floor.

Aidan and I rush to keep up as we turn down another white hallway, and finally slam through a door at the end of the hall.

I skid to a halt as I get inside the ritual room, my breath catching in my throat.

The room is warm, and the walls are painted a burnt orange. Candles burn all around the space, hundreds of them that cast a soft glow. Aries lies on a large stone slab, waist high and made of bloodstone, a dark green speckled with red, in the center of the room. His body is motionless with his arms folded gently over his chest, and his scarlet robes hanging over the edge.

I stare at the Zodiac, and for a moment I wonder if we're too late. If I didn't know that he's immortal, I would swear he's dead.

Aries rolls his head to the side and locks his red eyes on Zoe.

Aidan walks up to the Zodiac and gently sets Zoe on the ground, leaning her against the slab.

"What happens now?" I whisper to Capricorn, but he only shakes his head.

Aries reaches down, clasping Zoe's hand, the pink flames still burning on her fingertips. She rises to her knees, twisting to face him, and they lock eyes.

The room is completely silent. No one breathes. Even the flames on the candles seem to hold their breath.

Aidan takes slow steps backward until he stands by my side. I slip my hand in his and we wait.

Zoe drags herself into a standing position, and she

probably would've fallen over if it hadn't been for her grip on Aries's hand. She holds up her free hand, fingers spread apart, and pink flames jump to life on each tip. Her hand remains motionless as the flames grow taller until her whole hand is engulfed.

Aries takes a labored breath, and I can see how pale he is from across the room. I don't know exactly what the spell did to him, but he's definitely seen better days.

Zoe pulls her hand from Aries and holds it high until her second hand is completely covered in pink flame. She reaches down with her left thumb and places it squarely on his forehead.

His body stiffens, his back arching off the stone slab. As Zoe removes her thumb, a piece of the flame still burns on his head.

Zoe moves her right hand to his chest, again placing her thumb in the center of his body, leaving another piece of the pink flame.

A red line of light connects from his forehead to his chest, and the small flames roar into larger fires.

She moves to his feet, placing her hands over both legs. The red light splits from the chest, connecting each ankle to form a glowing red triangle. Pink flames ignite from the middle of the triangle, shooting so high into the air that they graze the ceiling.

I duck my head a little to shield my eyes from the bright glare, but I can't tear my gaze away from what's happening in front of me. I have no idea how Zoe knows what she's doing or if she knows what she's doing.

Zoe waves her hands through the flames, and they swirl around her hands and begin to spin. Her breathing comes in quick pants and her skin glows with the same pink light of the flame coming from inside her body. Her copper hair blows around her face as the flames spin faster.

Aries's body locks, straight and stiff like a board, floating an inch off the slab. His dark hair whips across his face as the hem of his robes flap against his body. His head tilts back and his mouth opens wide as he exhales fire.

A scream rips from Zoe's throat as she hangs on to Aries.

Her boots catch on fire, and the pink glow of her body intensifies.

I step forward, afraid for her safety, but Aidan's gentle squeeze on my hand makes me hesitate.

Aidan leans close, whispering in my ear. "Let it be."

I chew on my bottom lip as I watch the fire creep up Zoe's legs. It's not the pink flames but actual flames. "But she's on fire."

Aidan shakes his head at me as his jaw muscles twitch, and I know he's as worried as I am.

I look to Capricorn, his expression unreadable as he watches the healing ritual.

The fire from Zoe's boots spread across the floor even though it's made of marble and has nothing to burn. A ring of fire circles the slab and it splinters off, drawing burning magical symbols across the floor.

Zoe screams again and it trails off into a whimper as the fire continues to work its way up her legs.

"Is this the way it's supposed to be happening?" I tug on Capricorn's sleeve when he doesn't look at me. "She's hurting. You said she'd be okay."

"This ritual has never been performed before, so I cannot say. I can see she's hurting." Capricorn tugs on his goatee.

"I'm going to help her." I pull my hand free from Aidan's grip.

"You might disrupt the ritual." Capricorn's eyes stay glued to the flames.

"She's my friend, and it's a risk I'm willing to take." Before anyone can stop me, I dash to the center of the room, careful to cross the magical symbols without stepping on them, and leap over the ring of fire.

"Can you help me?" Zoe's jaw is clenched so hard she almost can't speak.

I'm already sweating thanks to the intense heat, and I wipe my face. "I'm going to try."

"I'm burning up. I think I'm dying." A tear slips down her cheek and instantly dries.

I move up behind her, placing my hands on her shoulders, and it's all I can do to hang on to her burning skin. "That's not going to happen."

My eyes close as I reach into the marble beneath my feet. I can still feel the earth inside the stone as the magic runs through the floor, and I funnel it into Zoe's body.

Fire burns. It's that simple. It destroys and it heals, and that's the way it has to be. But fire needs something to burn, and unfortunately the earth is often the victim. Zoe needs to channel the fire before it consumes her.

Zoe relaxes beneath my hands as the grounding energy fills her body. I feel her thoughts slow, able to focus instead of racing through her mind. She concentrates on sending the healing flames deep into Aries.

I grit my teeth as the heat seeps into my body, and I gasp as it makes it hard to breathe.

The flames at her feet and on her legs extinguish, and Zoe breathes a sigh of relief. She tilts her head back as her hair whips around her face and the flames above Aries grow in intensity.

I push more energy into her, keeping her grounded. My

face burns and sweat covers my entire body, and I'm not sure how much longer I can hold on.

The flames of the candles flare then just as quickly return to normal. The fire covering Aries and the floor goes out, leaving scorch marks on the floor.

I stumble back and Aidan is behind me in a flash, holding me tight in his strong arms.

Zoe's knees buckle and Aries jumps up, catching her before she falls. He scoops her up, holding her close. Her head rolls back, her breathing soft but steady.

Aries has color in his face again, and the brightness is back in his red eyes. He smiles at me, and it's genuine, and for the first time I feel at ease in his presence. He locks eyes with me and tilts his head in a slight nod.

"Thank you for saving her life. The fire would've taken her if you didn't step in when you did. I'm sorry we didn't get off to a better start, so thank you for helping me." He walks past us but stops near the door, turning back around. "You really are special."

They slip through the door before I have the chance to say anything, not that I know what to say to that. I stare at the door. "Where is he taking her?"

"To rest and get food. She needs her strength, and you need to get back to Earth. I'll take you to do the same." Capricorn wraps his arm around my shoulders, giving me a quick squeeze. The simple gesture brings tears to my eyes. "He's right. You are very brave and very special. Your instincts and heart amaze me."

He heads for the door, and I'm grateful he can't see the blush on my face.

Aidan gives me a quick wink and pulls me out of the room.

Aidan and I walk up the front steps of my house, hand in hand as I smile at him. "It's good to be home. Next time you want to show me around your realm, I vote no monsters."

Aidan chuckles. "Deal. But just so you know, there really are some beautiful places that I would love for you to see."

I plant a quick kiss on his cheek. "I think that sounds amazing. We'll put that on the bucket list for after we beat the mages."

Aidan frowns at me as he takes the key from my hand and slides it in the lock. "What's a bucket list?"

I shake my head, laughing. "Never mind."

He shrugs his shoulders as he pushes open the front door, guiding me inside with a hand on the small of my back.

As I step into the living room, Doran and Jocelyn jump up from the couch. They were sitting very close together, and Doran refuses to look at me.

"What's going on here?" I can't keep the smile from my face.

Jocelyn rushes over, wrapping her arms around me, and it feels good to hug my friend. "I can't believe you're back already. How did it go?"

I roll my eyes at her. "It went fine. How are things here?"

Jocelyn glances at Doran, and when she turns back around, her cheeks are flushed. "Good. It's been quiet. We haven't seen any mages, and your house is perfectly safe. Tell me about Polaris."

"Quit changing the subject." I laugh as her mouth drops open and turn my attention to Doran. "How was your stay here on Earth? I see you met my friend."

Doran's face turns completely red as he rocks back and

forth on his feet. That fact that he's so uncomfortable makes him look adorable, and I enjoy watching him squirm.

"Earth is good. You have some great food here, and yes, your friend was kind enough to keep me company."

"I'll bet she did." I giggle even as Jocelyn digs her nails into my arm.

"Earth has the best food, doesn't it? It's not like Polaris, right? Did you try some chips?" Aidan practically glows as he talks about food.

Doran lights up, a broad smile across his face. "I tried chips. You were right about them."

Aidan waves him toward the kitchen. "Come with me. There's something in here called donuts."

"What are donuts?" Doran practically runs after Aidan. "You're in for a treat, and before you go, we'll order something called pizza, and maybe even some potato sticks. They call them fries here. You're never going to want to eat on Polaris again." Aidan laughs as they disappear into the kitchen.

I look at Jocelyn and I can't help but smile. "What just happened?"

"I have no idea," Jocelyn giggles. "Seriously, how did it go?"

"It was crazy, and I'll tell you the full story over dinner. I almost died a few times. Zoe almost died. Aidan did die. There were lots of crazy creatures and fairies. Oh, and we found another piece of Leo's birthstone."

Jocelyn frowns. "Aidan doesn't look dead."

I roll my eyes. "Really? That's all you got out of that?"

"Fine. Where's the stone?"

"We'll get it tomorrow. Zoe has it." I glance into the kitchen to make sure the boys are occupied. "What's going on with you two?"

The blush creeps back into her cheeks. "I don't know. Maybe nothing. Maybe something. He's really sweet, and cute, too."

"Well, I hope something works out." I start toward the kitchen but stop as a thought pops into my head. "Hey, how was your ritual?"

"I didn't go through it yet," she mumbles.

"What? Why not?" I glance back into the kitchen as my voice sounds too loud.

Jocelyn turns to look out the window, a deep frown creasing her brow. "My ritual was supposed to take place on Mt. Rose, but something is wrong on the mountain. The mages are doing something, and Mierna was afraid my ritual wouldn't go right."

I stare at my friend as a cold chill races down my spine. "When Aidan and I were leaving to go to Polaris, I saw shadows on the mountain. I had a weird feeling looking at it. Do you know what it is?"

Jocelyn shakes her head. "No. Mierna said we had to wait for you. There's a storm coming, and we don't know what it's going to bring."

The cheery mood I felt coming home quickly disappears. "What are they up to now?"

Jocelyn shrugs. "Who knows, but it's bad this time."

I snort. "What do you mean this time? It's been bad every time."

"I know, but there's something different." She shakes her head and turns her eyes to me. "By the way, Sarah called while you were gone. She said it's important."

"I'll call her tomorrow. I want to relax tonight." I slip off my jacket and toss it over the back of the couch as questions tumble through my mind. What can the mages possibly be up to that it can ruin the magic of Jocelyn's ritual? What are they doing on that mountain?

Aidan steps out of the kitchen and stops behind me. "Jocelyn, Doran wants you to teach him how to make coffee."

Jocelyn giggles as she rolls her eyes. "Why can't you show him?"

"He asked for you." Aidan wraps his arms around my waist. "Besides, I need to talk to Ciara for a minute."

"Fine." Jocelyn heads into the kitchen.

"We'll be in there in a minute and then we'll order pizza," I call after her.

Jocelyn waves over her shoulder to let me know she heard me and disappears into the kitchen.

Aidan grips my waist and turns me around to face him, planting a soft, slow kiss on my lips. "I've been wanting to tell you something since we were in the first cave, when you passed out on the mountain."

My body tingles and my breath catches in my throat. I want to say something, anything, but I can't make my brain work as I stare into his blue eyes.

"We almost lost each other more than once, and I don't want to wait anymore. I know we haven't known each other very long, but we've been through so much. I just want you to know that I love you."

I can't feel my body anymore. I'm not even sure I'm still breathing. All I know is the blue of his eyes and the pounding of my heart.

Aidan raises his eyebrows, a smile tugging at his mouth. "Can you say something? Please?"

"I love you too." My words are soft, barely above a whisper, but I know he hears me.

The smile that lights up his face warms my heart. He

wraps his arms around me, holding me tight as he kisses me.

Jocelyn clears her throat behind us. "The pizza is on the way."

I groan, peeking around Aidan. "You interrupted for that?"

"Sorry." She skips back into the kitchen, giggling. "Come on. Tell us about your trip. I want to know what it's like to be dead."

Aidan frowns at me. "You told her?"

I shrug, wrapping my arm around his waist. "I might have mentioned it."

"I don't want to talk about it tonight. Let's just have a quiet night with good food and good company." He kisses the top of my head, pulling me toward the kitchen.

"Deal. Jocelyn said a storm is coming, and I want to relax, even if it's just for one night."

We join our friends in the kitchen, laughing as we wait for our pizza to get delivered. It feels good to have a normal night, but I know it isn't going to last. The shadow hanging over the mountain tugs at the back of my mind.

It's only a couple of weeks before the wheel turns into the house of Taurus, and that makes me wonder what Sarah wanted. I haven't heard from her in a few months, so whatever she wants probably isn't good. I'm also not looking forward to seeing Taurus again. I still don't trust him, and I'm not sure I ever will. I push the questions out of my mind and focus on the conversation as Aidan explains what a hamburger is to Doran.

So many questions, but I know I'll have my answers soon enough.

21

Deep in the marble city.

Kyrell paces across the floor, his leather shoes barely making any sound as he walks with his hands locked behind his back. Every few seconds he locks his almost white eyes on the door, but no one comes. He summoned them hours ago and they'd do well not to keep him waiting any longer.

Finally, he hears the echo of footsteps in the marble stairwell, slowly ascending to the top of the tower where he waits. Kyrell walks over to the window, staring out at the city below.

The streets are empty, and every marble building is quiet and dark. No one would ever know that hundreds of his fellow mages live here, ready to serve his every need. Willing to give their life if that's what it takes to defeat the Zodiacs.

Most of the mages are away from home, preparing for the coming war. Some of them collect creatures from Polaris, while others do his bidding on Earth. The Zodiacs will fall, and their precious Guardians will be the cause.

The door scrapes as it's pushed open from the outside, but Kyrell doesn't bother turning around. He knows who's there. "Why did you keep me waiting?" His voice is dry and brittle, like autumn leaves blowing across the ground.

"I'm sorry, master." The voice shakes, and it brings a smile to Kyrell's lips.

Kyrell turns from the window, slowly circling the mage that kneels in the center of the room with his head bowed low. "You may stand, Draven."

Draven slowly rises but keeps his eyes glued to the ground.

Kyrell makes another pass around the mage. "I am disappointed in you."

Draven flinches as if he's been slapped. "Yes, master."

"Do you know why I'm disappointed in you?" Kyrell reaches up and runs a finger down Draven's cheek.

Draven narrows his eyes but quickly clears his features. "Because I haven't brought you the Capricorn Guardian."

"And why haven't you brought her to me?"

"She has magic that no one knows about. She's strong, and she has a lot of people helping her." Draven tucks his hands deep into the pockets of his black robes.

"You are weak! You are a coward," Kyrell shrieks, causing Draven to jump with each sentence.

Draven finally looks Kyrell in the face. "Why her? Why not one of the other Guardians who isn't so well protected? Let's start with them and draw her in."

Kyrell returns to the window, staring out over the buildings, the white marble glowing blue in the moonlight.

Warm air blows in through the window, causing his platinum hair to flutter around his face. "She owes me her life. She is the reason I need the Zodiac magic. I will have what is mine."

"Yes, master."

"And what of your other task?" Kyrell reaches into his pocket, running his finger over the smooth stone that makes up part of the Leo birthstone.

"It's on track. The storm is brewing over the mountain and the mountain is dying. We'll be able to cut the Zodiacs off from their portal, and they won't be able to go to Earth. Layre is standing by, so when we redirect the portal, he can send over his shadow creatures."

"Good." Kyrell's word is more of a hiss.

Footsteps echo in the stairwell, and Kyrell and Draven turn around as the door scrapes open. In walks a short man, portly with a ruddy face.

"Welcome, Brother." Kyrell crosses the room and lays a hand on Kage's shoulder.

Draven stares at Kage. "What are you doing here?"

"I've been summoned to make sure you do your job and bring in the Guardian." A smile plays across Kage's face, but his eyes are hard.

Draven returns a sneer. "I thought you were part of the resistance."

Kyrell lashes out, slapping Draven hard across the face. "You will not speak to him that way. He is my family."

Draven clears his throat, giving Kage a sideways glance. "I'm sorry, master."

Kyrell flicks his wrist and a flash of red light flies from his fingertips.

Draven drops to the ground, growling as he writhes in pain. He slaps his hand over his neck and sucks in a sharp breath through his teeth. He pulls his hand away as the red line burns an intricate pattern of loops on the side of his neck. The light flares and disappears, leaving a pink scar.

"What was that?" Draven asks between gasps.

"That mark will allow me to track you and kill you if I choose. Kage will keep me informed. Do not fail me again. Get out of my sight." Kyrell watches as Draven drags himself to his feet and bows before heading for the door. "Oh, Brother, do you have something for me?"

Kage reaches into the pocket of his robes as Kyrell holds out his hand. In his open palm, Kage drops a heavy golden ring with a sapphire at least an inch long in the center, surrounded by diamonds and emeralds.

Ready for the next book in the Turn of the Zodiac series? The Second House is coming soon!

You can sign up for my newsletter for to get all the updates on new releases and behind the scenes info.

Also, if you loved this book, I'd really appreciate it if you could take the time to leave an honest review. They really help and it would mean a lot!

You can scan the code below to sign up for my newsletter and get all my book links!

ABOUT THE AUTHOR

Ashley R Scott lives in Reno with her boyfriend, Buzz, and fur babies, Zeus and Jordy. Even though she misses certain things about her home state of Texas, she loves the area and everything it has to offer.

When she isn't writing, she spends her time reading, working on video projects, and enjoying adventures and travel with her favorite boys.

To see a complete list of books and the reading order, visit www.ashleyrscott.com

Don't forget to join her on social media!

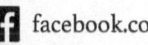 facebook.com/AuthorAshleyRScott

 twitter.com/ashrscott

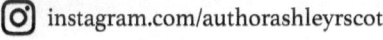 instagram.com/authorashleyrscott

ALSO BY ASHLEY R SCOTT